SAFE HARBOR

THE JACKSON CLAY & BEAR BEAUCHAMP SERIES
BOOK 5

B.C. LIENESCH

THE JACKSON CLAY & BEAR BEAUCHAMP SERIES

JOIN LIQUID MIND PUBLISHING'S MAILING LIST

Follow the link to join our newsletter and stay up to date with Liquid Mind Publishing!

https://BookHip.com/GTQPXSQ

You'll receive a **free** copy of

A Dangerous Game: A Jackson Clay Prequel.

CONTENT WARNING

The subject matter in this novel is intended for mature readers and may not be suitable for children and young adults. Please note this novel contains explicit language and depictions of violence. Reader's discretion is advised.

For my mother and father, who gave me my love for Chincoteague.

I'm sorry I used it as a hunting ground for a deranged killer.

PROLOGUE

STEPHIE MEACHEM STOOD on the dock watching the fireworks overhead. Mortar shots fired into the late evening twilight burst into red, blue, and yellow chrysanthemums. She could feel the explosions as they rippled through the air and onto the water beneath her. It was late July 1999, and the hot, humid air hung on to the smoke from the pyrotechnics with a vice-like grip. She brushed her blonde hair off her shoulder and picked at the peeling sunburn there. At seventeen, she was quickly growing into her leggy body, one that had darkened from sunning over school break, but remembering to put on sunscreen was a habit she was still working on.

The dock stood on the far tip of the Meachem family's property on Chincoteague Island, where Oyster Bay joined Assateague Bay, tucked up behind Assateague Island. When Stephie's English ancestors had settled the plot of land in the mid-seventeenth century, Chincoteague itself had been a Virginia barrier island. The earth had changed over centuries, but the Meachems remained a constant. Stephie wondered if that would still be the case once everyone learned the truth about what had happened.

A pontoon boat wrapped in neon lights sailed through the bay between the two islands, pop music thumping. Today had been the pony penning, an island tradition and tourist attraction where Chincoteague's firefighters got on horseback and corralled Assateague Island's wild pony herds, swimming them across the channel for some to be auctioned off in order to manage the population on the island. The town's population ballooned from thirty-six hundred to over forty thousand in the days around the swim. The boaters whooped and hollered as more fireworks exploded overhead. Everyone nearby always enjoyed the show Stephie's father put on, even if it wasn't entirely legal. She doubted the chief of the small town's police force would ever discipline one of his poker buddies.

Stephie wrapped her hands around her belly, cradling the secret within her. She turned, looking back at her family's property. Three large houses—some of the largest on the island—stood on their squat, wide foundations and glowed like ornamental lanterns on the flat grasslands, each with a much more substantial dock running out to a small flotilla of personal watercraft. One McMansion for each of the three siblings. Together, the family was having their own pony penning celebration, and Stephie could see little black silhouettes moving in between windows or underneath the lights on the wrap-around decks.

She watched the dark shadows move back and forth like ants when she heard the rapid pitter-patter of running feet in flip-flops. More fireworks burst overhead, and now Stephie saw her brother, Zach, sprinting toward her, his figure changing in the sporadic, colorful flashes.

"Stephie!" he shouted. "Stephie!"

Zach ran full speed as he hit the dock, then pulled up just feet short of his sister. Stephie flinched as if he were about to knock two of them into the water. Zach doubled over, dropping his hands to his knees, trying to catch his breath.

"Russell's here," he said in between heavy breaths.

Stephie felt her heart lurch into her throat. She stared at Zach, hoping this was some sort of joke. But Zach just stared back at her, his chest heaving under his tie-dyed tank top. Sweat matted the edges of his short, sandy hair, dropping in beads across his angular face.

"Did you hear me?" Zach asked. "I said Russell's *here*."

Stephie shook her head. "Dad..."

"Dad knows." Zach took another gulp of air. "He knows about all of it. Steph, when I saw him, he was going upstairs to get his gun."

Stephie could barely hear her own voice. "Oh, God. We have to stop him."

"I know. Come on."

Zach held his hand out, but Stephie just looked at it. Her feet were like cinder blocks beneath her.

Zach huffed in through his nose. "Steph, you have to be brave now. There's no more hiding this. You have to face it. I'll do it with you, but we have to do it *now*. Before the wrong people get hurt."

Stephie nodded. She reached out and took Zach's hand. Together, they began running for their house nestled between the two others. The mortars across the way began firing off their grand finale. In rapid succession, starbursts of every color painted the dark world around them, strobing with their flashes. Green, white, red, blue, red, yellow. Stephie's legs began to burn, but she pushed the pain out of her mind. Zach was right. She had to stop this before it went too far. They reached the first house and kept going. Their cousin, Adam, stood on the deck corner nearest them, two stories up.

"Hey!" he called out. "Where you all off to? A hot date? You know that family thing is frowned upon now." He cackled at his own joke.

Stephie thought she was going to be sick. Not from the morning sickness, which had started a couple of days earlier. From the fear that clawed at her insides. Fear of the truth that was about to come out. Fear of what it would do to her, to her family. Fear of what the town would think when they heard. The rumors, the gossip. Most of all, she feared her life as she'd known it was seconds away from ending.

They crossed the footbridge over the swampy marshes between

their aunt and uncle's house and theirs. Amidst the thunderous bombardment of fireworks came another pair of blasts. They were sharper and snare-like.

Gunshots.

"Oh, god," Stephie cried out.

"Come on!" Zach shouted.

Over the tall marsh grass, Stephie could see Russell's red Dodge Dakota in their driveway. She collapsed to her knees, fearing the worst, and began sobbing.

"Get up!" Zach begged. "We can't stop! You have to get up!"

The cab light on the Dakota clicked on as the driver's door opened. Stephie stared, mouth gaping, relieved to see Russell unharmed.

Russell looked over at them, his eyes narrowed and brow furrowed. "Stephie? What the hell is going on?!"

Before Stephie could find the words to answer, her father stepped out onto the driveway with a shotgun nestled under his arm.

"Russell!" Stephie screamed. "Go! Please!"

"Not until you tell me what is going on."

Over the fireworks, a third gunshot rumbled into the night.

PART ONE
CHASING SHADOWS

"The past can tick away inside us for decades like a silent time bomb, until it sets off a cellular message that lets us know the body does not forget the past." -Donna Jackson Nakazawa

ONE

JACKSON CLAY DROPPED his head and looked down the sights of his Benelli Super Black Eagle shotgun. He watched his target until it was inside the forty-yard marker he'd placed, moving fast. Jackson estimated it to be thirty-seven yards. *Definitely a makeable shot.* Following the target, he took a deep breath in, held it, then let it out. His heart rate slowed to the optimal sixty beats per minute. *Good to go.* Jackson slid his index finger down from the body of the shotgun and onto the trigger.

A metallic snap came from over his right shoulder, followed by a thud.

"Sonofabitch!" Bear grunted.

Jackson turned and looked just in time to see Bear fall off the back end of the duck blind and into the water below. He turned back to his shotgun. The duck had banked left and flown back out to Calfpen Bay. Jackson frowned and lowered the gun.

Bear began splashing somewhere beneath. "Help me up, dammit!" he said. "I'm not a strong swimmer."

"It's three feet of water, Bear," Jackson said. "Stand up."

Bear stopped floundering and got his feet underneath him. "Goddamn chair snapped on me."

Jackson snorted. "You don't say. Use the ladder to pull yourself up."

Bear reached out for a wooden rung built into the blind and hoisted himself up. The blind itself was crudely constructed but effective. A two-foot-by-four-foot platform stood a couple of feet over the shallow bay, with a wooden pen on the back end big enough to slip in a small to medium-sized boat. Harvested vegetation and branches camouflaged the structure on all sides.

The blind itself was tucked away on a tiny estuary called Will's Creek on the north end of Assateague Island, where it cut into the thin strip of land like a sickle-shaped knife. Tall southern pine trees shot up from the marsh grass and lowlands on either side, creating the perfect corridor for waterfowl to swoop down into.

Jackson took off his Piedmont Ammo & Supply ball cap and ran his fingers through ash-brown hair that was just long enough to show its natural curls. A lot longer than it had been during his Army Ranger days, or even in his time as a father and a husband. Those were completely different lives from the one Jackson lived now.

Putting the hat back on, he scratched at his beard, watching Bear struggle to climb out of the empty boat pen. Jackson was in his forties, but his athletic frame made him look ten years younger. The tapestry of scars that covered his body, however, told the true story of a life lived harder than most.

Beneath him, Bear had managed to get himself onto the ramshackle ladder. He'd just begun to climb it when the rotted rung holding his foot gave way and sent him back into the bay.

"Godfuckingdammit!" Bear stammered.

Bear was a few years younger than Jackson but looked older with his six-and-a-half-foot frame and bourbon-barrel physique. His legal name was Archibald Beauchamp, but he embodied his "Bear" nick-name in every way. From his unkempt chestnut hair and his long, bushy beard to the way he had a habit of growling when he got excited, one could be forgiven for thinking he'd descended from the population of black bears that called the Old Dominion State home. They'd met five years ago as Jackson tracked a missing girl across Virginia. Bear had backed him up in a bar fight, and the two had watched each other's backs ever since.

A staticky voice came from a radio in one of Jackson's coat pockets.

"Jackson? Bear?" the voice said. "I see y'all moving around out there, didn't hear a gunshot, though. Y'all got a bird down?"

It was their boat driver and hunting guide, Captain Terry Yarbrough. He waited a quarter mile away, on standby, with the twenty-foot Carolina Skiff they'd ridden in on.

Jackson pulled the radio out and keyed the mic. "Negative. Bear fell in the drink."

"He fell in? How?"

"He's talented."

Bear huffed as he took a second go at climbing the wooden ladder. "Let me get back up there and I'll show ya talented."

Captain Terry radioed again. "Well, y'all have been at it ten hours now. What do you want to do?"

Jackson looked at the sun dipping over Chincoteague Island to the west. They had a half-hour more of daylight tops.

He keyed the mic again. "Yeah, we better call it. Get Bear here into some dry clothes."

"Copy that, I'm on my way."

Bear got the top half of his body up to the platform, then flopped forward and rolled onto it.

Jackson scooted his own camping chair out of the way. "You look just like a fish I caught once."

Bear rolled onto his back, his camouflage waders and drab green hoodie dripping wet, and gave him the finger. "Help me up."

Jackson did as Bear asked. Minutes later, Captain Terry came gliding down Will's Creek and eased the boat into the hunting blind. The paunch-bellied skipper had gray hair and a clean-shaven face as round as his gut. He pulled a pair of glasses out of the breast pocket of the plaid flannel shirt he had on and examined the damage Bear had done to his blind.

"I'm going to have to run to Ace and get me some two-by-fours to fix that ladder," he said.

"Make sure you send Bear the bill," Jackson said.

"I din' do shit," Bear countered. "Those boards were rottin'!"

Captain Terry's belly jiggled as he chortled. "I'd have to agree with you there."

A few minutes later, Jackson and Bear had their gear in the boat, and the three men pulled out of the duck blind. As Captain Terry whisked them down the Assateague Channel, Jackson took in the wildlife refuge to their left. The squat white oaks dotting the marshlands reminded him of the fig trees he'd seen on the Serengeti when he and a couple of Army buddies backpacked across Tanzania a lifetime ago. The brisk autumn air whipping into his face, though, reminded him of anywhere but Africa.

Captain Terry cruised wide of a small island. On the other side, a ramshackle cottage nestled on one of the several fingers of land that jutted into the channel. Jackson looked back at Captain Terry, then nodded at the cottage.

"What's that?" he asked over the roar of the engine.

"Old hunter's club cabin," Captain Terry said. "Back in the day, the guys who owned it would come out here with a month's worth of supplies and hunt to their heart's content." He shook his head. "Been abandoned for a coupla decades now."

It took another forty-five minutes to get back to the small harbor on the extreme south end of Chincoteague Island. No more than a few hundred feet wide, with fishing trawlers, tour boats, and personal yachts bobbing in slips laid out in a square horseshoe. Beyond it on all sides was a vast blacktop for trucks and trailers. Captain Terry eased them over to the dock they'd left from. On the other side of it, a handful of men were unloading one of the fishing trawlers. Captain Terry waved to one of the men, dressed in orange waders and a long-sleeved tee. The man waved back.

"How's it going, Bert?" Captain Terry said.

"Not bad, how 'bout yourself?" Bert replied.

"Oh, can't complain."

Jackson tied a line around one of the dock posts before he and Bear grabbed their gear. Bert stood over them on the dock. He was tall and slender with a sharp jawline and salt-and-pepper hair.

"You boys been out fishing? That's what they pay me for, you know," he said, chuckling.

"Hell no," Bear said. "I ain't got time for some damn pole and string."

Bert nodded back at his thirty-foot trawler and grinned. "Same."

Jackson stepped out of Captain Terry's boat. "Duck hunting, actually."

Bert's eyebrows lifted. "Bag anything?"

"Few of them." Bear held up the day's take.

Captain Terry laughed as he climbed out of the boat as well. "It cost them a chair in the process, though."

Bear huffed.

"It buckled under my friend here," Jackson explained. "We own an outdoor rec store in Martinsville. Figured we could put some R&R on the company card as long as we do some product testing while we're out here. I guess we won't be recommending that chair."

Bert laughed. "Where you all staying?"

"We have a rental over on the west side of the island," Jackson said.

"Very nice. You boys here all week?"

Jackson nodded. "Got a couple more trips with Captain Terry here on the calendar, including tomorrow."

Captain Terry finished securing the boat and joined them. "Not if I can't get that ladder fixed early tomorrow morning." He checked his watch. "Shoot, I got to get over to Ace before they close."

One of Bert's crew members stepped off the fishing trawler but slipped and knocked into Captain Terry. Captain Terry caught the young man and righted him.

"Whoa, easy there," Captain Terry said.

The man looked back at the group. "My bad," he muttered sheepishly before heading toward the parking lot.

Bert rolled his eyes before turning back to the others. "Sorry about that. New guy." He shook his head. "I don't think they come any greener than that."

"New guy? You lose another member of your crew?" Captain Terry asked.

Bert nodded. "Sam Cutter. A crabbing crew out of Norfolk lured him away."

Captain Terry shook his head. "Ah, that's too bad."

Bert shrugged. "Can't say that I blame him. Fishing here isn't what it used to be. I don't recognize half the faces on the boats these days. I'm just lucky to scrounge together enough warm bodies at this point."

"Ain't that the truth." Captain Terry checked his watch again. "I really do gotta get to Ace, though." He waved at Bert and then Jackson and Bear before heading up the dock.

"See you tomorrow," Jackson said. He turned back to Bear. "Ready to roll?"

Bear grabbed his shotgun and the day's take. "If I hear one more quip about the damn chair, you're cleaning the birds."

Jackson ignored him and smiled at Bert. "You have a good night."

Bert smiled back. "You all do the same."

TWO

THE BULL SHARK stalked his victim as morning dawned, watching the man slip out of the harbor in the early light. He'd heard others call him Captain Terry, a doughy geezer that earned his keep ferrying tourists around. The Bull Shark had watched him for days. Now it was time to hunt.

Of course, The Bull Shark had a real name of his own. He wasn't, in fact, a sleek-bodied fish, swimming around with fins and gills. He was a person. A man, seemingly like any other, but The Bull Shark had always been different. Yes, he had a name, but it meant nothing to him. Nothing more than a random assortment of letters, as foreign to him as the people who gave it to him. A moniker claiming no lineage or ancestry. A permanent reminder of the discarded bastard he was.

But ever since The Awakening, that night two weeks back, he'd come to know himself as The Bull Shark. It was representative of his newfound purpose in this world. Bull sharks were notoriously aggressive, lone hunters that could live in fresh and saltwater alike. They adapted to their environments to survive. No, to *thrive*. They hunted not just to nourish but because they could. Because they were good at it. That was what The Bull Shark was doing here. Who he was. He chased his prey until he caught it. Because he had to. Something in him wouldn't let him quit, like a primal instinct.

He waited until Captain Terry turned north up the channel, then put his own boat in gear. Following him from a distance, they passed under the bridge over to Assateague Island and continued all the way to Will's Creek. When Captain Terry pulled into a duck blind just off the inlet, The Bull Shark killed his engine and waited. The blind was like several that dotted the waterways around Chincoteague, a boat slip and an elevated shooting platform covered with branches and brush. Only carrying his serrated hunting knife, he wondered if the hunting blind meant the boat captain was armed.

Minutes went by, and Captain Terry never appeared in the blind above the boat slip. This piqued The Bull Shark's curiosity. Slowly, he approached. His engine little more than idling, he floated up to the boat slip and found Captain Terry kneeling over the side of his boat near its bow, hammering away at the base of the duck blind. Inside the boat, at his feet sat a bin full of hardware supplies. As if sensing his presence, Captain Terry turned, startled at the sight of him.

"Good heavens!" Captain Terry said, falling onto his backside and clutching his chest. "You damn near scared the piss out of me."

The Bull Shark flashed his teeth, but with his head buried inside a hoodie and ball cap, he doubted Captain Terry saw it. "Sorry about that," he said. "I was going by and saw you deep in here. Wanted to make sure everything was okay."

"Ah, yeah, just fine." Captain Terry rolled back over onto his knees. "I took a coupla guys out hunting yesterday. Big fella did a number on my ladder here. Just trying to fix it up before I take them back out again today."

The Bull Shark got up from the outboard motor on his boat and put a foot on Captain Terry's. "'Early bird gets the worm', as they say."

"Yup, that's what they say."

"You need a hand with that?"

Captain Terry shook his head. "Oh, no. Just nailing a coupla planks is all. Wish the sun wouldn't take its damn time rising, though." He hammered at a nail, missed it, and clipped his thumb. "Ow! Dagnabbit!"

"You sure you don't need a hand? I don't mind."

Captain Terry looked over his shoulder, studying him for a moment. "Alright, sure. Go on and just hold the boat steady there if ya don't mind."

Stepping completely onto Captain Terry's boat, he got behind the steering console a few feet from the stern and gripped the outer post of the blind, holding the boat in place.

Captain Terry finished nailing in one rung, then replaced the one just above it. The last one needing work was the top one just before the platform deck. He got a fresh two-by-four and a handful of nails from the bin at his feet, then stood to finish the job. When his weight shifted, the boat rocked underneath him.

"Hold her steady," Captain Terry said. "I'm almost finished here."

Not saying anything in response, The Bull Shark looked down at the steering column. The keys were in the ignition. He had everything he needed to strike. He turned the key and the console beeped. The engine rumbled to life.

"Hey!" Captain Terry said. "What are you doi—"

The Bull Shark jerked the throttle back, and the boat jutted in reverse. Captain Terry lost his balance and fell backward. His rear hit the front lip of the boat and his momentum carried him over the bow. Tumbling backward, his upper half flipped over into the water. The Bull Shark shoved the throttle the other way and the boat shot forward, slamming into Captain Terry and pinning him upside down underwater.

Grinning, The Bull Shark watched as Captain Terry's legs kicked erratically in the air, trying desperately to right himself. The shark had to give the boat captain credit for being a fighter, even if it was all in vain. At this point, it was simple physics. With that much force pinning him in place, Captain Terry didn't have the strength to fight it. After almost a minute, the splashing stopped. His legs gave one last kick of spasmodic protest, and then Captain Terry was gone, his life washed from his body in the ebbing tide.

The Bull Shark cut the engine and looked out at Calfpen Bay, listening. Only the tall grass, rustling in the early morning breeze, mourned the life the shark had just snuffed out. The bay was tucked away in a corner of Assateague Island, with Will's Creek a separate nook off of that. At the busiest times of the year, this place could still pass for secluded. But here, at the dawn of a mid-autumn day, it might as well be on a different planet.

The Bull Shark stepped back over to his own boat, fired up his outboard motor, and twisted the throttle. The boat bucked high as it cruised out of Calfpen Bay, leaving Captain Terry's body and boat behind.

When the sun finally rose over the small dunes of Assateague Island, not a living soul was around.

THREE

JACKSON AND BEAR arrived in Bear's old firetruck-red Chevy Suburban five minutes before nine, their planned launch time with Captain Terry. They parked along the same stretch of pavement near Captain Terry's boat slip and noticed the slip was empty. Jackson and Bear got out, went down to the slip, and surveyed the harbor.

"Maybe he took the boat to prep it," Bear offered. "Get fuel, something like that?"

"Or he's not back from fixing the ladder on the blind," Jackson said.

Bear frowned.

Jackson and Bear stayed on the dock, waiting for Captain Terry to show. When the bottom of the hour came and went, Jackson became uneasy. Captain Terry had never been anything but early for their previous outings. He looked back at the thin strip of tarmac just off the dock. "Something's wrong," Jackson said. "His pickup, that white Silverado, is here, which means he's here. He knew we were meeting here at nine."

Bear shrugged. "Maybe it's like you said. He's out working on the blind."

It was possible, but Jackson wasn't buying that. "You still have his cell, don't you? From booking with him?"

Bear nodded. "Sure do."

"Give it a call."

Bear pawed at his phone for a minute, then put it to his ear. Almost immediately, he shook his head. "Straight to voicemail."

When Captain Terry was officially an hour late, Jackson decided it was time to get others involved. He walked over to the harbormaster and explained the situation. A stocky man named Stephen Gaines, likely in his fifties with short brown hair and a long face, took in Jackson from behind an L-shaped desk inside the harbor office. Papers covered the desk, and a computer sat in the corner.

"I know Terry," Gaines said when Jackson was done. "It's not like him to be late, let alone leave you all hung out to dry."

"I figured as much," Jackson said. "Which is why I'm here."

Gaines sat forward in his chair. "I think we've got Terry's home number on file here. One sec." He typed away at the computer. "Yep, right here. I know he's married. Let's see if his wife knows what's up."

Shuffling some papers over to reveal a phone on his desk, he punched in a number and put the handset to his ear. "Good morning. Mrs. Yarbrough?" A pause. "Yes, this is Stephen Gaines down at the harbor. How are you doing?" Another pause. "Doing alright. Listen, Terry's got some hunters waiting on him here at the harbor. You don't know where he is, do you?" Gaines met Jackson's eyes as he continued the phone conversation. "He left this morning to go out and repair a blind, huh? Well, I'm sure that's it. It must be taking him a bit longer. Alright, thank you, ma'am." One more pause. "Uh huh, I will. You have a good day."

Gaines hung up the phone. He sat back in his chair, thinking.

Jackson hadn't heard the other end of the phone conversation but could imagine what Terry's wife had said. "I think it's time someone goes looking for Captain Terry, don't you?"

Gaines looked at Captain Terry's information on the computer one more time before rocking forward and popping out of his chair. He stepped around Jackson and into another room. It was similarly cramped with office furniture, but windows overlooking the massive parking lot along the outside made it feel less crowded. A curio stood against the back wall stacked with equipment, including a radio.

Jackson followed Gaines into the room as Gaines grabbed the handheld mic. Jackson noticed the radio was set to Channel 16, the international distress and safety calling frequency.

"Channel Pony, Channel Pony, Channel Pony, Curtis Merritt Harbor. Over," Gaines radioed.

Silence.

After a moment, Gaines keyed the mic again. "Channel Pony, Channel Pony, Channel Pony, Curtis Merrit Harbor. Over."

Again, silence.

"This is Curtis Merritt Harbor calling Terry Yarbrough. Over."

When there was still no response, Gaines shook his head in frustration. "Attention any boats near the northern point of Chincoteague Island or Calfpen Bay, this is the harbormaster," Gaines said into the radio. "Come in, over."

A garbled transmission Jackson could barely understand came back from a boat saying they were near Calfpen Bay.

"We have a possible boater out of communication out that way, last reported to be headed for a duck blind at the mouth of Will's Creek. Over."

"Yeah, I know the one. Over."

"You mind running over that way and see if you can spot him? Over."

"Roger, no problem. Give me five. Over."

Jackson and Gaines stood in silence, waiting for the boater to get back to them. Jackson stepped around a desk and over to one of the windows. He looked out to see if Captain Terry had come back. He hadn't. Bear stood alone on the dock, looking out to the mouth of the harbor.

When the same voice came back over the radio, it was louder and more frantic. "Mayday, mayday, mayday! I have a boater in distress. I say again, I have a boater down!"

————

JACKSON WAITED with Bear by the Suburban as emergency vehicles streamed into the harbor over the next few hours. First, a Chincoteague Police cruiser. Then a second, followed by an engine truck from the fire department and an ambulance from the town's EMS. Everyone stood by, knowing what was to come. Finally, just after noon, a Virginia Marine Police boat cruised into the harbor and docked at a boat slip in front of the harbormaster's office. The paramedics from the ambulance wheeled a stretcher down to the dock and assisted the officers on board in transferring Captain Terry's body, shrouded in a black bag, onto it. When his body was secure, they wheeled him back up to the ambulance and loaded him in.

"I can't believe the guy's just ... gone," Bear said.

Jackson didn't say anything, but he felt the same.

As the paramedics climbed in and the ambulance pulled out of the harbor, a Chincoteague Police officer walked over to Jackson and Bear, a couple of papers in his hand. He introduced himself as Officer Andy Birch. He had a baby face with a buzz cut and green eyes.

"I'm sorry about your guide," Birch said to Jackson and Bear. "Did you know him well?"

"We'd spent the last couple days together," Jackson answered. "That's about it."

"Well, my condolences, anyway."

Jackson gave a slight nod. "What exactly happened?"

"They said he was found flipped over his boat in the water. He was apparently pinned between the boat slip and the blind. They're calling it an accidental drowning for now."

Bear's brow furrowed. "How does that even happen?"

Officer Birch shrugged. "Can't say for certain, but this sort of thing occurs from time to time, terrible as it is."

Jackson and Bear didn't say anything.

Officer Birch handed them one of the sheets of paper. "Here's a copy of the incident number and case number in case you need it for any reason. My card is also clipped to the top there."

Jackson took the paper and looked it over. "You said they're calling it an accidental drowning *for now*. What does that mean?"

"That's what the Marine Police concluded from their initial investigation. The Medical Examiner's office will likely conduct an autopsy. If they find reason to change the cause of death, they will."

Jackson gave a slight nod. "Alright, thanks."

Officer Birch shook Jackson's hand before turning and leaving. Jackson and Bear watched the young officer rejoin the cluster of first responders huddled across the parking lot.

"I know that edge in your voice," Bear said. "You're not buying that story."

"I'm thinking we spent most of the last forty-eight hours with the man, and he seemed like a very capable waterman. Not the type to accidentally fall and drown."

Bear kicked at a pebble on the ground. "Shit happens, you know? To good folks, just the same as bad ones. You yourself are proof of that."

"And sometimes things aren't the way they first seem." Jackson turned and met Bear's eyes. "I'm proof of that, too."

Bear cocked his head to the side, conceding his point. "So, then, what do you want to do? I'm guessing you don't want to find another way to go out hunting today."

Jackson checked his watch. It was almost one. "No, today's shot. Let's go back to the house and drop our gear off."

Bear closed the back of his Suburban before they both climbed into the front. As Bear fired up the SUV and backed out, Jackson spotted another boat coming into the harbor. It was a Coast Guard boat with a rounded red hull and a silver cabin in the middle of it. Behind it, in tow, was Captain Terry's Carolina Skiff.

"You want to grab some food on the way back?" Bear asked.

"Sure," Jackson said. But he'd barely heard Bear. His head was miles away, out at that duck blind they'd spent the past two days in. The one where Captain Terry had been found dead. A singular nagging question pinballed around in his head.

What the hell happened out there?

FOUR

JACKSON AND BEAR spent the rest of the day doing very little at the house they'd rented, a two-story cream-colored stilt house tucked away amongst the winding gravel roads and towering pines on the north end of the island. Out back, a long boardwalk passed over swampy marshlands and out to a dock on Chincoteague Bay, giving a stunning view of the landscape beyond the house.

Jackson, unusually quiet even for him, spent the afternoon alternating between burying himself behind his laptop and going out for runs. Bear processed everything that had happened in a different way. On the couch, his feet up on the coffee table, with a beer in his meaty mitt as he watched the talk shows on ESPN.

When evening came, Bear cooked them some steaks and baked potatoes. The inside of the house looked like it'd last been decorated in the 90s. The kitchen was all light-stained wood with white countertops and a matching bar. The dinner they shared at the dining table was the most time they'd spent in the same room since watching Captain Terry's body be carried away. Bear gave Jackson his thoughts on the ESPN commentators' hot takes. Jackson listened, quiet as ever. Bear wanted to broach the subject of what was on his friend's mind but also knew how Jackson operated. Behind that steely exterior, the gears were churning fast. The best thing he could do for his friend was to wait and see what the machine cranked out.

Bear awoke the next day and found Jackson gone again, giving the rental an eerie feeling as the last remnants of night were chased out of the sky across the bay. Bear ascended the stairs from the bedrooms to the kitchen and living space on the second floor and brewed a pot of coffee. When the machine had finished, he poured himself a mug and stepped out to the elevated gazebo just off the house. Octagonal in shape, it was a freestanding structure connected to the second floor of the house by a short walkway.

The gazebo reminded Bear of a World-War-II-era watchtower. He liked that. A table and deck chairs had been set up inside. Bear took a seat and spun around to face the rear of the property before settling in.

He took a sip of his coffee. Steam wafted off the top in the brisk fall morning. Behind him, he heard a car pull up on the crushed shell driveway. *Jacky boy is back.* The sound of a car door closing cut through the air, followed a moment later by footsteps up the front stairs. Shortly after, the door to the gazebo opened and Jackson joined Bear on the porch, a plastic shopping bag in hand.

"Figured you'd gone for another run," Bear said without looking over at him.

"Different kind of run," Jackson replied. He dropped the bag onto the table.

Bear looked over at it. "What'd you get?"

"Local newspaper." Jackson fetched it out of the bag and tossed it to Bear. "I wanted to see if they had any info about Captain Terry that the online outlets didn't."

Bear studied the front page of the newspaper. It had a large photo of Captain Terry's boat being towed into the harbor. Next to it was a headshot of the man, flashing a bashful smile. Bear skimmed over the article.

"Anything?" he asked.

"Not really, no," Jackson said. He pulled a chair out from the table and moved it next to Bear before sitting down.

Bear looked over at Jackson's fingers tapping impatiently on the armrest. "We're not letting this go, are we?"

Jackson met his gaze. "You're telling me him drowning feels right to you?"

Bear took another sip of his coffee and pondered the question. "I don't know. On the one hand, you're right. Captain Terry seemed to be able to hold his own. But even experienced folks make mistakes. You make the wrong one at the wrong time ..." Bear shook his head. "That's it for ya."

Jackson shook his head. "It still doesn't add up to me."

Bear knew this side of Jackson, the part that couldn't let the feeling of something being wrong go. It's how he had met the man. Truthfully, it's what he loved about the man, and Jackson had fought for strangers as much as those he cared about. That Bear was more skeptical about a malicious cause behind Captain Terry's death was beside the point. If Jackson wanted – *needed* – to see this through, Bear would have his six. "Okay, so what do you want to do?"

Jackson gazed out at the marsh. "I want to go down to the police department. This morning. They must have a detective or someone assigned to the case by now, or maybe someone assigned from the State Police."

"State Police?" Bear raised an eyebrow. "You thinkin' of callin' lady cop?"

"Special Agent Bailey?" Jackson shook his head again. "No, not yet. Let's get down to the local station and see if anything's changed. Then we'll decide how to play it." He sprang out of the chair and snatched the newspaper out of Bear's hands. "Grab a shower and get ready. We leave in twenty." He opened the screen door to the gazebo and headed for the kitchen.

"Can I finish my coffee at least?"

"Do what you've got to do, but we leave in twenty."

"That's not enough time!"

"I'll buy you a fresh cup on the way. And breakfast."

Bear groaned and rocked himself out of the chair begrudgingly. "This was supposed to be a damn vacation."

———

DESPITE IT BEING Bear's SUV, Jackson insisted on driving. As they headed out, Jackson scanned the radio channels for any local news. One anchor was talking about what to expect at the upcoming Oyster Festival before the program switched over to the weather. A tropical storm, Margaret, had formed off the coast of Florida, just east of the Bahamas, and computer models were forecasting it to come up the eastern seaboard. No mention of Captain Terry, his death, or the incident yesterday.

The Chincoteague Police Department occupied a single-story building off Deep Hole Road, about a half mile from the main business strip on Maddox Boulevard. Its metal siding was painted parchment yellow, and the roof hunter green. Jackson, with Bear in tow, walked through its double glass doors just after nine. Jackson explained who he was and asked to speak with whomever had been assigned Captain Terry's case. Minutes later, a man in a suit came to the front and greeted them.

"Investigator Joshua Bowden," he said by way of an introduction.

Investigator Bowden was of average build but looked stockier due to his chubby face. He was clean-shaven, and his dark brown hair, cut short, matched his eyes. Jackson figured him to be in his late thirties.

"Jackson Clay," Jackson said.

"Bear," Bear said.

Bowden's eyebrows scrunched together at Bear's single-name introduction, but when Bear gave him nothing more, he turned and led them back to his office. He gestured for Jackson and Bear to step in, then closed the wood-paneled door behind him.

The office was unremarkable in every sense of the word. Thin carpeting spread out to beige walls adorned with the occasional award or reference information for the town of Chincoteague. A desk bisected the space with two armchairs on one side and a computer chair on the other, all of which looked like it could've been ordered from a catalogue called *Acme Office Furniture*.

Jackson and Bear sat down in the two armchairs as Bowden eased into the computer chair opposite them.

"So, what can I do for the two of you?" Bowden asked.

"We wanted to know if there'd been any updates on Captain Terry's case," Jackson said.

Bowden raised an eyebrow. "From when you were kicked free from the scene less than twenty-four hours ago? No. That is, unless you all have some new information."

"We don't. I take it that means you're still treating it as an accident then."

Bowden folded his hands and placed his elbows on the table. "I know this can be tough to accept, that you want some sort of bigger explanation for what happened. But there's simply no evidence of that."

"No evidence *yet*, you mean."

"I don't know what evidence you think will come to light, Mr. Clay."

Jackson's eye twitched. "My understanding is you're waiting to hear back on the autopsy from the medical examiner."

"We are, but we looked at everything ourselves. There's nothing to suggest foul play. If you're banking on something like poison coming up in his system, I'd say that's a possibility, but I don't see it. By all accounts, Mr. Yarbrough was a beloved member of our maritime community. There's no motive for someone to do such a thing."

"You have to admit it doesn't add up, though. Captain Terry wasn't some tourist on a joyride. He grew up on the waters here. Worked his whole professional life on them. To simply fall over and drown doesn't make sense."

Bowden turned his palms out in front of him. "Maritime accidents happen all the time and not just to the ignorant or inexperienced. Just the same way good drivers get in car accidents, good watermen have accidents, too. It's a tragedy, sure, but that doesn't make it any less true."

Jackson shook his head but didn't say anything.

"Look, you seem like a smart guy. Do you want to know what the numbers say? The sheer odds of what you're insinuating? We average less than one criminal death a year. Statistically speaking, we are one of the safest towns in the state, and that includes during tourist season when everybody comes in. The last criminal death we had here was two years ago, and that was a DUI down on Main Street. The last time something like you're talking about? I'd have to look it up, and I've been the investigator here for a decade."

"One might say you all are due then."

Bowden shook his head. "That's an awfully cynical take."

"What about the duck blind? Are Bear and I free to go out to it, or do you have it taped off?"

Bowden shrugged. "Again, we have no reason to suspect a crime occurred there. Why would we tape it off? It was his blind though, and I guess by extension his wife's, so you all might want to do the right thing and ask for permission before messing around with other people's things."

There came a knock at the door, and it opened. Officer Birch leaned in. He looked surprised for a moment to see Jackson and Bear there before he refocused his attention on Investigator Bowden.

"Chief Diaz is asking for you," he said.

Bowden nodded. "Alright, thanks." He looked back at Jackson. "As you heard, I've got to run." Bowden pulled a business card out of the breast pocket of his suit and handed it to Jackson. "If you all have any more information, please reach out."

Jackson stood and took the card. "Thank you for talking with us."

"No problem. And I'm sorry for your loss, truly."

Bear rose as well, and the two filed out of Bowden's office and left the police headquarters. As they walked to Bear's Suburban in the parking lot, Jackson studied Bowden's card.

"What do ya think?" Bear asked.

"I want to go look at the blind," Jackson said. "But Bowden's right. We should ask for permission first."

Bear scratched at his head. "I don't know, Jacky Boy. The woman's husband just died. Is it right, you know, going over there and troubling her with all this?"

Jackson turned back and met Bear's eyes. "Trouble her with how her husband might've died?"

Bear held his hands up. "She must be going through a lot right now is all I'm saying. I'd hate to add to it."

"If you're wife died and someone thought they knew something about it, wouldn't you want to know?"

Bear didn't say anything.

"I'm not going to go over there to make things harder for her, Bear. But if the police and everyone are wrong on this, I imagine she'd want to know." Jackson got to the driver's door and hopped in.

Bear sighed. "I hope you're right about this, Jacky Boy."

———

THE YARBROUGHS LIVED IN A QUAINT, two-story cottage on East Side Road, across the street from marshlands, with sweeping views of Assateague Channel and the Assateague Lighthouse. White wooden siding ran up to the red metal roof and matched the white picket fence that traced the edge of the property. Beside it, a gravel driveway ran up to a detached garage, also white, tucked away behind the house. When Jackson and Bear arrived, a navy blue and yellow bow was tied to the fence post nearest the driveway. Nestled below the bow's knot was a photo of Captain Terry.

On the drive over, Jackson visited the same drugstore he'd stopped at earlier in the morning to buy a newspaper. This time he'd bought a small bouquet of geraniums. He now cradled the bouquet in his arm as he and Bear walked up to the house.

The Yarbroughs had a screened-in front door. The inside door was open, allowing Jackson and Bear to see inside. Jackson mounted the couple of steps and knocked. A moment later, a woman appeared. She looked to be about Captain Terry's age, with sun-kissed skin that was practically the same shade as her strawberry blonde hair. She was wearing white Bermuda shorts, a blue hoodie, and sandals. Seeing them, the woman came to the screen door and opened it.

"Hello," she greeted.

"Hello, ma'am," Jackson said. "Are you Mrs. Yarbrough?"

"That's right."

"My name is Jackson Clay, and this is Bear. We were the men your husband had been taking around the island the last couple of days. We're so very sorry for what happened, ma'am."

"Please, call me Susan." Susan opened the door and stepped back with a familiarity that said she'd done it a dozen times in the last day or so. "Come in, won't you?"

Jackson nodded and removed his ball cap as he stepped in. Bear smiled, following behind him. The two of them entered a living room filled with sunlight from windows that faced south and east. With the interior painted white, the room practically glowed in the midday sunshine.

"Would you guys like something to drink? Coffee? Water?" Susan asked.

"No, thank you," Jackson said. "We really don't want to impose on you."

"It's no imposition at all. I used to love fixing Terry his thermos of coffee in the morning. He'd gotten up so early yesterday I wasn't able to. And now, this morning..." Susan's voice drifted off before she shook her head, bringing her back to the here and now. "I'm sorry. Please, have a seat."

Susan gestured to a papaya-colored sofa and matching loveseat.

Jackson sat down on the end of the sofa as Bear filled in more than his fair share of the loveseat. Susan eased into a navy-blue armchair facing them across a wooden coffee table.

"We saw the ribbon out on the fence," Jackson said. "It's very nice."

Susan nodded. "Some of the boys from the football team at the high school put that together. Terry would help out coaching every once in a while. They wanted to do a black bow and drape the fence in ribbon." She shuddered. "I thought that was too morbid. Blue and gold are the team's colors. I think Terry would've liked that."

"That was mighty fine of them," Bear said.

Jackson, still holding onto the bouquet, leaned forward and offered it to Susan. "These are for you."

Susan smiled politely. "Thank you. This is very sweet of you."

"It's the least we could do." He sat back on the sofa. "We just wanted to come offer our condolences. We had only recently met Captain Terry, but he seemed like a great guy."

Susan held her smile, but her lips trembled as she swiped at the corner of her eye. "I'm just going to put these in water real quick." Susan stood, stepped into the kitchen, and began running the faucet. She tilted her head and talked loudly. "Terry was a wonderful man. I'll miss him dearly." She shut the faucet off and came back into the living room with two cups of water, placing one in front of Jackson and then Bear before returning to her seat.

Jackson smiled in thanks but didn't drink the water. "How long were you two married?"

"Thirty-nine years. It would've been forty next month."

"That's a hell of a thing," Bear said. "Not that you didn't make forty. I mean..."

Jackson shot him a look.

Susan gave them a soft smile. "It's okay. I know what you meant and thank you. Between dating and marriage, we had more than forty wonderful years together, and I'm grateful for that."

Jackson looked around them. "This is a beautiful home you two made." He eyed an iron spiral staircase off the hallway. "That's quite the staircase. Did you all put it in yourself?"

Susan looked back at it. "No, it came with the house." She turned back to them and laughed. "Terry hated it from day one. The primary bedroom is supposed to be upstairs, but Terry insisted we sleep in the bedroom down here just so he could avoid the thing. If and when he needed to go up there, he'd take the stairs off the back deck outside. I turned the room up there into an art studio. I paint oyster shells and sell them at local shops and special events around town. I was supposed to do the Oyster Festival later this week, but I don't know anymore."

Jackson and Bear nodded solemnly and a silence fell over the room. When he couldn't think of anything else to say, Jackson leaned forward, putting his elbows on his knees.

"It must be the last thing on your mind right now, but Bear and I wanted to go back out to the duck blind where we'd been going the last couple days. We didn't want to do anything without your blessing, though," Jackson said.

Susan shook her head as if it were silly of her not to think of it. "Yes, I guess those blinds he's built up and down the channel are my responsibility now." She looked down as if another weight had been placed on her shoulders. "Please, by all means, you guys continue hunting. I think Terry mentioned he had you on the calendar for a few more days."

"No, we would never continue in light of what's happened."

Susan looked up. Her eyes moved between Jackson and Bear. "Then why do you want to go back out there? Did you leave something?"

Jackson looked at Bear before coming back to Susan. "We just wanted to see for ourselves, to try and understand what happened."

"The police said what happened. He accidentally fell and drowned."

"I know." Jackson shifted, uncomfortable in his seat. "We just want to see for ourselves. Call it closure, I guess."

Jackson watched as the confusion on Susan's face shifted to understanding and then worry. She scooted forward in the armchair and wrapped her arms around her midsection.

"Do you think the police are wrong?" Susan asked, her voice lowered as if they were sharing a secret.

Jackson gave a single shake of his head. "Like I said, I just want to understand for myself. Captain Terry struck me as very capable. For him to fall and drown… I don't know… I'm trying to understand."

"Do you have reason to think it wasn't an accident, ma'am?" Bear asked.

Susan gave a dismissive wave. "What did I tell you about that ma'am business? And, no, I don't have any reason to doubt that it was an accident." She looked at Jackson. "But you're not wrong, either. He'd spent his whole life on the water. My first thought when the officers came to me was that it didn't sound like him."

"So, you wouldn't mind us going out there?" Jackson asked. "Taking a look?"

Susan shook her head. "No, of course not."

Jackson cleared his throat. "Then, I hate to ask on top of that, but we don't have our own ride out there."

It took Susan a moment to understand, but when she did, she sprang up from the armchair, energized with purpose. "Yes! Please take one of Terry's—*my*—boats. We have one on a trailer in the garage." Susan went into the kitchen.

Jackson raised his voice so she could hear him. "Actually, we saw them bring the boat Terry went out on yesterday back to the harbor. If it's all the same with you, we'd like to just use that."

Susan came back to the doorframe between the kitchen and the dining room, poking her head out to look at him over on the sofa. "Yes, that's right. They brought me the key yesterday. Hold on, I put it in here somewhere."

She disappeared back into the kitchen. Jackson and Bear could hear drawers open and close erratically, utensils and gadgets clinking around. Finally, with one last drawer closing, Susan came back into the living room, key in hand. A red and white fishing bobber attached to it. She held it out and offered it to Jackson along with a Post-it note.

"Thank you," Jackson said, taking both. He studied the note.

"That's my cell number," Susan explained. "If the police or the harbormaster or anyone hassles you about using Terry's boat, you give me a call and have them talk to me."

Jackson smiled and nodded. "Thank you, I'll do that."

Both he and Bear rose to leave.

"Just promise me one thing," Susan added.

"Sure, anything," Jackson said.

"If you learn anything, you tell me. Whether I want to hear it or not."

Jackson nodded, a serious expression on his face. "I promise."

FIVE

BY THE TIME Jackson and Bear got down to the harbor, got the boat ready to go, and took it up the Assateague Channel back to Will's Creek, the sun hung low in the sky over Chincoteague. Jackson, behind the wheel, eased the boat into the quiet inlet. Seeing the blind after everything that had happened since they were last here gave him an eerie feeling.

Jackson circled the blind once from the outside, looking it over. Nothing seemed different about it. When they came back around to the open end of the boat slip, Jackson guided the boat in and killed the engine. Bear went over to the ladder and observed it.

"He replaced the boards just as he said he was going to," Bear pointed out. "Missed the last one up top, though."

"Did he miss it, or is that when it happened?" Jackson asked.

Bear looked around the inside of the boat, seeing the hardware and tools still in it. "Well, let's MythBusters it. They say it was an accident. So, he's over here replacing the ladder rungs. He had to be working from inside the boat. You couldn't really do it leaning down from atop the platform."

"So, what?" Jackson asked. "He loses his balance, falls back toward the front here and then on over into the water?" He gave a slight shrug. "I don't know." He came to the front lip of the boat and stepped up to it, standing next to Bear in his waders.

"What are you doing?" Bear asked.

"Falling in."

Jackson placed one foot in the tiny gap between the boat and the blind's wall, then let the other slip off. In a split second, Jackson's bottom half disappeared below. The sudden commotion rocked the boat and Bear grabbed one of the freshly replaced ladder rungs to brace himself. Standing in waist-high water with the front of the boat up to his shoulders, Jackson peered over the bow at Bear.

"Well, you're in," Bear said. "There's only one problem. They said Captain Terry was found upside down like he'd tumbled over. You fell in the wrong way."

"It doesn't matter," Jackson replied. "Look. The boat gave way, allowing room for me. I even have a little space. Captain Terry is bigger than me, which means his weight going over would've been even more force pushing the boat back. It wouldn't have pinned him."

"Maybe him falling over caused it to shift in an odd way? Like wedging the back of the boat against one of the front posts of the slip or something? That'd stop the boat from giving way like it just did."

"Then why'd no one mention the boat was stuck like that?"

Bear shook his head. "I don't know. You're the one with law enforcement connections. Aren't they always holding back information and stuff?"

"If they think a crime was committed, maybe. But they're convinced this was an accident."

Bear scanned their immediate surroundings again. His eyes landed on the steering column of the boat. "Maybe Captain Terry had the throttle slightly forward while he worked? Pushing the boat into the slip to hold it in place?"

Jackson gripped the front of the boat and thrust himself up into it. He swung his feet over and sat on the side of the boat opposite

Bear. "Seems pretty unsafe. Every time he brought the boat in here, first thing he did was kill the engine. There's no reason he wouldn't have done the same yesterday morning."

Bear raised an eyebrow. "That we know of."

"So, you think they're right? It was an accident?" Jackson met his eyes.

Bear paused a beat. "I think the only person who will ever know for sure what happened out here yesterday is Captain Terry and the big man upstairs. And no amount of looking at this thing is going to change that."

"Captain Terry, the big man upstairs, and whoever else may have been here."

Bear took a deep breath in and sighed. "Then, what? Someone came across Captain Terry all the way out here and decided on a whim to kill him?"

"Or maybe there was a mishap and they panicked. Or maybe... any one of a dozen other things."

Bear shook his head again. "All I'm saying is you're out here chasing shadows. I don't know what you're expecting to find."

"That's the thing about shadows, though. There's someone behind them."

———

WHEN JACKSON and Bear got back to the harbor, Bert's fishing trawler was once again moored to the dock opposite the slip for Captain Terry's boat. His crew looked to be wrapping things up for the day. Bert, standing on the bow of the trawler, did a double take as Jackson and Bear came in. As they got closer, Jackson saw Bert glancing back and forth between Bear and him before his shoulders dropped. He came around the side of the trawler and stepped onto the dock as Jackson and Bear pulled in.

"I saw Captain Terry's boat out on the water," he said. "For a moment there, I thought maybe everything I'd heard wasn't true. Just some bad rumor."

Jackson fastened a line to one of the dock posts and shook his head. "Captain Terry is gone, I'm afraid."

Bert shook his head. "You all just carried on without him? Using his boat?"

"Of course not." Jackson stepped out onto the dock with a second line and slipped around a dock post. "We went to see Mrs. Yarbrough and asked for permission to take the boat out to the blind where they found Captain Terry."

Bert's eyebrows scrunched together. "What for?"

"To see for ourselves, I guess," Jackson said. "It seemed hard to think an accident like that could take him out."

"I know what you mean." Bert sighed. "I didn't want to believe it myself at first."

Jackson didn't respond. He looked back at Bear, who stared at him.

Bert stepped closer to them and lowered his voice. "You guys are thinking there's more to it than that."

Jackson turned back to him. "You tell me. You must have as many years out here as Captain Terry did. What do you make of the idea that Captain Terry drowned pinned between his own boat and duck blind?"

Bert crossed his arms and cocked his head to the side. "You do this long enough, you're bound to see things go sideways once in a while. I've seen people get hurt in ways you wouldn't believe." He paused. "But with Terry? Maybe, I don't know."

"It'd be helpful to confirm if he was out there alone," Jackson said. "Do you know if the harbor has any cameras?"

Bert shrugged. "There used to be a webcam livestreaming the harbor on its website, but I'm not sure if it's still running. You'd have to check with the harbormaster."

"Thanks, I'll do that."

Bear exited the boat and joined the group on the dock. He looked at Jackson expectantly.

"Ready to roll?" he asked. "I'm hungry."

"Yeah, just one second," Jackson said. "I want to ask the harbormaster something real quick."

Jackson started up the dock to the parking lot. As he did, he turned back and waved at Bert. "Good seeing you again," he said.

Bert nodded. "You all be safe now." He turned back and helped his fresh-faced boat hand unload a couple of coolers from the trawler.

Jackson led Bear to the harbormaster's office. Gaines sat inside. When he saw Jackson, he rose from his desk and came over to him.

"Don't tell me you've got another missing friend, now," he said.

Jackson shook his head with a polite smile. "No, I wanted to know if the harbor had any CCTV cameras."

The man's eyes narrowed. "We do. Why?"

"I was hoping to take a look at their recordings. The last few days, if you have them."

"What for?"

"Captain Terry obviously departed from here the morning he died. I just want to review the video of it. Make sure there isn't anything the police might be missing."

The man's eyes became thin slits. "Police told me the whole thing was some kind of accident."

"Exactly. We just want to confirm that."

Gaines pursed his lips. "Don't know how video from the harbor's going to tell you anything about what happened out there at Will's Creek. You a cop yourself or something?"

Jackson shook his head. "Nope. Just a concerned citizen."

The man studied Jackson a beat longer. "Fine, you'll have to access it in my office. This way."

Bear grumbled. Jackson stepped even closer to the man and spoke in a hushed tone. "Actually, we were hoping maybe to get those video files to go. My friend is getting hangry."

Now it was the man who grumbled. "Fine. But if anyone catches you with these, I'll deny ever giving them to you."

"Deal," Jackson replied.

The man stepped back into the windowless rear office and reemerged a few minutes later with a thumb drive. He gave it to Jackson.

"I'm serious. I never gave you this."

"Understood."

SIX

JACKSON AND BEAR went back to their rental to get Jackson's laptop, then doubled back to the main drag of restaurants and shops on Maddox Boulevard for dinner. They settled on Captain Zack's Seafood, a casual eatery with a screened-in, open-air dining room to keep the infamous mosquito population at bay. What walls it did have were adorned with large televisions and nautical knick-knacks. Buoys hung from the exposed timber beams above, and the center bar had been built to resemble a deadrise boat. All in all, it was the kind of place in which Jimmy Buffett would've felt right at home.

The two of them perched on stools at a colorfully painted high-top table near the bar's bow, overlooking the parking lot. Jackson focused on his laptop, while Bear nursed a Sam Adams and bemoaned the fact that the place didn't have his beloved Miller High Life.

Jackson ran through the footage from the harbor's cameras from the previous morning, then ran through it again two more times. Each time, he saw the same thing. The harbor lay dormant when Captain Terry arrived in his pickup truck just before five. He spent about an hour prepping the boat and loading gear into it, then pulled out of the slip and motored out of the harbor. As Captain Terry and his boat disappeared out of view for the third time, Jackson groaned and rubbed his eyes.

"Maybe if you watch that screen long enough, Jimmy Hoffa and Bigfoot will appear," Bear quipped from across the table.

Jackson shot him a vexed look.

Their server, a round woman with curly, ruddy hair, came over and brought their food to them. "Okay, we have the mahi-mahi, blackened, with corn and green beans for our IT guy over here," she said.

Bear chortled.

The server shifted his way. "And we have the Waterman's Feast with fries and extra hush puppies for his friend."

Bear's face scrunched up. "Except no oysters."

"You know the island is famous for its oysters."

"Yeah? And I can go to a doc known for giving mammograms, doesn't mean I'm getting one."

The server looked at Bear's ample chest, then met his eyes with a scowl. "Mmhmm. Well, there's no substitutions."

"It's fine," Jackson interjected. "I'll have his oysters. Thank you."

The server shrugged and walked away. When she was gone, Jackson gave Bear another irritated look.

"What?" Bear asked innocently. "The hell use do I have for some sea snot in shells?"

Jackson reached over, took an oyster from Bear's plate, and shot it into his mouth before returning his attention to his laptop.

He played the video again.

Captain Terry's boat cruised out of frame just as it had three times before, and Jackson was just about to close out of the video altogether when a cluster of grainy pixels caught his eye. He backed the video up thirty seconds and played it once more. The pixels shifted unnaturally again. Something in the darkness out on the water beyond the harbor started to head for the Assateague Channel shortly after Captain Terry left the harbor. Jackson allowed the video to continue playing longer than he had previously. The pixels floated like a specter across the dark waters.

"I'll be damned," Jackson murmured.

Bear raised an eyebrow. "You got something?"

"Maybe." Jackson poked at his laptop and set the video back again. "A few minutes after Captain Terry heads out, something the size of a small boat moves in the darkness out on the water. It seems to wait for Captain Terry to leave the harbor, then follows him."

Bear shook his head. "There're only two sides to the island. Only two ways to go. Could be a coincidence."

"Or it could be something." Jackson hopped off his stool. "I'll be right back."

"Where are you going?"

"I need someone to clean this video up better than I can. I'm calling Bailey."

Jackson left and walked out the front door of the restaurant. He crossed the gravel parking lot to an array of picnic tables and sat on top of one, his feet on the bench. The sun had dipped below the pharmacy cattycorner to the intersection, leaving a tangerine sky in its wake. The occasional car hummed past Jackson on Deep Hole Road.

Jackson found Bailey's number and called it. Jen Bailey was a special agent with the Virginia State Police. She'd been the first to aid Jackson in his new life, helping those he'd seen slip through the cracks of society. She'd also recently been promoted to Special Agent-in-Charge of the Western Virginia Human Trafficking Task Force based out of Roanoke. More personally to Jackson, though, she was watching his recently adopted dog, Josie.

Bailey picked up on the second ring. "Clay."

"Evening," he greeted.

"I didn't expect to hear from you until you were on your way back."

"Just checking in. How's my pup?"

Bailey sighed into the phone. "Terrorizing the shit out of my cat. It'll be a minor miracle if one of them doesn't need a visit to the vet before you get back."

Jackson snorted. "You agreed to watch her. Happily, I might add."

"Well, she's wearing out her welcome."

An awkward silence fell between them.

"You're not the type to just 'check in'," Bailey finally said. "What's up?"

"I need your help with something."

Bailey yelled at someone four-legged, then came back to the phone. "You're supposed to be on vacation. What could you possibly need from me?"

"Our hunting guide was found dead yesterday morning."

Bailey paused. "Jesus Christ."

"Yeah."

"What happened?"

"They found him unresponsive at the duck blind we'd been hunting from the previous couple days." Jackson's eye twitched. "They're calling it an accident. Drowning."

"Let me guess, you're not buying it."

Jackson scratched his beard. "I was with the guy for the better part of two days. He was a skilled waterman. The way they're saying it happened reads like a Three Stooges act."

"Anyone out there seen with him?"

"No."

"Anyone with an obvious motive to hurt the man? He have a hefty life insurance policy or anything?"

Jackson shook his head. "I spoke with the wife. She seems genuinely upset. I haven't looked at that, but I imagine she'd be the beneficiary of anything. These are normal, kind people."

Bailey paused again. "I don't know, Clay. Sounds flimsy."

Jackson grunted. "Well, there's plenty of room on the skeptics' bandwagon over here, too."

"It might be worth listening to us, then."

Jackson shook his head once more. "I'm telling you, Bailey. It didn't happen the way they're saying it did. I don't know if there was some kind of accident with someone else or if someone killed the man, but I know in my gut he didn't just simply fall off his boat and drown."

"Okay. But I don't know what you want me to do. It's a local case. A local *accident*, according to authorities. There's no reason for State Police to get involved unless we're asked. And even then, it won't be me, obviously."

"I got video from the harbor. I need someone—"

Bailey sighed. "Of course you did."

"I need someone to analyze it better than I can. Minutes after our guide, Captain Terry, leaves the harbor, it looks like something out on the water turns to follow him. But the image is grainy. Cleaning it up is beyond me and my laptop."

"Clay..."

"I think Happyland bought me one or two favors."

Jackson was referring to an exclusive resort on the Virginia-West Virginia border. The locals had called it Happyland. Bailey brought Jackson in as a source to get inside the resort and aid their investigation into the resort's ties to human trafficking. Jackson, along with Bear, had been integral in shutting the place down.

"Well, it didn't take you very long to play that card," Bailey said.

"You left me no choice," Jackson replied. "Can I send you the video or not?"

"Fine. Send it over. I'll see if someone can take a look at it."

"And see what's in the databases on the accident. His name was Terry Yarbrough. The drowning happened off Assateague Island. Coast Guard and Virginia Marine Police responded."

"You give a mouse a cookie," Bailey muttered.

"And the body. It'll be going to the County ME for an official autopsy. See if you can get that, too."

Bailey hissed through her teeth. "Anything else, your highness?"

"That'll do for now."

"Always the charmer."

Jackson hung up. He hopped off the picnic table and returned to finish his dinner with Bear.

SEVEN

TAYLOR JENSEN WOKE up an hour before the alarm on her phone was set to go off at six-thirty. She made herself a cup of coffee with the Keurig machine in her hotel room, then stepped out onto its third-floor balcony. Still dark, the muggy morning clung to the remnants of yesterday's unseasonal heat. Today was supposed to be another hot one. All the more reason to get her run in early again.

Taylor didn't mind. She was naturally an early riser. There was something magical about being awake before most everyone else, like sneaking down early on Christmas morning to see what gifts the day would bring.

Across the street, the McDonald's hummed with life, the golden arches atop the tall sign beckoning anyone awake this early for McMuffins and coffee. A minivan pulled into the lot and a young boy skipped exuberantly toward the door of the restaurant. Taylor smiled.

Let's go take on the day with that kid's kind of energy!

She went back into her room, shed her pajamas, and pulled on a pair of black running tights and a pink sports bra. She stepped to the mirror and checked herself over as she pulled her long, blond hair back into a ponytail. Dropping to all fours, she got in a few quick yoga poses. Contorting her five-foot-six athletic frame, she straightened her arms and arched her back, coming up and looking again at her own reflection. Her deep blue eyes looked back at her, then narrowed as she grinned.

Time to rock and roll!

She popped up, put in her earbuds, and hit play on her phone. The White Stripes began thumping in her ears. Her grin widened.

Leaving her room, she rejoined the muggy world outside and jogged down the steps to the hotel lobby. Inside, the clerk at the desk, a young woman with purple hair, smiled and waved. Taylor waved back and headed out the main door. She jogged at an effortless pace across the parking lot, then stepped it up a notch as she turned east on Maddox Boulevard. Her hotel was just before the bridge over the Assateague Channel to the wildlife refuge on Assateague Island.

As Taylor crossed the bridge, she stepped up her pace to a full-on run. The White Stripes ceded the stage in her earbuds to Paramore, and Taylor ran in sync with the frenetic drums of Zac Farro. The road headed deeper into the island refuge before zigging southwest, then zagging back southeast. Rays of the rising sun shot in spurts through the tall loblolly pines as a herd of ponies grazed on the flat marshlands in the distance. The morning, humidity aside, was shaping up to be idyllic. Twenty-five minutes in, Taylor had already logged two and a half miles and was only just beginning.

The road hooked due east, heading out to the beach. Taylor came through the island's woodlands and out onto the thin isthmus that divided Swan Cove from Little Toms Cove when she became enshrouded in a thick bank of fog. She slowed to a jog and looked around her. She couldn't see more than ten or twenty feet in any direction. The road below her simply appeared from one direction before disappearing in the other. The world around her ceased to exist. Kendrick Lamar, in her ear, told her to be humble. The eerie setting didn't creep her out. In fact, just the opposite. She dug it.

Taylor sped up into a run and continued on toward the beach, taking on the world as it came to her twenty-foot pieces.

Three minutes later, she came to the traffic circle at the head of the parking lot. She rounded it and took the walkway over the small dunes out onto the beach. When she saw the shoreline, she turned left up the beach and even deeper into the fog.

EIGHT

USING the early morning darkness for cover, The Bull Shark prowled the beachhead. He'd taken his boat up into Janey's Creek on the western side of Assateague Island and slipped into a small estuary only accessible by boat at high tide. From there, he hiked his way through the sandy woodlands and out to the Wildlife Loop trail, where it linked up with a different trail, and followed that into the thick canopy of fog that enveloped the beach.

Even in perfect conditions, he'd be invisible. This early in the morning and nearly a mile from the parking lot further south, the area was deserted. Wild. His dominion. He hoped someone was foolish enough to wander into it.

The Bull Shark fancied the idea of finding his next victim on the beach. He'd read about how the species was most dangerous in murky waters. There they were hard to see coming until it was too late. The gray mist around him now brought a menacing, tooth-filled smile to his face. He stood in his murky waters. His hunting ground.

In the distance, over the noise from the leisurely waves rolling onto the shore, came the pounding of footsteps. Someone was running his way. He crouched low and unsheathed the twelve-inch hunting knife he had on his hip. Based on their approaching footsteps, the runner had a fast pace, increasing the chances that they wouldn't expect him. He would attack even before his victim knew he was there.

A dark apparition formed in the dreary gray void. A woman, slim and taller than average, running straight up the beach, feet from the surf. The Bull Shark launched. In one swift motion, he sprang forward and thrust the knife into the woman's side. She shrieked as she jerked sideways, causing the knife to cut even deeper into her. Pulling it out, he brought his arm back for another blow. The woman defensively threw her arms in front of her. He swung down, slicing them, then drove the blade into her leg. Again, the woman screamed in agony. She collapsed to the sand, the knife ripping out of her as The Bull Shark held it firmly in his grasp. She grabbed both her leg and her side as she looked up at her attacker.

"Please! Stop!"

The Bull Shark merely showed his teeth.

He stood over her, watching. With her one good leg, she tried to kick herself back and away from him. When her efforts proved futile, she flipped over and started crawling with her bloodied arms. The Bull Shark allowed her a few feet, then jabbed the knife into the hamstring of her uninjured leg. The woman cried out yet again, then began to sob into the sand in front of her.

"Why are you doing this?" she asked, her voice muffled by the sand.

He didn't give her an answer, simply walked around her, watching. A predatory animal playing with the fruits of its hunt. Killing the boat captain had sent surprisingly few ripples through the small town. It had failed to register as the grand act he'd hoped for. This time, The Bull Shark wouldn't leave any doubt.

The woman made it several more feet, crawling with just her hands. She was stronger than he thought. In a fair fight, she could probably even take him. But predators like him didn't fight fair. This wasn't a sporting match, this was nature. Survival of the fittest. Of the fiercest. And in nature, there were only beasts and the poor souls they preyed upon.

"Help!" the woman screamed.

It was time to end this. The Bull Shark came over to her, then dropped down, placing one knee on each of the young runner's outstretched arms. He grabbed the hair at her scalp and yanked her head back. A guttural moan bellowed out of her just before The Bull Shark plunged the knife sideways into the center of her neck, then thrust it forward until it came free.

He rose and walked calmly into the surf to rinse off his knife, his hands, his arms. When he was done, he slipped it back into its sheath and prowled back to the woman's body. The Bull Shark stood for a moment, admiring his work. A sandpiper wandered through the bloody trail behind the body and tracked tiny scarlet footprints up the beach. People would talk about this one. He imagined them conjuring up some monster. A Boogeyman. Some malevolent spirit so evil it couldn't possibly be human.

They had no idea The Bull Shark was one of them.

NINE

JACKSON AWOKE the next morning to find Bear on the couch in their rental's living room. He had the television on The Weather Channel. Jackson read the flashy chyron on the bottom of the screen.

TROPICAL STORM MARGARET NOW A HURRICANE, GAINING STRENGTH

The TV showed a reporter broadcasting live from a beach in Bermuda. She looked out of place in her Weather Channel windbreaker amidst the brilliant sunshine and cerulean waters, her presence foretelling the impending storm.

Bear looked over his shoulder at Jackson, standing at the top of the stairs, and pointed to the television. "Mornin'," he said. "Looks like this storm out in the ocean's gaining strength."

Jackson nodded at the television before heading for the kitchen. "Is it going to hit Bermuda? That why that reporter is out there?"

Bear grunted in the affirmative. "They say it's eventually going to hook back toward the US, maybe even Virginia."

Jackson didn't say anything. He had zero time or mental space for a storm five hundred miles away. He grabbed the pot of coffee in the kitchen and poured himself a cup, then eased into an armchair next to Bear. His eyes were on the television, but he didn't pay it any mind.

"I figured you'd be out on the deck you like so much," Jackson said.

"Ah, it's already too damn hot and humid to enjoy it," Bear griped. "I thought it could get muggy in Martinsville, but it's a whole other level of swamp ass out here."

Jackson went back to pretending to watch television.

Bear looked between him and it. "So... last full day here. What's the plan?"

Again, Jackson didn't say anything. Truthfully, he had a whole to-do list in his mind. But ever since Bear's skepticism over Captain Terry's death, even after they'd visited the duck blind, Jackson had become less enthusiastic about sharing how much it still occupied his mind.

"First, I want to go back to the pharmacy," Jackson said. "Grab another paper."

Bear raised an eyebrow. "I don't think the paper's going to have any more in it than it did yesterday."

"Maybe, maybe not." Jackson sipped his coffee. "There's only one way to know for sure."

Bear took a beat then rocked himself up from the sofa. "Well, I assume we're leaving sooner rather than later. I ain't going to be the one holding us up two days in a row."

———

TWENTY MINUTES LATER, Jackson and Bear pulled into the pharmacy. As Jackson climbed out from behind the wheel, he clocked a Chincoteague Police patrol car driving unusually fast down Maddox Boulevard. Bear watched him eyeing the police car.

"What is it?" Bear asked.

Jackson watched the patrol car until it disappeared from view. "Nothing," he replied.

They went into the pharmacy and fanned out. Jackson found his newspaper and flipped through it near the counter as Bear perused a shelf filled with knickknacks and souvenirs. When he returned to Jackson at the front of the store, he held a pirate flag that read 'Surrender Ye Booty'. Jackson looked at it before looking up at Bear.

Bear grinned and winked. "What?" he asked.

Jackson ignored him and went to the clerk to pay for his newspaper. Bear paid for his flag and the two of them headed out. As they left, Bear turned to Jackson.

"Anything in there?" he asked, referring to the paper.

"No," Jackson said flatly.

He went over to the driver's door and opened it as a fire truck, followed by another patrol car, hurried through the intersection, lights flashing and sirens wailing. They were headed in the same direction as the first patrol car. The parade had others on the street looking on as well.

Jackson glanced at Bear, who raised an eyebrow.

"Come on," Jackson said. "I want to see what's up."

The two of them hopped in Bear's Suburban and followed in the direction taken by the emergency vehicles. The patrol car raced past the McDonald's and headed over the bridge to Assateague Island where the cops were immediately waved through the entrance stations to the wildlife refuge. Jackson and Bear were forced to stop at the booths.

Jackson rolled down his window, and a young park employee waved at him.

"Good morning," she said, smiling.

"Morning," Jackson replied. "Just for the day, please."

"That will be ten dollars."

Jackson grabbed a credit card out of his wallet and handed it over to her. "Deal." He watched the rear end of the patrol car disappear around the bend up ahead. His finger tapped impatiently on the steering wheel. He nodded at the road in front of him. "Something going on down the road?"

The woman shrugged as she processed the payment. "Something out on the beach. You never know. They cut funding for lifeguards this year." She shook her head. "It's begging for disaster." She turned back to Jackson with his credit card and a paper receipt. "There you go. You need a park map?"

"Yes, please."

The woman handed him one. "Enjoy."

"Thanks." Jackson drove off. As he got back up to speed, he handed the map to Bear. "Figure out how we get to the beach."

Bear unfolded the pamphlet until it consumed his half of the front row. "This road goes out that way. You just stay on it."

Jackson did. The road cut right, then left through a mix of marshy grasslands and tall, thick woodlands before emptying out onto a thin strip of land surrounded by water. Sand dunes marked the beach up ahead. A cluster of emergency vehicles were parked just in front of them.

They crossed the tiny isthmus and pulled into a parking lot bedded with crushed seashells. Jackson found a parking spot just before the mess of first responders and pulled in.

He and Bear got out and climbed the stubby sand dune in front of their car. Farther up the shore, the police had the entire beach taped off. Jackson began hiking up the beach, Bear reluctantly following.

"I hate the goddamn sand," Bear grumbled.

"Hurry up," Jackson said, already several paces ahead.

"Not all of us are G.I. fuckin' Joe, Jacky Boy."

Jackson came up to the taped-off area. A nearby officer stepped toward him with his hand out. Jackson stopped at the tape, heeding the officer's warning. He took in the scene beyond. The beach was crowded with everyone from paramedics to firefighters to police officers and park rangers. Several canopy tents with blue tops had been erected at the center of them, with screens put up on the sides facing Jackson and the other onlookers that were amassing.

Bear, sucking wind, got to Jackson and leaned against him. "What's with the tents?"

"Something they don't want people to see," Jackson said. "A body, I'm guessing."

"A young girl," said a voice next to them.

Jackson looked to his left. An older man, scrawny with thinning gray hair and skin like tawny leather, kept his gaze focused out at the tent.

"Heard it on the police scanner this morning," he explained. "Some poor girl ended up sliced and diced like a damn bait fish." He shook his head. "Terrible. Just terrible."

A helicopter flew by low overhead, shaking the earth. Jackson watched it as it came up the coastline, then banked hard just past the scene on the beach to come back the other way. He recognized its bright red fuselage and enclosed tail rotor as one of the MH-65s that the Coast Guard used for Search and Rescue and Medevac Response.

Jackson looked over at Bear, who met his eyes.

"Still think I'm chasing shadows?" he asked.

PART TWO
THE REFUGE

"We don't live in some kind of crazy, accidental universe. Things happen according to certain laws, laws of nature." -Sharon Salzberg

TEN

IZZY SHAW STOOD on the beach, the scene splayed out before her so strange that a part of her questioned if she was dreaming. Fifty feet away lay the bloodied body of a young woman. The authorities had erected tents and screens to keep people from snapping and posting gruesome photos on social media or less scrupulous news platforms, but they did nothing to block her as she stood on the other side atop one of the small sand dunes.

It was early enough in the morning that Izzy wasn't completely uncomfortable in her Federal Wildlife Officer uniform, a tactical vest emblazoned with her Department of the Interior badge over a tan short-sleeve polo tucked into brown rip-stop pants. She'd taken her copper hair and tied it back in a tight bun that sat just below her Federal Wildlife Officer cap. The cap sat low on her head, blocking the rising sun, as she stared at the body of the dead woman on the beach. Who was she and what had she done to deserve this violent death? The two questions danced around each other like a double helix twisting through her mind. The honest answer was that the woman had done nothing to deserve this. No one could warrant such a death. And still, it had come to this poor woman all the same. Perhaps the real question was why?

FWO Thomas Bridger, Izzy's supervisor, joined her on the dune. Six-foot-four with a husky frame, he stood a whole foot taller than Izzy and nearly twice as wide.

Bridger tilted his cap up just enough to scratch his receding hairline. "This your first dead body?" he asked.

Izzy nodded. "On the job, anyway."

Bridger looked at her, an eyebrow raised.

Izzy met his eyes. "I just meant, I've seen friends and loved ones at wakes and funerals. Never anyone…"

"Murdered?"

"Yeah."

Bridger nodded. "Same for me. Awful thing. It looks like she went through a hellish ordeal."

Izzy scanned the throng of emergency responders before her. "Who takes the lead on something like this?"

"I imagine OLE will send a special agent out, possibly a team," Bridger said, referring to the Office of Law Enforcement within the U.S. Fish and Wildlife Service. "Maybe the National Park Service or FBI will assist. I don't know, honestly."

"Chincoteague Police?"

Bridger pursed his lips. "The town manages the refuge in tandem with us, so I guess it's not out of the question. This all may be above their pay grade, though, quite frankly."

"Do we know who she was yet?"

"A couple of girls at the Driftwood Motor Lodge apparently reported their friend missing. Said she usually went out for a run when she woke up but never returned this morning. The description they gave matches our victim, but we're still waiting for confirmation."

"Christ, a tourist?"

"Yup, it's going to be a real shit show when the news breaks. We've been asked to canvas the area for anyone who may have seen something." Bridger snorted. "This far up the beach? At the crack of dawn? I guess we're supposed to ask the damn seagulls."

Izzy shook her head. "We should still do it. Cover our bases." She started down the dune toward the beach.

"It's a fool's errand, Iz," Bridger called out as she walked away.

Izzy turned back to him. "Then I guess I'm a fool. Grab my truck. We'll rendezvous at the beach parking lot."

"I'm pretty sure I'm supposed to give the orders."

Izzy ignored him, continuing down the beach, weaving her way through emergency personnel. When she got to the tents, she stopped for a moment to look at the young woman up close. She wore running tights, a sports bra, and running shoes nicer than any pair Izzy had ever owned.

She thought about the girls who had reported their friend, a runner, missing. There was no way this wasn't her, which meant their world was about to be shattered into a thousand pieces. Izzy didn't know if anything could put those pieces back together, but closure might help. If Izzy could, she wanted to play a role in giving them that.

She approached a group of onlookers clustered at the yellow police tape that Chincoteague Police had stretched across the beach.

When Izzy got to them, she began asking questions.

———

JACKSON AND BEAR stood on the threshold of the police tape for another half hour. The man who told them he heard about the grizzly scene over the police scanner also stayed. Hank Willis, as he'd introduced himself, lived in a modular home off Ridge Road. He was talkative and all too eager to offer up his life's story, as well as his many opinions about various things around town. Most notably, he couldn't stand the "yuppie shops that've popped up everywhere" and remembered when "NASA, not billionaires" sent up rockets from the nearby Wallops Island Flight Facility. He was also keen to give them his theory of what had happened to the dead woman.

"Drugs, most likely," he said. "To get done like that, she pissed someone off, someone that wanted to send a message. Drug dealers do that. I see it all the time on TV."

Jackson listened to the man's baseless thoughts with a curt smile. "This sort of thing happen here a lot?"

"No, no. I'm just saying... that's what you see. No, this island is damn near allergic to violent crime. Hell, I can't think of another killing here since the Hanz boy." Hank shrugged. "I've left my door unlocked every night for thirty years, never thought twice about it."

Jackson wasn't sure if the man's insight was based in fact or simple conjecture, so he let it go. A Federal Wildlife Officer wandered over to the crowd they'd become part of and began asking if anyone had seen anything. Jackson read the last name embroidered on her vest. Shaw. When she asked him the same question as everyone else, Jackson explained that he and Bear had only come over out of curiosity and hadn't been in the refuge earlier in the morning. The officer noted their statements and handed them a business card.

"If you think of anything else, please reach out," she said.

Jackson nodded and filed the card away in his back pocket. He turned with Bear in tow and headed back to Bear's Suburban. Behind them, Hank laid out to the officer the vicious narcotics-driven retribution murder that almost certainly hadn't happened. As Jackson and Bear walked away, Jackson did catch that Hank had heard the name of a young woman reported missing from a nearby hotel, Taylor Jensen.

It was almost ten now, and the seashore was filling up with beachgoers. Most seemed to ignore the scene unfolding just up the beach from them, but Jackson saw a few throwing wary glances in that direction.

He and Bear made it back to the parking lot when a gray SUV with dog dish hubcaps that screamed "law enforcement" pulled up behind the mess of emergency vehicles. Investigator Bowden exited and stared curiously at them. Jackson walked over to him. Bear reluctantly followed.

"Morning," Jackson said. "You catch the case?"

"It's federal land, I'm only here to assist," Bowden said. "What are you guys doing here?"

"We were out on a hike. Just made our way back when we stumbled across the action."

Bowden shook his head. "I see. Well, if you'll excuse me…"

He moved to step around them but Jackson mirrored him.

"That girl out there makes two dead in three days," Jackson said. "You mentioned the odds of things happening when we met yesterday morning. You tell me, what are the odds of that sort of thing happening in a place where, as you put it, you couldn't remember the last criminal death there'd been?"

Bowden flashed a grin, his eyebrows raising. "You can't possibly be implying this has anything to do with Terry Yarbrough's accident."

Jackson was stone-faced. "You tell me. I'm just asking questions."

Bowden held an open hand in front of him. "Look, I get you want the guy's death to mean something. But you strike me as a smart guy. So, what's the angle here?"

"Like I said, I'm just asking questions."

"If you have anything *material* to add to the investigation, please reach out. Otherwise, I have work to do." Bowden shook his head again, stepping around him.

This time Jackson let him walk by. He watched the man as he walked away, then continued to Bear's Suburban. Bear hurried to catch up to him.

"Do you really think this is connected to Captain Terry?" he asked.

"I think exactly what I said," Jackson replied. "That's two bodies in three days. And I'm not one to believe in coincidences."

"What could Captain Terry possibly have to do with some girl found stabbed to death on the beach?"

"I don't know," Jackson said. "But I'm going to find out."

Jackson climbed behind the wheel of the Suburban and called Bailey as Bear climbed into the passenger seat. She picked up almost immediately.

"I don't have anything yet, Clay," she answered with an edge to her voice.

"Things have changed," Jackson said. "A young woman was found dead on the beach this morning on Assateague Island."

Jackson heard rustling on Bailey's end. "Jesus, really? Any connection to your boat captain?"

"That's what I need to find out."

Bailey sighed. "So, that's a no."

"It just happened. The woman's body isn't even off the beach yet."

"Still, it sounds flimsy. Don't waste your time going down rabbit hole after rabbit hole."

"It's my time to waste. I just need the files on the case. Assateague is federal land, which means it's got to be a federal agency that ends up investigating. You have some federal guys on that task force of yours, don't you?"

"I'll see what I can do, Clay. No promises."

Jackson hung up. He dropped the phone on the bench seat between them, tapping his fingers on the steering wheel as he thought.

"Penny for your thoughts, Jacky Boy?" Bear asked, looking over at him.

Jackson didn't say anything. He picked up his phone again and searched for Taylor Jensen. One of the first results was an Instagram account. Jackson opened it and tapped on the most recent photo. It showed ponies grazing on a wide swath of grassland with tall pine trees in the distance. As if he needed confirmation, the post was tagged with Chincoteague National Wildlife Refuge as the location.

He flipped to the next post, a video. When it started playing, Jackson's heart sank. He watched a montage of her running on what was clearly the road out to the beach.

He turned his phone so Bear could see the screen. "Did you hear Hank out there mention the missing girl, Taylor Jensen? This is an Instagram account with the same name. With a post from two days ago."

"Holy hell," Bear muttered. "I bet you dollars to donuts that's the girl out on the beach."

"I think so." He slipped the phone into his pocket and fired up the SUV.

"But what would she have to do with Captain Terry?"

Jackson cocked his head to the side. "I don't know. But I know who might."

———

WHEN JACKSON and Bear pulled into Susan Yarbrough's driveway, she was out front tending to a bed of flowers. Recognizing them immediately, she stood and waved. Jackson waved back as he climbed out of the SUV.

"We came to return your boat key," he said.

Susan brushed the dirt off her knees. "Oh, thank you."

Jackson came around the SUV and handed her the key. "Thank you again for letting us go out there."

"I was happy to." Susan put a hand over her eyes, blocking the sun. "Did you find anything?"

"Nothing definitive, I'm afraid."

Susan nodded. "Well, why don't you come in and tell me about it anyway. I made some fresh lemonade this morning."

"Sure, that'd be great."

Jackson and Bear followed her into the house where they took the same spots on the sofa and loveseat they had the day prior. Susan disappeared into the kitchen for a few minutes, then returned with three glasses of lemonade on a little wooden tray. Before sitting down opposite them, she moved a different tray of painted oyster shells onto the coffee table.

"Those are pretty," Jackson said. "New ones?"

"Yes, I decided to do the Oyster Festival after all. You all should come out tomorrow. It's not as big a deal as the pony-penning in the summer, but it's a good time."

Bear scrunched his face in disgust.

Jackson ignored him. "Today's our last day, actually."

Susan flashed a sad smile. "Ah. That's a shame." She paused. "So, the duck blind?"

Jackson reached for a lemonade and took a sip. "Like I said, nothing was definitive."

"But... there was enough that you still don't think it was an accident."

Jackson took a beat to choose his words carefully. "We tried some things and couldn't recreate the way the authorities are saying they think everything happened."

Susan's eyes were fixed on him. "You're saying the police have it wrong."

Jackson shook his head. "I'm simply saying that we weren't able to recreate it according to their theory. There are a number of reasons that could be."

"But one of those reasons would be that they're wrong."

"Yes, that's possible."

Susan's gaze drifted off into the distance. Jackson could see her mind churning. She rubbed her hands on her knees.

Jackson leaned forward. "I want to be clear. I'm not saying they are wrong."

Susan nodded. "But you have doubts."

"Some. Have you heard about what happened out on the beach in Assateague this morning?"

"No. What happened?"

"A young woman was found dead out there. Almost certainly

murdered."

Susan put a hand up to her mouth. "Oh my goodness. Did they say who she was?"

"We think her name was Taylor Jensen. Does that sound familiar to you?"

Susan thought for a moment, then shook her head.

"Any reason she might have known your husband? It sounds like she was visiting from out of town. Could Captain Terry have taken her on a boat tour or something?"

"I can check his logbooks in the garage, but the name doesn't ring a bell."

Jackson pulled his phone out of his pocket, thumbed it a couple of times, then held the screen up for Susan to see, showing her a picture of Taylor from her Instagram. "This is a picture of her from her Instagram. Do you recognize her?"

Susan took the phone and studied the picture closely before shaking her head. "I don't. Sorry."

Jackson filed his phone away. "Okay. Well, thank you for answering my questions."

"You say she was murdered out on the beach?"

"That's what it sounds like, yes."

"My gosh. That's awful. I can't even think of the last time something like that happened around here."

Jackson recalled what Hank had said. "We heard something about someone named Hanz?"

"Russell Hanz, yes." Susan shrugged. "I suppose if you believe he was killed."

Jackson rubbed at his beard and looked over at Bear, who was already halfway through his lemonade. "What do you mean?"

"Well, he disappeared. They never actually found him, dead *or* alive. It was a whole thing way back." Susan took a beat and thought. "Twenty, no, twenty-five years ago, actually. Gosh, how time flies."

"Was it also out on the beach?"

"No, nothing like that. It had to do with the Meachems. One of the big family names around here. They used to practically be Chincoteague royalty."

Jackson nodded. The conversation had petered out, and he couldn't think of anything else to ask, so he stood to leave. "Well, like I said. Thank you. For everything." He offered his hand. "And I'm sorry we couldn't get you all the answers you were hoping for."

Susan rose with him, taking Jackson's hand and shaking it. "Thank you for trying. Most people would think 'Oh, what a tragedy', and then move on with their lives. So I appreciate you caring about Terry."

Jackson gave her a solemn nod as Bear rocked out of his spot on the loveseat. As he and Jackson filed out of the room, he gave Susan the same gesture. She smiled in return.

Jackson and Bear got into the Suburban, fired it up, and backed out of Susan Yarbrough's driveway. As they did, they rounded the post with the blue and yellow ribbon memorializing Captain Terry. Someone had placed a toy shark on the fence post next to it.

ELEVEN

RETURNING TO THEIR RENTAL, Jackson spent the afternoon once more buried in his laptop. He knew anyone he tried to talk to in law enforcement would be tight-lipped this early on in the case, so he decided to focus his efforts on what he could find himself.

Taylor Jensen's social media showed her as a resident of Herndon, Virginia, just outside Washington, DC where she'd worked as a law clerk for the Fairfax County Government. She'd graduated from Virginia Tech the year before and had moved to the DC area with her boyfriend. Jackson was tempted to look into him but also knew that would be the first place investigators would go. He wanted to cover whatever they might turn a blind eye to.

A Google deep dive on Terry Yarbrough yielded no connections to any of those information points about Jensen. True to what the man had told Bear and him first-hand, real estate records showed him and his wife purchasing their current home in 1988, long before Taylor Jensen was born. The only social media account either he or Susan Yarbrough had was a Facebook page for their boat guide and tour business. The posts, mostly filled with photos of ponies or hunters holding up their bounty, were of little use to Jackson. As he clicked through them, he wracked his brain for every possible angle. Could Jensen have had family that went out on a tour or hunted with Captain Terry? He regretted not asking Susan Yarbrough to search her husband's logbooks for anyone with the last name Jensen, not just Taylor.

Jackson pinched the bridge of his nose, then got up from the table to stretch his legs. He paced around the main floor of the house, then leaned against the kitchen island next to the dining table and stared at his laptop. He replayed every conversation he'd had that day over in his mind, looking for another lead to pursue. Both Hank Willis and Susan Yarbrough had been familiar with the Russell Hanz case, one that, according to Susan, had happened a quarter century ago. Something about it must have been memorable, like finding a young woman from out of town stabbed to death on the refuge's beach. Jackson sat back down and decided to run with it.

Russell Hanz had disappeared in July of 1999. An article showed him in his high school football uniform. He'd had a sharp, clean-shaven jawline with black hair spiked up. He'd last been seen heading to the Meachem family property on the north end of the island. Apparently, the Meachems were one of the most well-known and wealthiest families on the island. The three siblings—two brothers and a sister—each lived with their families in their own houses on the shared property. Russell Hanz had apparently been dating Stephie Meachem, the daughter of Mark Meachem, one of the two brothers. When police tried to question any of the Meachems, they'd been stonewalled by a small team of lawyers. They'd eventually been able to secure a warrant to search the property for Hanz's missing Dodge Dakota pickup, but when it wasn't found, the investigation had stalled and the case went cold.

Jackson rubbed his eyes and sighed. Another path going nowhere. He opened up Google Maps, brought up the island, and plugged in the Meachems' address. True to the article, they were on the northernmost property on the island. About a mile further was Wildcat Point, the actual northernmost point of the island, and a mile beyond that was Will's Creek and the blind where Captain Terry was found dead.

The Meachem property being close to Captain Terry's blind was sort of interesting, but not exactly a smoking gun. Jackson thought about the boat he'd seen on the harbor CCTV. Perhaps the Meachems had cameras of their own. If he could get a hold of their recordings, he might be able to confirm the boat seen just beyond the harbor was, in fact, following Captain Terry. Any video might even have a better look at the boat.

Another quick Google search yielded no contact information for anyone with the last name Meachem, and it was too common a name to search through social media. Jackson stood and stretched again. This time he stepped to one of the large windows overlooking the marshes out back and Chincoteague Bay beyond. The sun teetered just above the tree-lined horizon on the mainland in the distance. Jackson spotted Bear's plump silhouette in a chair on the small dock over the marsh. The cooler beside him meant he wasn't empty-handed. A beer with the sunset sounded really good to Jackson in that moment, and he went out to join his friend.

As he came down the boardwalk, Bear glanced over his shoulder. He reached into the cooler, fetched a fresh beer, leveraged the cap on his wooden armrest, then slammed his fist down and popped the cap off. He offered the open beer to Jackson.

Jackson took it and took a seat on the cooler. "I wish you wouldn't do that," he said, nodding to the armrest. "One day it'll cost us a security deposit."

Bear chortled. When silence fell between them, he looked over at Jackson. "So, did you crack the case?"

Jackson took a sip of his beer. "Not so much."

"Well, we still got tonight and tomorrow morning if you want to do something." Bear looked back out at the bay.

"Yeah." Jackson paused. "I wanted to talk to you about that."

Bear grinned and shook his head.

Jackson looked at him. "What?"

"Jacky Boy, I know you like the top of my pecker."

Jackson winced at the crude metaphor. "And?"

"*And* I called the renter two hours ago. Asked if we could stay a few more days. He said he's got no renters 'till the holidays and to be his guest. Literally. For the same nightly price, of course." He took a swig of his beer and met Jackson's gaze. "I knew the second you called your cop lady friend you weren't going to let this go."

Jackson nodded his thanks. "If you've got to get back and mind the shop, it's all good. I can rent a car or…"

"You lose your hearing on one of your deployments back in the day? I said *we* are staying a few more days. I called Jake, that bean-pole of a kid I left in charge, and asked him if he could keep running things a little while longer."

Jackson gave the slightest of smiles.

Bear tilted his beer and looked down the mouth of the bottle. "This Hurricane Margaret could give us some trouble, though. I saw an update earlier when I was scrolling through my phone. They're expecting it to hit the eastern seaboard."

Jackson looked out at the setting sun. "We'll cross that bridge if and when we come to it."

Bear shook his head. "Poor choice of words out here on an island."

———

IZZY SHAW PULLED onto her slab concrete driveway just after seven. In the dusky twilight, her headlights illuminated her one-car garage in front of her. She killed the engine and let the world around her fall into a quiet darkness. She'd had some tough days at work, but never something like this. A park visitor brutally murdered.

After canvassing the beach for the better part of two hours, she drove over to the Driftwood Motor Lodge to speak with the girls who had reported their friend missing. She asked the two women to show her a picture of Taylor. When they did, Izzy felt herself go numb.

Through the dried blood and bruises, the resemblance was unmistakable. The same piercing blue eyes from the girl on the beach now looked at Izzy from her friend's phone.

Izzy opened the door to her service truck — a dark gray F-150 with the US Fish and Wildlife Service logo printed on the front doors and black bull bars installed over its front fender — and walked up the path to her house. She lived in a Colonial-style cottage on a cozy quarter-acre plot on the south end of Chincoteague.

Inside, stairs ran up to the second floor next to a hallway that went straight to the back of the house. In the hallway stood a coat rack and credenza with a gun safe bolted to the top of it. Izzy shed her vest and hung it on the coat rack before stepping to the safe to file away her service weapon—a .40-caliber Glock 22—and two spare magazines. When she was done, she went down the hall to the kitchen, where she pulled a bottle of vodka from the freezer and a rocks glass from the neighboring cabinet and poured herself two fingers. She cocked her head back, slammed back the shot, then poured a refill.

Slapping the little cork back into the bottle, she placed her hands on the kitchen counter and closed her eyes. Dead Taylor Jensen stared back at her, shock and fear forever frozen on her face. She took a slower, more deliberate sip of her vodka, allowing the burn to linger as she swallowed.

What kind of monster left you like that, Taylor?

Izzy was just about to polish off her second glass when her phone buzzed in her pocket. She pulled it out and looked at the screen. Bridger.

"Hey," she greeted. "What's up?"

"I didn't get a chance to catch up with you at the end of the day," Bridger said. "Just wanted to check in, make sure you're okay."

Izzy swirled the glass in front of her. "Yeah, I'm good. Just a hard day."

"Heard that. Well, I just got word NPS ISB is going to take the lead on this thing with the assistance of the FBI if needed. Chincoteague PD will consult, too." Bridger referred to the Investigative Services Branch of the National Park Service.

Izzy shook her head. "Why NPS?"

"They know hunting season is heating up and we're already spread thin as it is," Bridger said. "ISB is better equipped to handle something like this than we are."

Izzy hissed through her teeth. Bridger made them sound like school hall monitors. "So, what does that mean for us?"

"For the most part? Back to work like usual."

"Just pretending some poor woman wasn't stabbed to death in the refuge?"

"NPS runs the Maryland side of the island, Iz. You know that. It's just as much their backyard as it is ours. Besides, we're all on the same team here."

"Mhm." Izzy cocked her head back and finished her drink.

Bridger paused for a moment. "Are you sure you're okay?"

"Yeah, I'm fine. Like I said, long day and all."

"ISB taking the lead on this doesn't mean it's getting swept under the rug. Just the opposite, actually. Them coming in means this is being taken seriously."

Izzy rubbed her temples. "I know."

"Okay. Well, I'm supposed to tell you to have your reports ready for tomorrow. Whoever ISB is sending is supposed to arrive in the morning."

"Will do."

"Have a good night, Iz."

"You, too, Bridge."

Izzy hung up, uncorked the bottle of vodka, and poured herself a third glass. It was probably more than she should have, but she decided the news that the Jensen murder was being taken out of their hands warranted it.

She re-corked the bottle and put it back in the freezer, then took the glass upstairs with her to her bedroom. She traversed the mine-field of scattered clothes and set the glass down on her nightstand before changing into sweats and a T-shirt. Finally comfortable — or as comfortable as she'd get tonight — Izzy lay sideways on her bed and turned on the television across the room.

FOX21 Delmarva, named for the peninsula made up of parts of Delaware, Maryland, and Virginia, was running its evening news program and covering the discovery of Jensen's body. The show rolled B-roll footage of the scene taken from far back behind the perimeter Chincoteague PD had roped off. All you could really see were the two blue canopy tents with little first responder ants walking around them. Izzy guessed one of them was her.

"The victim was identified as twenty-three-year-old Taylor Jensen of Herndon, Virginia," the broadcaster said.

The screen image shifted to a photo of Jensen, practically glowing as she flashed a brilliant smile. She wore a black graduation gown with a maroon and orange stole around her neck. The newscaster explained that Jensen had graduated from Virginia Tech just a year ago.

Izzy took a sip of her drink, then rolled onto her back and closed her eyes. She tried to reconcile the happy, hopeful Taylor Jensen from the TV with the one she'd seen on the beach. Someone had taken her life in every sense of the word. She opened her eyes and stared at the ceiling. The glow from the television washed across the darkness like an electric blue ocean on a black beach. Lying on it was Taylor Jensen's body, staring back at her. Izzy asked herself the same question again.

What kind of monster left you like that, Taylor?

But Taylor Jensen didn't respond. She just stared down at Izzy, challenging her to find the answer.

TWELVE

JACKSON WAS UP BREWING a pot of coffee when Bailey called him the next morning.

"Any news?" he asked.

"Good morning to you, too," Bailey said. "And yeah, your dog now has my cat spraying all over my goddamn house."

Jackson grabbed a mug from the cupboard. "It's probably stressed."

"Well, that would make two of us then. What time are you going to be here?"

Jackson turned around and faced the interior of the house as if Bailey were standing there. He'd been so hyper-focused on everything going on, it hadn't occurred to him to let Bailey know they were planning to stay longer. "About that…"

"No!" Bailey said. "Don't you dare."

"Something's not right here, Bailey."

"You're not the police, Clay. There are investigators for that sort of thing."

"That's an interesting take, given our relationship."

Bailey huffed. "Isn't there a hurricane coming up the coast? You're not worried about that?"

"We'll worry about it if we need to. Right now I'm focused on Terry Yarbrough and Taylor Jensen."

Bailey didn't say anything.

"Our boat captain and the woman found on the beach."

"I know, Clay. I was thinking." She groaned. "Alright, I was going to tell you when you got here, but since that's apparently not happening, I was able to run down the autopsy on Yarbrough. Cause of death was drowning, as expected, but that wasn't all. His pelvis was fractured."

A chill coursed through him. "It'd be hard to fracture your pelvis just falling overboard."

"Hard, but not impossible. Especially considering he was older. There was bruising on his back near the fracture, as well, but it's pretty easy for bruising to occur."

"So the ME is also calling it an accident."

Bailey took a beat. "They've ruled it inconclusive. But, Clay, that doesn't mean..."

"I know. It doesn't mean homicide. But it also means there's evidence to suggest it wasn't an accident." The brewer finished percolating and Jackson poured himself a cup. "Anything on the boat on the CCTV?"

The sound of paper rustling came over the line. "Yeah. I was able to get some techs to clean it up for you. It's not enough to positively ID anyone, but it's more than you had before. It looks to be a single individual operating an outboard motor on a small craft. From the scale size of the operator, they put the boat at ten to twelve feet in length."

"Can you send me that image and information?"

"It's little more than a silhouette, Clay."

Jackson waited for her answer.

Bailey groaned again. "Fine."

"What about the Jensen girl?"

"I had some of my guys from the FBI make a couple of calls. The National Park Service's Investigative Branch will be running point on the investigation."

Jackson went over to his laptop on the dining room table where he'd been jotting things down on a notepad. He copied the information Bailey had given him. "Do you have a name?"

"I do not."

"Copy that. Anything else?"

"I think the words you are looking for are 'thank you', Clay."

"You know I appreciate it."

"It still wouldn't kill you to say it every once in a while. I take it this means I'm still on the hook for watching your dog?"

Jackson waited a moment, the guilt rising in his chest from how much he was asking of Bailey. "I can see if I can make other arrangements if she's becoming a problem."

Bailey let out a long sigh. "No, I guess I can watch her a little while longer. Just... don't make me regret this, okay?"

"I'll do my best. You'll send that info on the boat?"

"Uh huh."

Jackson ended the call. He finished jotting down what Bailey had told him as Bear came ambling up the stairs from his bedroom below. His beard was particularly disheveled even by his standards, and his hair was matted down on its left side.

Jackson didn't care. He said, "That..."

Bear grunted at him and held up a finger as he lumbered toward the coffeemaker, grabbing a mug from the sink as he went. He filled the mug, then downed half of it in three large gulps. He growled when he came up for air.

"I had a nightmare I was in a fishin' tournament out on the water here," Bear said.

Jackson looked at him, an eyebrow raised.

"I hate goddamn fishin'." Bear took another hearty gulp of coffee.

Jackson held his phone up. "That was Bailey. Captain Terry had a broken pelvis. The ME is ruling his death inconclusive."

Bear blinked twice. "That's something."

"It is. And what's more is we have a lead on our mysterious boater. I want to talk to Bowden this morning. I'll make some breakfast and we can roll out."

Bear growled again. "He's going to love this."

AS JACKSON PULLED onto the road for the police station, Bear riding shotgun, he spotted Bowden walking down the sidewalk from the parking lot. Jackson sped up to catch him, then slowed to a crawl as he pulled up alongside him and rolled down his window.

"Morning, Investigator," Jackson said.

Bowden gave him a cursory look as he walked. "That it is." He looked forward again. "You know, I had this dream that you left town and I had one less thing to worry about, but I guess that's all it was. A dream."

"Tell him about the fishing nightmare I had," Bear said from the passenger seat.

Jackson elbowed Bear back and leaned out the driver's window. "Terry Yarbrough had a broken pelvis. Seems pretty unlikely for a guy just falling out of a boat."

At that, Bowden stopped walking. He turned and stepped toward the SUV. "Who told you that?"

Jackson shrugged. "Call it a little birdy. But it's true, which means there's a pelvic-sized hole in your accident theory."

Bowden rubbed his eyes. "It doesn't mean anything. People break bones falling all the time."

"Tumbling out of a boat into water? We went out there ourselves and tried to recreate it. Even with me going over the side, a guy half Captain Terry's size, the boat gave way. It didn't come close to pinning me."

"So what's your theory? Someone went out there and killed Yarbrough? Just for the hell of it?"

"It's adding up a lot more than your theory is right now."

Bowden brushed back his suit coat and put his hands on his hips. He licked his lips. "What do you want then? For me to look into the case as a homicide?"

"That'd be a good start. You could also tell me about the Meachems."

Bowden's expression grew incredulous before he glared at the ground and muttered, "This day just keeps getting better and better." He met Jackson's gaze. "What *about* the Meachems? I suppose they killed Yarbrough?"

"I don't know. But I do know they're the last property on the north end of the island, closest to Will's Creek and the blind where Yarbrough was found."

Bowden shook his head. "Okay... and?"

Jackson pulled his phone out of his pocket, tapped at it, and showed the screen. "I have a lead on a boat that looks like it followed Captain Terry out of the harbor that morning. If I can prove it followed him all the way to the north end of the island, we may have a solid lead. From what I understand, the Meachems are a big deal, the kind of people likely to have security cameras of their own. Not only could any video they have prove this boat was tailing Captain Terry, it might also give us a better look at the person in that boat. I'm happy to go up there and ask myself, but it might be more persuasive coming from someone with your authority."

Bowden's eyes widened and his jaw went slack as he shook his head. "I'm not... your errand boy. And I'm definitely not opening up the can of worms that is the Meachem family."

"So that's a 'no'."

"Correct. No."

"Why not? If I'm wrong, it's a half-hour out of your day. Forty-five, tops. But if I'm right..."

"Because I have real casework to do. Real casework that doesn't involve escorting you around town to play Sherlock Holmes."

Bowden stepped away from the SUV and turned toward the door to the police station.

Jackson let Bowden get far enough away so he'd have to speak louder for Bowden to hear him. Loud enough that others outside would hear him as well.

"The Chincoteague Police Department wouldn't be protecting the Meachems, would they?"

Bowden stopped in his tracks, did a one-eighty, and stomped back to the SUV. "You really are a paranoid individual, aren't you?"

"I just know what people are capable of."

"There's no grand conspiracy here, Mr. Clay. Just real police working real cases. And I have way too much on my plate for you to be spouting any kind of nonsense about the Meachems." Bowden huffed. "That's the last thing this town needs."

Jackson didn't say anything more.

"Now, I don't care what you do. Go down to the movies on Main Street, go over and check out the Oyster Festival, or better yet, go home like I hoped you had. But whatever you do, you stay away from anything to do with the Yarbroughs or Taylor Jensen. And if you don't think I'll put you in handcuffs for obstruction, you'd be mistaken." He slapped the open window frame of the driver's door. "Now, you all have a good day."

With that, Bowden turned and walked away. Jackson and Bear stayed there, the SUV idling on the side of the road, and watched him disappear into the police station.

"Well, all in all, I think that went well," Bear said. He looked over at Jackson. "What do you want to do?"

An idea came to Jackson. He reached into his back pocket and fetched the business card he'd slipped in there.

ISABEL SHAW, FEDERAL WILDLIFE OFFICER

"There's more than one branch of law enforcement here that can help us," Jackson said.

He dialed the number on the card.

THIRTEEN

SHAW HAD AGREED to meet Jackson and Bear at the Oyster
Festival. The Festival was held at Tom's Cove Park, tucked away
where the Assateague Channel took a swooping slice out of the
southern end of the island. Canopy tents dotted the grassy park
grounds with tall pine trees looming overhead. Jackson and Bear
could hardly take a step without bumping into someone.

Under the tents, vendors sold not only oysters but all sorts of
oyster-related products, including a local brewery that was tapping
their signature oyster stout. When Bear spotted a shirt that read
'Shuck Dynasty', he bought it on the spot and immediately threw
it on.

They made their way over to one of the paved walkways that
crisscrossed the park grounds where they found Susan Yarbrough set
up behind a folding table dressed with a gold tablecloth. On it were a
collection of painted oyster shells. Most of them were pony or beach-
themed, but others included birds and various flowers.

Susan's eyes flitted from person to person as they walked past
then widened when she spotted Jackson and Bear. "Hi, good morn-

ing," she said, giving a polite smile. "What are you two doing here? I thought you were headed home."

Jackson smiled back. "We decided to stay in town a couple more days," he said. He looked around them. "This is quite the event."

Susan wrapped her arms around herself. "It is. And it's usually even more lively than this." She shrugged. "It's still early though. Maybe it will pick up later on."

Jackson wondered if the news about Taylor Jensen had people worried. He looked down at the shells in front of Susan. "These are pretty incredible."

Susan gave a dismissive wave.

"No, I mean it." Jackson picked up one painted with a man riding a horse and swinging a lasso over his head. "I'm glad you decided to come out. People should see these."

Susan's hand drifted up to a locket around her neck. "That's very kind of you."

"Mr. Clay?" a voice said over Jackson's shoulder.

Jackson turned and recognized Shaw, the Federal Wildlife Officer he'd spoken to at the beach the day before. Once again, she was in uniform. In a sea of blue jeans and T-shirts, she was conspicuous and several passersby gave her a curious look.

"FWO Izzy Shaw," she greeted. "We spoke on the phone." She extended her open hand.

Jackson shook it. "Jackson Clay. Thank you for coming out." He gestured at Susan. "This is Susan Yarbrough."

Again, Izzy offered her hand. "It's good to meet you, ma'am. I heard about your husband. I'm so sorry for your loss."

Susan's smile ebbed into one tinged with sadness. "Thank you."

Jackson didn't want to keep prospective customers from Susan. "Why don't we walk and talk?" he suggested to Shaw.

Shaw nodded. "Sounds good."

They both waved goodbye to Susan and, with Bear following closely behind, began to stroll down the strip of pavement. Jackson explained why he'd asked to meet her and walked her through the discrepancies he and Bear had discovered with Captain Terry's purported accident. He then told her about the mysterious boater he'd spotted on the harbor's CCTV and showed her the cleaned-up image Bailey sent him.

"I told Investigator Bowden with Chincoteague PD that I aimed to find footage or images of the boat still following Captain Terry further north up the channel," Jackson said. "But he wasn't having any of it."

"I see. I've only worked with him a handful of times, but he's always seemed pretty buttoned up," Shaw said.

Jackson dodged a man balancing three trays filled with oyster po' boys. "Is that to say you're not?"

"No, not necessarily. I'm just saying it doesn't surprise me that he was hesitant to work outside normal channels."

A vendor left his tent and reached out to Bear, offering a tray of shucked oysters. "Fresh Teaguers! Would you like to try one? First one's on us!"

Bear grimaced and held his hands out as if the shellfish might suddenly lunge at him. "Some sea snot from the ocean? Hard pass, hoss."

"Bear," Jackson admonished.

Shaw chuckled. "So, Mr. Clay, you'd like me to act as an intermediary between you and the Meachems. See if they have any cameras facing the channel that might have a better look at your mysterious boater, assuming he went that far."

Jackson nodded. "It's just Clay. Or Jackson. But yes, I figured having the legitimacy of law enforcement might makes the Meachems more amenable to such a request."

Shaw was quiet for a moment before raising her eyebrows. "I don't know." She turned and looked at Jackson. "Why don't we find out?"

————

SHAW, Jackson, and Bear all rode in Shaw's service truck. They took Main Street all the way north, where it shrank to a small, rural road. As they continued, a black and yellow roadside sign read 'Private Road'.

Jackson, sitting shotgun, looked back at the sign as they passed it.

Shaw, seeing this, smirked. "Good thing I'm here," she said with a grin. "Someone might report you for trespassing."

Jackson turned forward. "I read some about the Meachems," he said. "It sounds like that whole Russell Hanz thing was kind of their fall from grace."

Shaw nodded, not taking her eyes off the road. "Oh yeah. It was big gossip here on the island for years. Still is, I guess."

"So, you remember it happening?"

Shaw smirked again. "How young do you think I am? I was in grade school, but yeah, I remember it for sure."

"What I read made it sound like one of the Meachems killed Russell Hanz and everyone knew it, they just never found the evidence to pin it on one of them."

"That was the feeling, anyway. Prosecution could never bring murder charges without a body, but this was 1999. OJ had happened just a few years earlier, and no one had a problem labeling the rich and famous guilty until proven innocent."

Jackson looked curiously at Shaw. "So... you don't agree with them then?"

"No, I'm just saying how it was. The Meachems became pariahs. Scott and Mark Meachem—Mark was the father of Stephanie, the girl who'd been dating Russell Hanz—left town in the months after. Only Emily still lives up this way. It was a whole thing when Mark Meachem and his family left town. I remember it plain as day. Think a parade, only with the opposite of a cheery atmosphere."

"And Scott?"

Shaw shook her head. "Also gone. When the whole family hid behind their lawyers, Scott never showed his face again. People guess he slipped away in the middle of the night with his family after the fanfare Mark's departure received." She shrugged. "Don't blame him, really."

Leonard Lane narrowed to a one-lane gravel road that cut a trail across grassy marshlands dotted on either side with pine and birch trees. The coastal tides formed little tributaries and ponds throughout. The trio took a small bridge over one, which dead-ended at a massive wrought-iron gate. On either side of it walls covered in thick vegetation stretched into the distance.

"Here we are," Shaw said.

She nosed the truck up to the gate where an intercom box extended from a brick post. Shaw rolled down her window and pressed the button for the intercom. The box began ringing, but the sound abruptly cut off after several seconds. Shaw tried it again. Again, there was no answer.

"Can they see us?" Bear asked from the backseat. "Maybe they're not a fan of cops. Wouldn't blame them."

Jackson turned and shot Bear a look.

Bear held his hands out. "What? I'm just saying..."

Shaw shook her head. "You friend's right. I guess they don't want to speak to us." She opened her door and climbed out of the truck.

Jackson followed suit. "Maybe they're not home."

"Unlikely." Shaw came around the front of the truck and stepped up to the iron gate.

Bear got out of the truck as well, and he and Jackson joined Shaw at the gate.

"What makes you say that?" Jackson asked.

Shaw pointed through the gate's bars. "You see that white Lincoln Navigator parked there?"

Jackson followed her finger. The road on the other side split in two about fifty yards in, with a marsh filling the space between the prongs. The road on the right curved out and away, running up to a large house. Just in front of it, Jackson could see the back half of the Navigator sticking out from behind some trees. He nodded.

"That's Emily Meachem's car," Shaw said.

"I assume you're not willing to just claim exigent circumstances and let yourself in," Jackson said.

Shaw snorted. "I'm afraid I value my job too much for that."

Bear wrapped his meaty paws around two of the bars. "You seem to know a lot about these folks."

Shaw cocked her head, ceding the point. "It's something of a guilty pleasure for many of us on the island. The Meachems are such shut-ins these days, they've almost become an urban legend. Those of us curious enough track their movements the same way others track the pony herds over in the refuge."

Bear gave a half-shake of his head. "They really oughta have a Federal Wildlife Officer or something for that."

Shaw laughed. "Yeah, well... it is what it is." She turned back toward her truck. "Come on."

Jackson and Bear exchanged glances before looking at Shaw, who climbed in.

"Come on where?" Jackson asked.

"Maybe we can't let ourselves in," Shaw said. "But we can see if they have any cameras facing the water."

———

NINETY MINUTES LATER, Jackson and Bear were riding on a U.S. Fish and Wildlife Service boat. A center console design with a T-top and a deep V-hull. Shaw stood behind the wheel, whisking them north up the Assateague Channel. As the Meachem houses came into view around a cluster of trees, she slowed down, then cut the engine altogether.

Unencumbered sunshine bore down on them as the boat bobbed lazily in the channel. Jackson took in the houses. One sat closer to them with two farther back on the property. The house nearest them was squat and wide, two stories tall with a cupola crowning the top of it. Parked beside it was the white Lincoln Navigator Shaw had identified as belonging to Emily Meachem.

Shaw came around from the steering console and joined them at the front half of the boat. She held two pairs of impressive binoculars, handing one to Jackson then lifting the other up to her eyes.

"The house nearest us is Emily's," Shaw said.

Jackson looked through his pair of binoculars. "I figured. What about the other two houses?"

"Those used to belong to Emily's brothers, Scott and Mark. Now, Emily's two children live in them."

Jackson shifted his focus to the two houses further back. They had a similar beach house design but were propped up on stilts and painted tan and gray, where Emily Meachem's house was a light blue. The tan one, closer to them than the gray, had a widow's walk facing the channel.

"They each live separately and alone? The children?" Jackson asked.

"As far as anyone knows," Shaw said.

Jackson studied the roof joints and support beams of each house closely, looking for a camera that might face out toward the water. He could see the outline of one on Emily Meachem's house, but it was pointed toward her SUV, most likely covering the driveway and the approach to the house. Jackson lowered his binoculars.

"I don't see anything useful," he said.

Shaw lowered her own pair. "Neither do I."

"No one thought to bring a third pair, so I don't see shit, either," Bear said.

Shaw shook her head and handed her pair to Bear. "By all means."

Bear took the binoculars and looked for himself. "That's a hell of a boat next to the tan house. Must've run someone at least a hundred grand."

Jackson could see the boat plainly without the assistance of the binoculars. It was a large cabin cruiser with a flybridge up top.

"If not more," Shaw said. "That was Mark Meachem's originally. He'd show it off all over the island. It's called *The Mother of Pearl.*"

"Like the crystal layers inside an oyster," Jackson said. "Cute."

"He never came back for it?" Bear asked.

"Never," Shaw said. "Everyone figured the farewell they gave him on the way out made him think twice about coming back for it."

Bear sighed. "Well, y'all are right. I don't see any cameras."

Jackson handed his binoculars back to Shaw. "Thanks anyway, I guess."

Shaw took them and returned to the steering console. "You said the blind where they found Captain Terry is a little further up?"

Jackson nodded. "At the mouth of Will's Creek."

"Show me," Shaw said, firing up the motor.

Jackson guided her further north up the channel, then into Calfpen Bay. As they approached Will's Creek, the blind came into view. Shaw eased up on the throttle, allowing them to coast past it.

"Captain Terry was found in between the front of his boat and the slip's wall," Jackson said. "It'd be hard to show you on this boat with its pointed bow, but the second anything pushes against the front of the boat, it yields and begins floating back. There's no way he would've been pinned without the boat being held somehow."

Shaw frowned. "And the engine was off?"

"From what I understand. You'd have access to more information than I would."

Shaw looked around. "Okay, so play it out. If it's like you said, someone else had to have been here. Where did they come from? Where could they have gone afterward?"

Jackson shrugged. "Only thing that makes sense is another boat, hence our interest in the one that seems to tail Captain Terry out of the harbor."

"Maybe, but what if they came on foot from the island? Did you look around?"

Jackson's mouth twitched. "No. As a matter of fact, we didn't."

Shaw scanned the nearby coastline. "It's pretty remote up here.

There's a good chance any evidence or proof someone was here is still intact." She turned the wheel on the boat hard, pointing it to a muddy bank just past the blind. "Let's take a look, shall we?"

————

JACKSON, Bear, and Shaw spent the remaining hours of daylight searching the shore in the vicinity of the duck blind. They started in the muddy marshlands to the northwest, made their way up the banks of Will's Creek as it snaked its way into a tight grouping of pine trees, then followed it out on the opposite side. Jackson was impressed by Shaw's eye and tracking skills as she caught animal tracks that even he missed. Bear, for his part, mostly tried not to get stuck in the mud. None of them found anything they thought could be related to Captain Terry's death.

With night rolling in from the ocean beyond, they all hiked back to Shaw's boat where she took the helm and led them out of Will's Creek. Taking Assateague Channel back south, she threw the throttle fully open. The boat bobbed and bounced as it glided over the rippled surface of the water. With the sun now gone, the air grew chilly. Jackson zipped up his pullover and tucked his ball cap lower.

Houses along the coastline flew by in a misty blur. Jackson had prolonged his and Bear's stay and had little to show for it. If he were perfectly honest, today had brought more questions than answers. But that didn't change that Captain Terry was dead and, separate from him, Taylor Jensen was as well. Those two pieces didn't fit together, which suggested a missing link between them.

Jackson set his jaw and looked out over the water, more resolved than ever to find that missing piece.

————

AS SHAW GUIDED them back into the harbor, she saw a second US Fish and Wildlife Service truck parked next to hers in the parking lot just off the docks. Leaning against its bull bars was Bridger. Seeing them coming, he came down onto the dock and waited for them to arrive.

Well, this couldn't be good.

Shaw eased the boat into its slip before coming around the steering console and tossing Bridger a line. Bridger took it and moored the boat to the dock as Shaw hopped out and did the same with another line off the boat's stern. Jackson and Bear both clambered out of the boat, and she introduced them to Bridger.

"Why don't you guys head up to the truck?" Shaw said. "I'll be right there."

Jackson nodded and led Bear up to the parking lot. When they were gone, Bridger stepped closer to Shaw, folding his arms.

"We missed you today," he said.

"Yeah, sorry," Shaw said. "Some things came up."

Bridger looked back at Jackson and Bear getting into her truck. "Giving out-of-towners boat rides?"

Shaw gave Bridger a cold look. "They knew Terry Yarbrough, the boat captain that died. They asked for my assistance in looking into something, so I helped them."

"Still, an awfully curious day to go AWOL with the ISB special agent coming in."

Shaw took a deep breath in, then out. "I forgot about that. How'd that go?"

"Fine. Seems like a solid enough guy." Bridger looked back at Shaw. "Determined, that's for sure. He was nonplussed when he learned you hadn't turned in your report for the day."

"*Nonplussed?*" Shaw said, raising an eyebrow.

Bridger grinned. "Charlene got me one of those word-a-day calendars for our anniversary last month. I've been trying to expand my *vocabulary.*"

Shaw shook her head with a smile. "Well, stick to small words. It suits you better."

Bridger chuckled. "No offense taken. Anyway, you missed the day's big development."

She dropped her smile as she met Bridger's eyes. "What's that?"

"Techs were able to recover a DNA sample. Skin cells under Jensen's fingernails."

Shaw shook her head again. The lapping water nearly drowned her words. "She was a fighter."

Bridger grunted in the affirmative. "She was. Let's hope it helps us nail the son of a bitch that did all that to her."

"Here's to hoping."

"Also, this Hurricane Margaret is apparently turning toward us. We may be asked to assist if an evacuation warning is issued, so no more unplanned field trips."

"Got it," she said, nodding.

"And whatever you do, please turn those reports over first thing tomorrow. There's not much of my ass left to chew out."

Shaw grinned. "Noted. I'll make sure the ISB special agent has them tonight."

"Lederer. The guy's name is Chris Lederer."

Shaw nodded again. "Lederer. Got it."

Bridger turned and started back for his truck. "I'll see you tomorrow." He waved at Shaw. "Have a good night, Iz."

Shaw waved back. "You, too."

She waited for Bridger to leave, then joined Jackson and Bear in her truck. After shutting her driver's door, she looked at Bear in the back seat, then over at Jackson riding shotgun, and finally straight ahead at the sleepy harbor.

"You didn't hear this from me," she said, "but they were able to pull a DNA sample from under Taylor Jensen's fingernails."

Jackson looked over at her. "How long for a possible ID?"

"I don't know." Shaw turned the key in the ignition and the truck rumbled to life. "And there's no guarantee it'll come back with a hit, either. This isn't TV. You'd be surprised how often the databases don't come back with a match."

"Mind if I make a phone call?"

Shaw pulled out of the parking lot. "Like I said, you didn't hear it from me."

Jackson pulled out his phone and placed a call. "Bailey, it's me. Give me a call back when you get this. It's important." He lowered the phone into his lap and tapped out a message.

"Bailey a girlfriend?" Shaw asked.

"She's a contact with Virginia State Police." Jackson continued tapping at his phone.

"Perhaps a contact with benefits?" Shaw smirked.

Jackson's words came out clipped. "It's not like that."

Shaw raised a hand off the steering wheel. "Didn't mean to pry. I just noticed you didn't have a wedding ring on." She looked at Bear in the rearview mirror. "You two aren't... together, are you?"

Bear guffawed. "Me and Jacky Boy?" He shook his head. "He should be so lucky."

The slightest of grins formed on Jackson's face. He slipped his phone into his pocket. "No, we are not together. I'm divorced."

She nodded. "Same. We got married too young. Didn't know the difference between infatuation and love. Then he tripped and fell on top of a woman who happened to be lying naked in our bed. That was that." Shaw looked over at Jackson. "You?"

Jackson remained quiet for a moment as he looked out the window at the dark world around them. "We grew apart after our son disappeared. She was killed a few years ago. Same guy who took and killed our son killed her, too, when she got too close to the truth."

A knot formed in her stomach as she struggled to find the right thing to say. "I'm sorry," she finally managed to get out in little more than a whisper.

"Yeah. Me, too."

They drove the rest of the way back to Bear's SUV in silence.

FOURTEEN

JACKSON FOUND sleep fleeting that night. It still bothered him that he hadn't thought to search the island around the duck blind before Shaw suggested it, and it bothered him even more that it hadn't yielded anything new. With nothing else to go on, he wondered what else he wasn't thinking of.

By five, he'd conceded sleep wasn't coming. He had too much restless energy, so he did what he often did at such times. He sweated it out. Throwing on shorts, a hoodie, and sneakers, he headed out for a run, taking the gravel road back to Main Street and toward the center of town.

The rest of the island, as well as the sun, had yet to wake, so Jackson ran on, alone in the early pre-dawn blackness. As he ran, he couldn't help but think about Taylor Jensen. The news reports said she'd left for a run when her friends had reported her missing. Had her day begun just like this?

He ran two miles to where Main Street intersected Maddox Boulevard and the drawbridge to the mainland, now raised to allow a fishing trawler to pass through. He turned onto Maddox Boulevard, down the main drag of shops and restaurants, and out onto the

Sheepshead Bridge toward the refuge on Assateague Island. He'd gotten half-way across it when his phone buzzed in his shorts. He stopped to check it and saw Bailey's name lighting up the screen.

"I tried calling you last night," he greeted. "You didn't pick up."

"I'm aware," Bailey said, already sounding annoyed. "I got your missed call and your message. For normal folks, Saturday and Sunday are called the weekend, and it's not often that I get one when I'm not on call."

Jackson began walking further down the bridge, catching his breath and allowing his heart rate to slow. "What is normal? Nine-to-five with 401k's and family cookouts? That's not either of us, Bailey."

"I get Deferred Compensation, but I get your point. What's up? Your text only said to call you and it's important."

Jackson looked out at the Assateague Lighthouse swinging its beams of light across the two islands, then out to the sea. "I got word they were able to pull a DNA sample from the Taylor Jensen scene, the young woman found on the beach."

Bailey groaned. "Do I even want to know how you came across this information?"

"A Federal Wildlife Officer down here. She's been about the only one with a badge that's been helpful."

"No offense taken."

The corner of Jackson's eye twitched. "You know what I meant. You said the National Park's ISB is running lead on her case, which means it'll be going to a federal lab. Do you think one of your bureau guys can make a couple more calls?"

Bailey didn't say anything.

Jackson checked his phone. "Bailey?"

"Even if they can, to what end? They'll either get an ID, in which case they'll find the perp faster than you, or they won't, in which case it'll be no use."

"Just humor me. Can you?"

Bailey sighed. "I've been doing a lot of that this week. Like I said,

I'll see what I can do. In the meantime, why don't you ingratiate yourself to whoever the ISB *did* send so you can be their problem and not mine?"

Jackson ignored her. "How's my dog?"

"Wearing my patience thin. Something you two have in common."

"I'll be back as soon as I can. I promise."

"Uh huh."

"*Thank you, Bailey.* I appreciate it."

He hung up and began walking back toward Chincoteague. The sky behind him was lightening with the oncoming day. Bailey did have a point about the ISB investigator or investigators. Jackson wondered if Shaw could make an introduction. He called her.

Shaw picked up right away. "This is Shaw."

"Shaw, it's Jackson Clay. I hope I didn't wake you," Jackson said.

"No, I was up. How can I help you?"

Jackson stepped off the bridge and back onto land. A large field of tall pampas grass rustled quietly in the breeze next to him. "The Taylor Jensen investigation, is ISB heading that up?"

Shaw took a beat. Her voice was wary. "They are. How did you...?"

"Educated guess. So, they must have someone on the island by now. An investigator or team of investigators?"

"They do."

"Do you think you could put me in contact with them?"

Shaw paused again. "I don't think that's a good idea. My supervisor wasn't exactly happy I disappeared pursuing your Captain Terry angle yesterday."

"Just let me make the case to him same as I did to you. If he doesn't buy it, I won't push it any further."

Shaw sighed. "Alright. Let me see when he can meet."

———

JACKSON, Bear, and Shaw met with ISB Special Agent Chris Lederer at the Educational and Administrative Center facility inside the refuge. A wood-and-glass mid-century modern building, it was impressive from the outside. The offices inside, though, were your average federally funded workspace.

As Shaw led the trio through the refuge visitor center and through the office door on the other side, Lederer came down an aisle between cubicles and greeted Jackson with an open hand.

"Chris Lederer," he said, stone-faced. "Thank you for coming in."

"Thank you for meeting with us," Jackson said, shaking his hand.

Lederer was tall and lean in an athletic way. He had short chestnut hair that matched his brown eyes and wore a blue polo with a Department of the Interior Special Agent badge embroidered on it. Jackson also clocked the large knife and service pistol clipped to his belt.

"Come on in," Lederer said. "I've requisitioned an empty office in the back."

He led them down the aisle bisecting the cubicles to an enclosed office with a glass door and two windows looking out at the bullpen workspaces. Inside, it looked as vacant as Lederer described, sporting only a desk, a couple of visitor's chairs, the man's laptop and a small stack of manila folders.

"I've only got chairs in here for two of you," he said. "I can see if we can find a third."

Bear shook his head. "You all talk," he said. "I'll see what kind of trouble I can get into."

The corner of Jackson's eye twitched, knowing with Bear that wasn't just a turn of phrase, but he didn't say anything. Shaw closed the door to the office after Bear left, and she and Jackson took the two armchairs opposite the desk.

"So, FWO Shaw here tells me you may have some information pertinent to the Jensen case," Lederer said.

"That's correct," Jackson said. "Are you familiar with the death of Terry Yarbrough?"

Lederer rested his elbows on the desk and clasped his hands together. "No, I'm afraid not."

Jackson walked Lederer through everything, from the local police's theory that it had been an unfortunate drowning accident to him and Bear being unable to recreate said accident to the boat that was seen on CCTV turning to follow Captain Terry out of the bay. Lederer, Jackson was relieved to note, listened closely, taking notes on his laptop.

"And you don't know of any connection between Ms. Jensen and Mr. Yarbrough?" Lederer asked. "They never met or anything like that?"

"Not that I've been able to find," Jackson said. "But the duck blind where it happened is at the mouth of Will's Creek, just several feet offshore from Assateague Island."

Lederer nodded. "No, I definitely agree it's concerning. But it's also *just* that for now. Concerning."

Jackson bit the inside corner of his lip. "So, you're not going to look into the possibility that the two are connected."

Lederer shook his head. "I didn't say that. I intend to look at every aspect of this case. But I have to go where the evidence points me first. And right now, there's nothing solid to connect the Jensen murder to your boat captain's death, whether it was an accident or not."

Jackson looked over at Shaw. He knew if he brought up the DNA sample it'd throw her under the bus, so he played dumb. "Do you have any evidence pointing elsewhere?"

Lederer opened his hands toward Jackson and Shaw. "I really can't comment on anything like that with an ongoing investigation."

Jackson bit his lip harder. Pretending he didn't know about the DNA sample was proving harder than he anticipated. Then, a different way to bring it up came to him. "What about Captain Terry's body?"

Lederer's brow furrowed. "What about it?"

"I know that his autopsy was ruled inconclusive by the local ME, which already pokes holes in the theory that it was an accident."

Lederer shook his head. "Inconclusive doesn't mean it wasn't an accident. It means exactly what it states, the results were inconclusive between natural death, accident, or foul play."

"You must be able to get his body over to some bigger, federal forensic lab. They could conduct their own autopsy, see if there is something the local ME might have missed. Maybe they pull DNA or something."

Lederer thought for a moment. "If his next of kin signs off on it, I'll see what I can do."

"That's all I ask."

"Fair enough." Lederer stood. "Then you better let me get to it."

Jackson stood and offered his hand. "I'll do just that. Thanks again."

Lederer shook it. "No problem. I'll be in touch if anything comes up."

Jackson and Shaw left the way they came and found Bear in the visitor center. He stood in front of a large diorama showing how waterfowl dive beneath the surface to hunt. Jackson joined him as Shaw stepped away to say hello to a park ranger.

"You think that bird imagined in all its time on earth it'd spend the rest of its days in some museum?" Bear asked.

"This isn't a museum, and I don't think that's a real bird," Jackson said.

"Not anymore."

"I mean ever."

Bear scratched his chin as he examined the model closer. "Who the hell do you think does these then? Is there a professional museum modeler somewhere?"

"Still not a museum, and probably some *rural lifestyle enthusiast* with too much time on his hands." Jackson turned and started to walk away. "Come on, let's go."

Bear snorted as he turned to follow. "How'd the meeting go?"

"About as you'd expect. Didn't exactly shut us down, but wasn't overly eager to help, either."

"So, I guess I shouldn't mention I overheard two park rangers talking out here about how they think whoever killed that girl came to the refuge by boat, huh."

Jackson stopped as the two of them rejoined Shaw. He looked at Bear. "They do?"

Bear nodded. "Yessir. Apparently, they've got cameras at the front gates. No one entered the park overnight, and the only two people who came in before that girl have been cleared." He mimed a boat cruising through water with his hand. "Short of swimming, there's only one other way to get to an island."

Jackson thought for a moment. "Will's Creek snakes its way into the island. Someone with a small boat and knowledge of the little waterways could move around virtually undetected. That could be the connection to Captain Terry."

Bear pursed his lips. "I'd buy it."

"We need a way to ID boats. The Coast Guard must have a database or something."

Shaw shook her head. "You wouldn't register a boat that small with the Coast Guard, but anything motorized in Virginia has to be registered with the Department of Wildlife Resources."

Jackson turned to her. "Do you have access to that registry? Is it searchable?"

Shaw pursed her lips. "You can but a small, outboard boat like that? You're talking about a needle in a haystack."

"It's still worth a shot. Can you see what you can find?"

"I need to hang around here today. If I have a minute, I can see what I can dig up."

Jackson nodded. "Thank you. And thanks for the meeting with Lederer."

"No problem." Shaw turned and headed back to the offices.

Bear came around to stand opposite Jackson. "What do you want to do in the meantime?"

"Let's go down to the marina. Shaw's right that the database will cast a wide net, but locals will know who's got what kind of boat out here. Maybe we get lucky."

Bear nodded. "Sounds good."

"And let's run by Susan Yarbrough's house again, see if she doesn't mind lending us her boat one more time in case we need it."

Bear headed for the lobby of the building, Jackson following behind him. As they left the exhibit they were in, he noticed a large quote on the wall attributed to the conservationist John Muir.

When we try to pick out anything by itself, we find it hitched to everything else in the Universe.

The murders of Terry Yarbrough and Taylor Jensen weren't two random tragedies, they were a cancer cluster. An anomaly cast against the serene backdrop of these picturesque islands. Like everything else in the Universe, they were hitched to one another.

———

SUSAN YARBROUGH HAD BEEN MORE than happy to give Jackson and Bear the key to Captain Terry's boat again and insisted they keep it until they actually headed out of town. With it in hand, Jackson and Bear drove to the harbor and canvassed the docks, asking anyone around if they knew anyone on the island who might have a ten- to twelve-foot outboard motorboat, showing them the profile of the boat and boater they were looking for from the enhanced image Bailey had provided them.

If finding the boat in the online register was going to be like finding a needle in a haystack, asking around proved to be a similarly futile task. Everybody Jackson and Bear asked could name at least a half-dozen people, and each person's half-dozen was mostly different from the next. In just under a couple hours, Jackson and Bear had a list of people almost fifty names long. When they'd talked to everyone they could find, they circled back to Bear's Suburban, parked nose-in to a parking spot directly overlooking the harbor. Jackson hoisted himself up onto the hood and sighed in frustration.

"We'll be here until next hunting season at this rate," Bear said as he rested his backside on the front fender.

"Hopefully Shaw gets back to us soon with names from the registry," Jackson said. "We can cross-reference her names with the ones we got and see where that leaves us. Names on both move to the top of our list."

Bear shook his head. "Seems like a lot of legwork."

"Two people are dead, Bear. There's no taking shortcuts."

"I know, I'm just saying." A silence fell between them. "So, you just want to wait around for Shaw to get back to us?"

Jackson looked out at Captain Terry's boat bobbing lazily in its slip when an idea came to him. "No, let's go cover the coastline."

Bear looked back at him, an eyebrow raised. "What do you mean?"

"We covered the harbor, but the island is lined with private docks and boats. We can start with the channel side between the north end of the island and the bridge where Jensen came across into the refuge. Seeing the boats for ourselves is more reliable than the accounts of others, anyway."

"I'm in, Jacky Boy, but it seems like a long shot."

"It beats sitting here on our hands." Jackson hopped off the hood of the Suburban. "Come on, let's go."

———

THE REST of the day was business as usual for Shaw. After meeting with Lederer and turning over her reports related to the Jensen case, she made her rounds in the refuge. By five that afternoon she found herself on the trail road that ran north and south up and down the island near a spot called Bow Beach, a grassy landform at the head-waters of a small estuary on the channel side of the island. Not a soul in sight, save for a herd of ponies grazing on the opposite bank. Finally, with a free moment, she used the laptop in her truck, equipped with a satellite internet connection, to search the DWR Boat Registry.

In total, the registry had information on nearly two hundred fifty thousand boats, almost a quarter of which had addresses on the peninsula that was Virginia's Eastern Shore. Shaw sucked at her teeth. Even if she limited the search to boats under sixteen feet, the number of matches was in the thousands. She slapped the laptop shut and rubbed her eyes. Her gaze went out to the Assateague Channel in the distance. A small motorboat cruised southward. There had to be at least a hundred boats fitting Jackson's description just on Chincoteague alone. There was no way to home in on any legitimate suspects.

Her phone buzzed in the truck's center console and she saw Bridger's ID on the screen. She answered it.

"Bridger, what's up?" she said.

"Hey, where are you right now?"

She scanned around her as if Bridger might be nearby, testing her for some reason. "I'm not AWOL again, if that's what you're asking. I'm out on patrol."

"No, I know. And Lederer mentioned you got your stuff to him. I appreciate that. Where are you at *on patrol?*"

"Bow Beach. I was just about to turn back and head south."

"Good. Yeah, head back to the office and hurry if you can."

The hair on the back of Shaw's neck prickled. "Something happen?"

"Well, in a manner of speaking. This Hurricane Margaret looks like it's going to hit here one way or another, it's just a matter of how direct a blow we take. Word just came down, and they're issuing an evacuation advisory for Chincoteague, Assateague, and coastal parts of the mainland."

Shaw rubbed at her temples. "Terrific."

"Yeah. So, double time it back here if you can. Things are going to get chaotic around here fast."

Shaw put her truck in gear. "Got it. On my way back now."

FIFTEEN

IT HAD BEEN NEARLY three days since he'd encountered the young woman in the fog on the beach, the longest he'd gone without taking a life since his Awakening. Seeing the news, reading what people were saying about him online had been exhilarating. But it also made his appetite even more ravenous. The desire had become unbearable, a kind of rush that was as euphoric as it was fleeting. The more he craved it, the more it slipped from his grasp. His very being ached for the moment when he watched a soul leave its body.

And so, he hunted. Taking his boat down Janey's Creek, he headed for the same inlet on Assateague he'd used before. He wanted to return to the Wildlife Loop trail at the heart of the island. A three-and-a-quarter-mile paved coil, the east end of which snaked its way through one of the island's many woodlands. There, The Bull Shark would have the perfect cover to attack his unsuspecting prey.

Nosing his boat onto the muddy shore, he hopped out and dragged it securely up onto the bank, safe from the rising water. High tide accompanied nightfall this evening, and the little tributary would be deeper and wider when he returned. He was just about to head off into the tall marsh grass when movement caught his attention out of the corner of his eye.

Paddling up Janey's Creek was a single kayaker, a man in a sit-in style model. The kayaker had definitely seen him standing there on the bank of the island. Maybe he wouldn't think anything of it, but it was a risk The Bull Shark couldn't take. This kayaker would have to be dealt with. Never mind his original plan, The Bull Shark thought, good fortune had brought him a new opportunity to fulfill the desire within him.

He moved to the water's edge and waved at the man with a toothy smile. His other hand wrapped around the handle of his knife.

SIXTEEN

TOM MARSHALL WAS ENJOYING his early evening kayak outing so much, he decided to take the long way back to the boat ramp off East Side Road he'd departed from hours earlier. The sun hung low behind the bridge across the channel in the distance, painting the sky overhead in shades of pink and fiery crimson. Juxtaposed with the dark silhouette of the tree-lined horizon of Chincoteague to the west, one could be forgiven for conjuring similarities to a devilish underworld. But no hell could be so beautiful.

He took a moment to take it all in, tipping his head full of raven-black hair back and dipping his tanned and toned arms into the cool waters below him. Refreshed, Tom headed back to where the meandering creek he'd taken rejoined the channel when he spotted someone several yards in on Assateague Island. Knowing everything this far south was part of the wildlife refuge, the sight piqued his curiosity. The person on the island now spotted him and came to the shore, waving. Tom turned and headed in his direction.

"Good evening!" the person said.

"Hey," Tom said. "I don't mean to be a Karen or anything, but I don't think you're supposed to go into the refuge like this."

The figure—a man, Tom now saw up close—shrugged. "Oh, yeah, I know," he said. "It's a little bit embarrassing, but I was fishing out this way and snagged a lure on the shore here." He grinned. "Maybe I'm cheap, but that darn thing cost me twenty-five bucks. I was hoping to find it."

Tom glanced over at the person's boat in the little tributary a ways back. He didn't see any fishing pole or gear sticking out of it. In fact, the only thing the person seemed to have with him was a knife sheathed on his belt.

The man followed his gaze to the boat and chuckled. "I doubled back after dropping off my friends with our things, of course."

Tom nodded. "Not very good friends if they weren't willing to help you out." He nosed his Kayak onto the island shore. "Here, I can give you a hand."

"Oh, no. It's bad enough I let this take up the rest of my day, I can't let it do the same for you."

"Nonsense. I really don't mind."

The person walked up to the bow of the kayak. "Really, it's okay. I'm losing light and about to call it, anyway."

Tom looked up at him. There was something about his presence that turned his skin to gooseflesh. "Fair enough," he said. "Just wanted to offer."

The person flashed another smile. "I appreciate it. Here, let me give you a push back out." He came around the front of the kayak, bent over, and began pushing it out into the creek.

"That's alright," Tom said. "I can manage."

The man started walking with the kayak, guiding it into deeper water. "Please, I insist."

Feeling like he was losing control, Tom put an oar in the water to resist their effort. "It's okay. Please stop."

He did as he said. Standing now in waist-high water, the two of them were nearly level with one another. The smile dropped from the person's face, replaced by a dark expression. "Your choice."

Before Tom could react, his kayak tipped underneath him,

plunging him into the water. Upside down, he became pinned under the capsized craft, his life vest pushing him up into the kayak's shell. He tried to wiggle himself free, but he could feel the person at his side, forcing him under. Tom flailed underwater, desperate to grab anything that might force the person to release him. He felt an arm brush him off, then slip around his head and hold it in place.

The last thing Tom Marshall felt was something slice into his neck.

SEVENTEEN

SEARCHING the coastline of Chincoteague for a boat matching the profile took the rest of the day. Starting at the north end near Captain Terry's duck blind, they circumnavigated the island and by sundown found themselves back where they'd started.

Their search had yielded few results. Jackson noted a couple possible matches scattered throughout, but most were docked in front of places with signs indicating they were rental cottages or cabins, meaning their owners likely weren't local and the establishments likely wouldn't provide any information about who was staying there. Jackson had snapped pictures of the boats, hoping the numbers on them might make them identifiable to Shaw and the DWR registry.

With dusk upon them, Bear turned to Jackson, who sat behind the steering column and raised an eyebrow in question.

Jackson took a deep breath, sighed, then nodded. "Okay, let's call it," he said over the rumble of the idling motor. "Back to the harbor."

Jackson put the throttle at full and whisked them down the Assateague Channel. The lights of houses on the shore to their right dotted the twilight horizon, adding to the stars appearing with the coming evening. Ahead and to their left, the Assateague Lighthouse beckoned them forth with its light. Jackson was watching it strobe around when a much smaller flicker suddenly caught his attention. He looked to his left and a chill coursed through him.

A faint but unmistakable glow emanated from somewhere inside the old hunter's cabin nestled on a muddy outcropping of Assateague Island.

Bear must have seen a change in Jackson's expression because he followed Jackson's gaze. Jackson eased back on the throttle and hung a turn so sharp Bear had to hold on to avoid being tossed overboard. They came about, lengthwise in the channel, twenty yards past the cabin. Jackson could just make out the shoreline and edged up to it, trying to get a different point of view on the cabin.

As he did, the glow shifted from window to window. Someone was inside, moving. Jackson found a little finger of water cutting into the land and guided the boat into it, getting a side view of the cabin. In the back, a small dock jutted out into the water. When the beacon light from the lighthouse whipped around once more, Jackson could make out the dark profile of a small outboard motorboat.

Jackson killed the engine and met Bear at the front of the boat. They kept low, crouching down. The beacon light came around again and, again, Jackson saw it.

"Tell me that doesn't look like a ten- to twelve-foot outboard motorboat," Jackson whispered.

"Sure as shit does," Bear said. "Didn't Captain Terry say this place was abandoned?"

Jackson nodded. "For decades, he said."

Bear shook his head. "Unless you believe in ghosts, that sure don't look abandoned to me, Jacky Boy."

They watched the cabin for several moments longer. The glow disappeared, then immediately reappeared as something or someone stepped in front of it. Jackson's pulse quickened, and adrenaline filled his veins. The supposed-to-be abandoned cabin was almost equidistant between Captain Terry's duck blind and where Taylor Jensen had been found on the beach. Moreover, a boat very similar to the one seen leaving the harbor on the heels of Captain Terry was moored to this cabin's dock.

"You want to call Shaw?" Bear asked.

Jackson shook his head. "No, we handle this ourselves." He stepped back to the steering column and reversed as quietly as possible.

Bear sat back on one of the boat's benches. "Back to the harbor to lay out a game plan?"

Jackson shook his head again. "We're going directly to the dock off our rental house. We load up and load out, then come back."

He backed the boat out into the open water of the channel before turning it north to head back the way they'd come. He gave the hunter's cabin a wide berth, staying close to the opposite shoreline. When they were far enough past it, Jackson revved the engine open once more. Bear looked back at him, holding onto his hat so it wouldn't fly off.

"Tonight," Jackson shouted over the roar of the motor. "We're going in there."

PART THREE
SINS OF THE FATHER

"To live in the body of a survivor is to never be able to leave the scene of the crime." -Blythe Baird

EIGHTEEN

JACKSON AND BEAR returned to their rental house to prepare and formulate a plan. The hunter's cabin sat on the tip of a thick finger of land off Assateague Island. Jackson would take them to the base of the finger, several hundred yards away from the cabin, on its north side. Bear would wait there for Jackson to cross on foot to the other side. When he was in position, the two of them would then move together, flanking the cabin.

They hadn't expected trouble while on their hunting trip, so their equipment was limited. Neither of them had body armor, and the only communications gear they had were the two-way radios they'd used with Captain Terry. Their only guns were an assortment of shotguns loaded with birdshot, and the pistols they always carried with them. For Bear, that was his Smith & Wesson .357 revolver. For Jackson, his silver M9 Beretta with a custom ebony wood grip engraved with his late son's initials, ERC. The only thing they had plenty of was hunting gear, which each of them changed into before loading up.

Just before midnight, they arrived at the hunter's cabin. Jackson did just as they'd planned, easing the nose of the boat onto a muddy bank far away from the cabin. Together, he and Bear pulled it in to make sure the rising tide didn't take it away, then Jackson crossed the finger of land.

On the other side, he radioed Bear. "In position."

"Copy," Bear radioed back. "On you, brother."

"Move now. Quiet from here on out."

With a shotgun slung around his chest, Jackson drew his pistol out in front of him and stalked toward the cabin. The cabin was completely dark, only the moon's light shining off the motor on the boat docked behind it. Jackson moved, slow and methodical in his approach, taking easy, sure-footed steps as he waded through the sea of waist-high pampas grass. To his right, he could just make out the inky, amorphous figure that was Bear moving parallel to him. As they converged on the cabin, Jackson signaled for Bear to stop short of the cabin's boardwalk. He stepped gingerly onto it, testing that it wouldn't creak under his weight, then moved quietly to the door. Jackson looked in one of the cabin windows. Inside was a black abyss. He crouched down out of view and signaled for Bear to move up to join him.

"Lights," Jackson whispered.

Each of them pulled a flashlight out of their coats. Jackson positioned himself in front of the door.

"I'm point."

In one swift motion, he raised up and kicked the door in. Pistol up and light on, he moved quickly inside. The first room looked like some kind of entryway or mudroom. Jackson cleared it and stepped into a hall. The hall ran to another door at the front of the cabin, facing the water. Two more doors branched off of it. Jackson moved to the first and checked it. It was a kitchen, empty. He stepped to the second and was just about to turn into it when an aluminum baseball bat came swinging out at him. Jackson ducked back as the bat smashed into the opposite wall.

A dark figure filled the doorway. Jackson's flashlight revealed portions of a man's physique. His torso twisted, winding up for another swing. Jackson ducked again and then launched himself into the man's midsection in a linebacker's tackle.

Jackson heard Bear thump into the hallway behind him and lock the hammer back on his revolver.

"Quit moving!" Bear barked.

Jackson rolled the man onto his stomach and twisted his right arm behind him. The man yelped.

"I've got him," Jackson said. "Get the bat he swung at me."

He heard Bear lower the hammer on his revolver and holster it, before he secured the bat. Jackson, controlling the man by his pinned arm and the collar of his sweatshirt, brought the man up and forced him into the room he'd come swinging out of. Inside, there was nothing more than a cot with a sleeping bag and several opened cans of food.

"Sit," Jackson ordered.

The man dropped onto the cot. Jackson stood over him, shining his flashlight on him. The man looked down at the ground, showing Jackson only his black hair, flecks of gray throughout.

"Look at me," Jackson said.

"Look, dude," the man said. "Whatever you want, just take it. I don't have anything worth a damn anyway."

"I want you to look at me."

The man took a deep breath in and out, then did as Jackson wanted. When he did, Jackson felt a tremor roil through him. He recognized the face looking at him. It was several years older, decades to be exact, but it was the same man he'd seen in a half-dozen articles.

Russell Hanz.

NINETEEN

RUSSELL LOOKED as though he'd lived a hard life since his high school days. Still thin, but he'd lost most of his muscle mass. His skin had become tan and weathered and pockmarked with sunspots. He now had a bushy beard, though it'd grown in patchy. It held specks of gray like the rest of his hair.

"Russell Hanz, in the flesh," Jackson said.

Russell sneered at Jackson. "That's not my goddamn name anymore," he said.

"Isn't it?" Jackson asked. He leaned against the wall opposite Russell and his cot. "I didn't realize dead men could change their names."

The disdain on Russell's face metastasized. "Do I look dead to you?"

"No, you don't. Something a whole town full of people across the channel outside would be surprised to learn."

Russell didn't say anything, he just looked down and shook his head.

Jackson looked at Bear, then nodded toward the hallway. "Toss the place."

Bear disappeared into the hall. A moment later, Jackson heard the sound of cupboards opening and shutting.

"I already told you," Russell said, "if you're looking for anything worth a damn, I ain't got it."

"We're looking for something that ties you to Captain Terry or Taylor Jensen," Jackson said.

Russell looked up at him, his face scrunched. "Who... or who?"

"The local boat guide and a vacationer. The two people that have been killed in the last few days. Both less than a couple miles from this very cabin."

Russell shook his head. "That doesn't mean shit. I didn't kill anyone."

"Maybe, maybe not. But a dead man hiding out in an abandoned cabin is a hell of a cover." He crouched down. "Easy to kill a few people when everyone thinks you're already dead yourself."

Russell stomped his foot. "God dammit! I already said! Do I look dead to you?!"

"And I told you no, which makes me curious about you showing up now in the wake of two people being killed."

"How many times do I have to tell you, I don't know what you're talking about."

"Prove it then."

Russell's eyes narrowed. "I don't have to prove shit to you. You're not the police."

"No, but I can get them if need be. They might be surprised to see you here."

Russell sneered again. "You wouldn't."

"Wouldn't I?" Jackson said, raising his brows.

Bear stepped into the room and looked at Jackson. "Jacky Boy, you're going to want to see this."

Jackson rolled off the wall and pointed at Russell. "Stay there." He stepped over to the corner of the room.

Bear joined him, his tone hushed. "Wasn't Captain Terry killed early in the morning on the thirteenth?"

Jackson nodded.

Bear held up a greasy receipt. "This was in a backpack next to a cooler in the kitchen. If he killed Captain Terry, then what was he doing at a 7-Eleven in Ocean City, Maryland buying a cup of coffee and a pack of sticky buns?"

Russell snorted. "Told you I didn't fucking kill those people."

Jackson shone his flashlight on the receipt, examining it. "This doesn't mean anything. You could've fished it out of a trash can after the fact to give yourself an alibi."

Russell's shoulders dropped. "Oh, come *on*."

Jackson came back and stood over him. "Then what were you doing in Ocean City?"

"I live there now. I've lived there... pretty much ever since I ran away from here."

"Just letting people think you were dead?"

"Well, I was half-sure if I poked my head back up, Stephie's old man would finish the job."

"Stephanie Meachem, whom you were dating. What do you mean by that, her father finishing the job?"

"That night!" Russell flung his hands up in front of him. "The night it all went to shit. The night I ran."

"When you disappeared. What happened?"

"Stephie had been acting weird for a few days. I thought she was going to dump me. Then my buddy told me he'd heard she was pregnant. I didn't know if it was mine or someone else's or what. So, I drove over there to ask her about it."

Jackson folded his arms. "And? What'd she say?"

"I was halfway down that long-ass driveway of theirs when I heard a gunshot. I stopped and got low in my seat, thinking her dad or someone was trying to shoot me. After a minute, there weren't any more gunshots, so I got out. Stephie came running up from her aunt's house across the way. Then her dad came walking out of theirs, gun in hand." Russell shook his head. "I barely had enough time to ask what was going on when all hell broke loose. Shots firing out one after another."

"Mark Meachem was shooting at you?"

"I don't know who the hell was shooting, but I didn't stick around to find out. I ran into the marshes, eventually found one of their jet skis tied to a dock, and got the hell out of there. My half-brother had a place in Greenbackville up near the state line. I went there to lay low. After a while, I realized everyone assumed I was dead. I figured with the Meachems actually trying to kill me, that might be for the best."

Jackson shook his head. "That doesn't make any sense. You could've gone to the police, or your folks, or the school, a dozen places."

"You don't get it. Everyone knows the Meachems. There isn't a mayor or town council member that gets elected that they don't approve. I'd already disappeared on paper. You think it would really be that hard for them to make me disappear for real?"

"And so... what? You've just been on the lam all these years?"

"Like I said, I found my way up to Ocean City. Working odd jobs for cash. Paying rent for a small place the same way. I go by Michael Hall now."

"That's not terribly imaginative."

"Yeah, well, a common name helps you blend in. People ask fewer questions. They forget about you."

Bear walked over and stood beside Jackson. "I don't understand. Don't you have folks in Chincoteague? Didn't you at least want them to know you were okay?"

Russell shrugged. "I thought about it, but not long after, my brother told me my parents brought a wrongful death suit against the Meachems. I guess it was clear no one was going to do time, and they wanted someone to pay in some way. He said the Meachems settled with them. I know how rich they are, it must've been a lot. I figured if I showed up, it would only get my parents in trouble."

"Except the Meachems became town pariahs after what went

down. Stephie's dad and uncle left town. Those that stayed apparently keep to themselves."

Russell shook his head. "I didn't know that. When I left, I tried as hard as I could to put everything that had happened behind me."

Jackson put a boot up on the cot. "Which makes it all the more curious that we find you here tonight."

Russell leaned back and folded his arms. "I come down a couple times a month this time of year to empty some peoples' oyster cages they've got out here. A few restaurants up in OC will pay me cash under the table for them."

"You mean you poach them."

Russell shook his head again. "Whatever. A man's got to eat. See for yourself, it's that cooler in the kitchen your friend mentioned."

Jackson took Russell up on his offer. He stepped around Bear and into the hall. Before he left the room, he looked at Bear and nodded at Russell. Bear tipped his head.

Russell rose to follow Jackson but Bear stepped in front of him.

"You know what happened to the dude that went quail hunting with Dick Cheney?" Bear asked.

Russell looked at him, his brows furrowing.

Bear unslung his shotgun from his shoulder. "You want to find out?"

Jackson left them to each other's company. He went into the kitchen and checked the cooler. Sure enough, it was filled with oysters and a couple bottles of water. Jackson took a deep breath in and sighed. He hated to admit it, but he believed Russell. Not enough to let him go, though, which gave him another problem. Jackson thought for a moment, then returned to Bear and Russell.

"Your boat," Jackson said, looking at Russell. "It's a pull start? No key needed or anything?"

"No," Russell replied. "Why?"

Jackson looked at Bear. "Let's go. You take his boat back to the house. I'll take ours back to the marina and get the Suburban."

Bear's face wrinkled in a skeptical look. "We're not really letting him go are we?"

"Letting me go?" Russell exclaimed, his hands out in front of him. "You're leaving me here, stuck."

"That's right," Jackson said, shifting his eyes to him. "You're not going anywhere. Of course, you could start hiking your way out or swim, but you're not dumb. You know it's only a matter of time before someone spots you, at which point you'll have a lot of explaining to do."

"So, what? You're just going to leave me here to rot or give myself up?"

"We'll come back tomorrow night."

"What the hell difference is a day going to make?"

Jackson shrugged. "We'll find out."

Bear stepped in close to Jackson. "We're not really doing this, are we? We can't just leave him."

Jackson didn't take his eyes off of Russell. "We can't bring him with us, and we definitely can't kick him free. This is our only option."

Russell scoffed. "I can't just stay here all day with no supplies."

"You've got clothes on your back, a roof over your head, and a cooler full of food and water. I'd say you've got everything you need." Jackson nodded to the doorway. "Let's go, Bear."

Bear filed out of the room, Jackson close behind.

"This is bullshit!" Russell shouted as they left.

Outside, Jackson stood on the boardwalk and waited to make sure Bear got Russell's boat started.

When he was gone, Jackson waded back into the tall marsh grass.

TWENTY

JACKSON DIDN'T SLEEP WELL AGAIN that night, this time from anxiety that he'd made a mistake leaving Russell Hanz out at the abandoned cabin unsupervised. He made sure it sounded to Russell like trying to leave was a dumb idea, but he wasn't so sure. If the guy was a strong swimmer, he could make his way back to the mainland, maybe even some place like Greenbackville. Did Russell still have family there? Anger pulsed through Jackson from the thought that he hadn't double-checked.

When he saw the sky lighten, he popped out of bed and threw on a fresh pair of sweats for another run. Bear still snored like a sputtering chainsaw in the room across the hall, so Jackson eased out the front door and shut it carefully behind him.

He had just begun stretching when a Chincoteague Police cruiser rolled down the seashell driveway to the house. It stopped several feet away as if Jackson were some sort of threat. The driver's door opened and an officer Jackson recognized got out.

"Good morning, Mr. Clay," the officer said. "Headed somewhere?"

"Officer Birch, isn't it?" Jackson asked.

Birch nodded. "That's right, sir."

"I was just about to head out for a run." Jackson's voice was flat and wary. "What's up?"

"The chief asked to see you." Birch nodded over his shoulder as if the chief were standing there with him.

"About anything in particular?"

Birch shrugged. "He just asked me to pick you up."

"Is this a sit-up-front or sit-in-the-back kind of ride?"

"Wherever you're most comfortable." He stepped away from the open car door and rested his hands on his belt. "You could run there if you'd like. Of course, I'd have to follow you."

Jackson thought about it for a moment, then started for the other side of the police cruiser. "You're driving me back, too." He opened the passenger door and slid in.

———

CHIEF BEN DIAZ'S office was in the far back of the police headquarters, walled in on two sides with a bank of windows across the third. The fourth held a door and two more windows looking onto the interior of the building. Officer Birch escorted Jackson into the office. Chief Diaz was slim with thick eyebrows and shaved head that made his ears look larger than they were. The sleek, hairless look also shaved ten years off his age, which Jackson guessed was somewhere in the fifties. Chief Diaz rose from his desk when Jackson entered and extended his hand.

"Mr. Clay," he said with a firm handshake. "Thank you for coming in."

"I didn't realize I had a say in the matter," Jackson replied.

He looked to his right. Inspector Bowden, a stern look on his face, leaned against one of the windows. He didn't offer Jackson a hand.

Chief Diaz gave a forced laugh. "Of course you did. You're not under arrest or anything. In fact, you're free to go at any time."

Jackson grunted.

Chief Diaz gestured to an armchair opposite his desk. "Please, have a seat."

Jackson did.

Chief Diaz sat down as well. "Mr. Clay, I believe most problems in life come about through miscommunication. Wires get crossed, someone says something and another person takes it the wrong way, that sort of thing."

Jackson didn't say anything.

"I understand you have concerns over the death of Mr. Yarbrough and Ms. Jensen. I also know Investigator Bowden here. I've worked with him the last four or five years, ever since I've had this chair. Investigator Bowden is a competent and diligent detective, but sometimes his tenacity can come across as ... ornery."

Jackson shifted his weight in the chair. "I'm still waiting to find out why I'm here."

Chief Diaz gave another forced laugh. "What I'm saying is, perhaps things seemed to you as though Investigator Bowden here and, by extension, the Chincoteague Police Department, were not taking both deaths very seriously and pursuing all leads in an effort to understand what really happened in each case."

Jackson let out a deep breath. "Okay..."

"But any outside or *private* attempts to look into things, even well-intentioned ones, can only end up impeding the real investigation."

"I'm not...*impeding*... anyone."

"I don't believe you mean to, but you are going around the island causing a stir. First, visiting Susan Yarbrough several times. Then there was yesterday, where we fielded a number of phone calls about two men lurking around people's docks, taking pictures of their boats."

Jackson rested his elbows on the armrests of the chair.

Chief Diaz leaned forward. "Care to explain yourself?"

"I like boats."

Chief Diaz smirked. "You do, apparently. As you've been taking the late captain's boat all around the area as of late. The interesting thing is, after getting all those calls, we checked with the harbor to see when you wrapped up your little excursion." He looked over at the computer monitor on his desk. "The CCTV video puts you returning at just after one in the morning... and curiously, your buddy that left with you is absent."

"It was a late night and he was tired. I dropped him off at the dock off our rental, then I headed back for our SUV."

"What were you two doing all night? It's got to be hard to appreciate people's boats in the dark."

"You'd be surprised."

Chief Diaz stared at him.

"We were looking into local lore."

Chief Diaz raised an eyebrow. "Local lore?"

"You know... history. Ghosts. Things like that."

Chief Diaz leaned forward. "Mr. Clay, for the sake of time and effort, can we just lay our cards on the table?"

Jackson shrugged. "Sure."

"We really are taking both Mr. Yarbrough and Ms. Jensen's deaths very seriously, but we're not a department of unlimited resources. So whatever time and energy I have to spend chasing down, say, two out-of-towners creeping out the locals takes away from those efforts. Now, I don't know if you've heard, but there is an Evacuation Advisory for the island. This Hurricane Margaret is shaping up to be a pretty nasty storm, and I don't want anyone else getting hurt if I can help it."

"Neither do I, but—cards on the table—I've come to your boy, Bowden, here three times already and each time he's brushed me off. So, I'm doing some looking around myself."

"And that's what I'm saying. I believe there's been some miscommunication between you and our department." He turned his palms out and smiled. "At the end of the day, we all want the same thing, so it doesn't make sense for us to work against each other."

"I'm not working against anyone except whoever killed Captain Terry and Taylor Jensen."

Chief Diaz's shoulders dropped. "Mr. Clay, I am politely asking you to heed the evacuation warning and head to the mainland. Leave the investigation to us and the other law enforcement agencies involved. You remain concerned, and I can appreciate that. You're welcome to call my office anytime and check in on how things are going."

"And you'll be completely transparent?"

Chief Diaz leaned back in his chair. "As transparent as we can be. We're talking about open investigations here. Serious investigations at that."

Jackson nodded as if he were expecting such an answer. "This evacuation advisory... it's just that, isn't it? An *advisory*? As in, a suggestion?"

Chief Diaz's head dropped. "Mr. Clay..."

"And even an evacuation warning... that's not legally enforceable, right? You can't *force* someone to leave the island?"

"Mr. Clay, I mean it when I say this will be a very dangerous storm."

"Sounds like it." Jackson rose. "I'll take that ride back to my rental now. I have a busy day of looking at boats ahead of me."

"Mr. Clay, I called for this meeting to be courteous. Since that's not working, let me be blunt. If you obstruct our investigation... *any* investigation... we will bring charges."

"Noted." Jackson turned and walked out of the office.

———

WHEN OFFICER BIRCH pulled into the driveway of Jackson and Bear's rental house with Jackson riding shotgun, Bear was sitting on the landing atop the steps leading up to the front door, a mug of coffee in his hand. Jackson got out of the cruiser and joined his friend to watch Officer Birch back out of the driveway.

"I was just about to head out and look for you," Bear said. He nodded at the now empty driveway. "What was that all about?"

"Apparently we spooked the locals with our trip around the island yesterday," Jackson said. "The Chief of Police wanted to have a heart-to-heart and encourage me to leave the investigating to the professionals."

"Did it work?"

Jackson looked down at him, his eyebrows raised.

Bear chortled. "Didn't think so." He took a sip of his coffee. "Do they know about our friend out in the hunter's cabin?"

Jackson shook his head. "I don't think so. The Chief seemed eager to show he knew about everything we'd been up to, but he didn't mention that." He leaned an elbow against the banister. "Still, we should be extra cautious about eyes on us. I don't think they'll bother trying to tail us — the chief made it a point to say how limited their resources are — but we're now squarely on their radar."

Bear took another sip. "Is that so?"

Jackson nodded. "The Chief encouraged us to heed this hurricane evacuation advisory that's been issued and head out of town."

"And I assume we're not."

"Not until we figure out what to do with Hanz, anyway. Speaking of, I need to call Bailey."

Bear got up, brushed off his backside, then stepped to the front door. "I assume we're on the move soon. I'll go grab a shower."

"Sounds good."

Bear opened the door and went inside. When he closed it behind him, Jackson pulled out his phone.

Bailey answered on the first ring. "The news says half of the Eastern Shore is under an evacuation advisory. Please tell me you're heading home."

"I'm not done here yet," Jackson said.

"This isn't some scumbag you can shoot or punch and kick. It's a damn *hurricane*, Clay."

"I know, but I'm in the middle of something here. And I need another favor. This one I need you to do yourself, though, and tell no one."

Bailey sighed. "How do I already know I'm not going to like this?"

"I need you to check for CCTV video from a 7-Eleven on Philadelphia Avenue in Ocean City, Maryland for the morning of the thirteenth, between five and seven. Someone else can get it for you, but I need you to review it yourself."

"How gracious of you."

Jackson sat down on the landing. "I'm serious. I'm going to send you a photo of a teenager from a while back. I need you to see if you can ID anyone that might look like the kid, just twenty-five years older or so."

Bailey snorted. "This is ridiculous. Just give me his name, I'll get his latest DMV photo and let you know if it's him."

"You won't find him in the DMV system."

"Why not?"

"Because he's been missing and presumed dead since '99."

Bailey was silent for a moment. "How does a missing person fit into your two deaths?"

Jackson rubbed his eyes. "I'm still figuring that out. But for now, I need to clear him of at least one of the murders. Captain Terry was killed the morning of the thirteenth. If this guy was up in Ocean City, he couldn't have been involved."

"But how does Ocean City fit into this? You had to have gotten this theory that the man was supposedly at this 7-Eleven from someone."

Jackson paused, choosing his words carefully. "From someone, yes."

Bailey put it together and hissed into the phone. "Clay, if you've found someone that's been missing for a quarter-century, you need to bring in the authorities. This isn't a game."

"If his alibi is bull, I will."

"Wait, please tell me you're not *holding* this person against their will."

"Not technically, no."

"Clay, I swear to god you're going to cost me my badge one of these days, if not kill me outright."

Jackson took a moment to let the tension simmer. "Will you help me?"

Bailey didn't say anything.

Jackson checked that the call hadn't disconnected. "Bailey?"

"Yes, fine. But only because I want you out of the path of this damn hurricane. I'll get you your information, but only if you promise you'll then get off that goddamn island."

Jackson could tell he was pushing Bailey to her limit. He couldn't betray her trust. "If you can review that footage for me, I'll do what I need to do here then be on my way. I promise."

"Good. Fine. And there's no more reason to keep me in the dark. Give me the guy's name, I'll see if I can ID him or not."

"Russell Hanz. He went missing in July 1999. Most everyone here believes he was killed by one of the members of the Meachem family. They were a big deal here until everything with Hanz ended in scandal."

"Wait, there's not someone in prison convicted for his murder, is there? Because I can't sit on that."

"No. No charges were ever brought forth. Hence, the scandal."

"Alright, got it."

"It goes without saying, if you want me out of here before this hurricane, it's got to be sooner rather than later."

Bailey clicked her tongue. "And yet, you said it."

"Just had to make sure."

Bailey hung up.

Jackson slid the phone into his pocket and went in to check on Bear.

TWENTY-ONE

SHAW GOT an email overnight that there would be a briefing about Hurricane Margaret first thing in the morning as it pertained to the refuge. She pulled into a spot in the administrative building's employee parking lot just before nine. Bridger and two park rangers were hitching a trailer with a rigid inflatable boat to his service truck. Shaw hopped out and walked over to them.

Bridger glanced up and waved. "Good morning."

"Morning," Shaw replied. "What's going on? I thought there was a meeting about hurricane prep."

"There is, but we've also got a missing kayaker. He went out alone yesterday evening and hasn't been seen since."

"Do we have a last known position?"

Bridger shook his head. "Not really. His fiancé called it in. They were supposed to go out together, but she wasn't feeling well and stayed behind. All she knows is he headed north from the Snug Harbor Resort marina on the south side of town."

Shaw raised her eyebrows. "That's like seven or eight miles of coastline on the channel. And that's assuming he didn't go farther north into the bay."

"Yup. And this damn storm is putting us on an accelerated clock. Coast Guard and Marine Police are assisting. They'll cover the main waterways, but it's on us to check that he didn't wander up any of the little tributaries and get himself in trouble."

Shaw nodded. "Send me what info you've got. I can assist as well."

"I'll take you up on that, but later." Bridger hiked a thumb over his shoulder, pointing toward the administration building. "I need you in that meeting for the both of us. Then, if they don't need you, I'll gladly take the help."

"Deal." Shaw started for the building. "Good luck."

"Thanks."

As Shaw walked inside, she weighed telling Jackson about this latest development. She didn't want him interfering with any search and rescue efforts, but she couldn't deny she too believed Captain Terry and Taylor Jensen's deaths were somehow connected. This kayaker had disappeared in the same area. If something had happened to him, that would make three people killed in nearly as many days.

She pulled out her phone and texted him.

> We've got a missing kayaker. Could be nothing, but he was last seen heading north up the channel. I'll keep you posted.

———

JACKSON AND BEAR were standing out in front of Sandy Pony Donuts when Jackson's phone buzzed in his pocket. Bear looked over at him as he pulled it out and read the message.

"What is it?" Bear asked, leaning against the order window of the pastry purveyor.

"Shaw," Jackson said, slipping his phone back in his pocket. "A kayaker went out last night and never came back."

They took in the people around them, engaging in lighthearted banter, before exchanging a look. Jackson shook his head.

The donut shop was little more than a single-story building with a covered porch and order window overlooking Maddox Boulevard. As Jackson waited for Bear to get his breakfast, he took in the scene before them. A steady flow of cars headed west on Maddox, queuing their way to the bridge and the mainland beyond. Half the vehicles had out-of-state plates. Vacationers unwilling to chance the hurricane.

He didn't love the idea that they were staying, but he knew he couldn't leave now. If not because of Captain Terry and Taylor Jensen, then surely because they were still basically holding Russell Hanz captive.

A Chincoteague Police patrol car headed the other way up the street. As it slowed for the traffic ahead of it, Jackson got a look inside its open windows. An officer he hadn't met yet was behind the wheel, giving Jackson a once-over. Jackson nodded hello. The officer nodded back before the traffic ahead of him moved, and he continued on.

The order window slid open and a woman their age handed Bear a box with a half dozen donuts.

"Here you go, hon," she said. "And two coffees." She put the coffees up next to the box.

"Thank ya," Bear said. He handed one of the coffees to Jackson before grabbing the other and the box of donuts.

They walked to their car in the lot at the back of the building without saying another word and climbed in. As soon as the doors were shut, Bear looked over at Jackson.

"You think the missing kayaker has anything to do with Hanz and his fortress of solitude?" he asked.

"I don't know," Jackson said. "It depends on when this kayaker went missing."

"Did Shaw say anything about that?"

Jackson sipped his coffee. "No. Just that it was last night."

"If he did something to that kayaker because of what we did, trying to get a hold of a boat to make a run for it or something, that's on us."

Jackson took another sip. "I doubt a kayaker would be out in the middle of the night. Most likely he went missing before we went in for Hanz."

"I hate to say it, but it didn't seem like Hanz had just attacked someone. And we didn't find any signs of a kayak or kayaker. If this missing kayaker is connected to the other two investigations, then I don't think Hanz is our guy."

Jackson simply nodded.

Bear opened up the box of donuts, pulled one out, and took a bite. "Jesus H. Christ, these are amazing." He took another bite and offered the box to Jackson.

Jackson shook his head.

Bear shrugged. "Suit yourself." He put the box on his lap and took another bite of the donut in his hand. He growled as he swallowed. "So, how do you want to play it then?"

Jackson stared straight ahead. "Let's wait for Bailey to get back to us on Hanz's alibi. We can't go back to the hunter's cabin until nightfall, anyway. If Hanz's alibi checks out, it doesn't really matter if this missing kayaker is connected or not."

Bear took a loud slurp of his own coffee before grabbing a second donut. "*If* Hanz's alibi checks out, we're basically back to square one... with a nasty storm on the way."

"I know."

"Well, we've got daylight to burn until we hear back from your lady cop friend. How do you want to use it?"

Jackson thought. "We were looking for a boat coming from Chincoteague headed toward the refuge, but it could've come from anywhere. The one data point we have is Jensen's attack." He fired up the Suburban.

Bear looked at him curiously. "Where're we headed?"

"To the beach." Jackson put the SUV in gear. "Let's start at the end and work backwards."

———

TWO DOZEN LAW enforcement officers from an alphabet soup of agencies, as well as a handful of park rangers, crammed into the conference room in the administration building. Stained wood panels lined three walls, with a bank of frameless windows flooding the otherwise dark room with natural sunlight. All the attendees were either standing or sitting around one half of the large, unremarkable conference table that filled the center of the room. Opposite them stood the manager of the Chincoteague National Wildlife Refuge Complex, Nathan Kerr.

Shaw stood just behind two people seated at the center of the table, listening to Kerr speak. He was a touch shorter than her, with gray hair combed back and a heavy salt-and-pepper shadow around his chin. Kerr was wrapping up the meeting when the door to his right opened and in walked Ben Diaz, the Chincoteague Chief of Police. He and Kerr conferred with one another before facing the room.

"Good afternoon, everyone," Chief Diaz said. "As you may be aware, Hurricane Margaret hasn't altered course much since the National Hurricane Center issued its watch. We now know that a hurricane warning for the entire Eastern Shore Peninsula is imminent. I've just wrapped up a call with the mayor, the town manager, and the town council. We have decided, when that happens, we will also be elevating the Evacuation Advisory to an Evacuation Warning for the entire island. This means all non-essential personnel should be prepared to leave."

A park ranger over Shaw's shoulder raised his hand. "Who is that, exactly?"

"We will have a skeleton crew of personnel who have volunteered to stay behind. They will set up an emergency shelter at the

Chincoteague Center for people who can't or won't heed the evacuation warning, and it will be up to them to decide when calls for emergency services are discontinued on the island. Everyone else should plan on evacuating when the warning is issued."

Shaw cleared her throat. "We've got a missing kayaker out there somewhere, sir."

Chief Diaz nodded. "I'm aware, and we are coordinating with all agencies here as well as the Coast Guard to expedite that search. With a little luck, hopefully we can find him and get him back safe before the evacuation warning goes into effect." He paused, looking around the room. "Any other questions?"

No one spoke.

Chief Diaz clapped his hands together. "Okay then. Everyone be safe out there."

The meeting adjourned, and people began filing out. Shaw snaked her way through the river of bodies and made her way out to her truck, eager to get on with aiding in the search for the missing kayaker. If it was Fish and Wildlife Services' job to search the interior of the island, few knew it better than she did. She pulled out of the employee parking lot and headed for the service road that ran up the western coastline of the refuge.

———

JACKSON AND BEAR entered the refuge and took the road out to the beach. The sky was a blanket of ashen clouds, and the parking lots were deserted save for a couple of cars, giving the area an eerie feel. They took the parking lot as far north as it would go, leading them to the same corner that had been cluttered with emergency vehicles on their last visit. From there, they got out, climbed over the small sand dune and continued on foot.

The wind gusted inland, pelting them with loose sand and sending large waves crashing onto the shore. Giant red signs, staked every thirty yards or so, cautioned beachgoers that the beaches were closed and absolutely no swimming was allowed.

Bear stopped at one of the signs and read it.

"Riptides," Jackson said. "Dangerous ones form ahead of any hurricane or tropical storm."

Bear nodded and they continued on, wind whipping at their clothes. Gone from the beach were any signs of a crime scene. Jackson led them to a point on the beach and turned back to Bear.

"This was about the spot where the tents were the other day," he said.

Bear surveyed the ground around them. "I don't see any sign they found a body out here."

"In this?" Jackson shook his head. "You wouldn't." He turned his back to the ocean, giving his face a respite from the scouring sand. The beach ended at a gentle incline covered with beachgrass like a head of hair. "So, if you're whoever killed Jensen, where'd you come from?"

Bear looked back the way they'd come. "You'd think Jensen came from the parking lot area, same as us. Maybe the person followed her."

Jackson cocked his head to the side. "Maybe, but then why wait until she's all the way up here?"

Bear shrugged. "Someone else out on the beach? Potential witnesses?"

Jackson shook his head. "Shaw would've said something about that." He scanned the top of the beach again. "Something brought him out here."

Jackson started walking to where the beach rose and met the grass. On the incline, he had a better view. Fifty feet further up the beach, he spotted a sandy trail cutting through the grass as it went further inland.

"There," he said, pointing at it. "There's a trail."

The two of them followed the edge of the beach to the trailhead, then looked down it. It cut a narrow path through the grass to the woods beyond.

"You think it goes all the way out to the channel?" Bear asked.

"Only one way to find out." Jackson started down the trail.

Bear groaned. "I wore the wrong damn shoes for this."

The two of them followed the trail through the tall grass and into the thick cluster of trees. The trail slithered its way out to a paved drive that cut through the woodlands.

"A road?" Bear asked.

"I think this is the wildlife loop we drive by as we enter the park," Jackson said. "Come on."

They took the loop, continuing deeper into the center of the island and headed for the channel on the other side. The loop cut through an open swath of marshland several hundred yards wide before turning sharply south and west, tucking up against more woods on the other side.

Jackson surveyed his options. Branching off the loop was what looked to be a service road. It had a cattle gate across it, barring unauthorized vehicles from entering and implying unauthorized hikers should likewise stay out.

"The channel is on the other side of these woods," Jackson said. "Whoever killed Jensen wouldn't have taken the wildlife loop back out to the beach road. Too much of a risk being spotted." He went to the cattle gate, climbed up, and swung his leg over.

"I don't think I have to remind you we're quickly wearing out our welcome with the law around here," Bear said.

"Hurry up," Jackson replied.

Bear got up and over the gate, albeit much slower and less gracefully than Jackson, and dropped down onto the other side. The two of them started down the service road, looking for any sort of clearing or path through the woods. They'd gone a quarter mile or so when the rumble of an engine grew louder behind them. Jackson slipped into the brush lining the road and squatted down. Bear, after making a gap big enough for himself, did the same.

"I guess this is a bad time to remind you we're probably somewhere we're not supposed to be," Bear said, his tone hushed.

"It's fine," Jackson cautioned. "We're just two hikers that got a little lost."

Bear shook his head. "And hiding?"

Jackson could see the vehicle as it approached. It was a Fish and Wildlife Service pickup like Shaw's. In fact, as it came closer, Jackson saw Shaw behind the wheel.

The truck rolled past them, then slowed to a stop. Shaw climbed out of it, shut her door, then looked their way.

"I hope you two were better at camouflaging yourself in the duck blind," she said.

Jackson and Bear climbed out from underneath the brush.

"Keen eye spotting us like that," Jackson said.

"It wasn't hard with Bear's big boot sticking out." Shaw countered.

Bear's face reddened.

"I'd tell you this area is for official park use only, but I'm guessing you know that," Shaw said. "In fact, the whole park is fixing to close to the public. Probably by the end of the day."

"We were following a trail from the beach," Jackson said. "We'd heard you all believe whoever killed Taylor Jensen got on the island by boat. It would make sense that they'd stick to small trails and keep out of sight. We were looking to see if we could find the spot where they came in." He nodded at her. "What are you doing back here?"

Shaw raised her eyebrows. "Besides the fact it's my job to be back here? I'm assisting with the search for the kayaker, checking the shore."

"You want to pretend you didn't see us? We'll see our way out the way we came."

"And risk you getting spotted by someone else?" Shaw shook her head. "I don't think so. Get in."

Jackson hesitated, but Shaw had already turned back to the

truck. Guess this wasn't up for discussion. He walked around the back of her truck and climbed into the passenger seat. Bear got in behind him, and they continued up the service road.

They drove on for several minutes in silence, the tall brush and trees enveloping them on either side giving way to more open marshland. Large, squat oak trees dotted the area like small islands on a verdant sea.

"What makes you think your missing guy would be all the way back here?" Jackson asked. "You can't even see the channel from here."

"There's dozens of little inlets and tributaries a small boat could wander up," Shaw replied. "It wouldn't take much for someone that didn't know what they were doing to get themselves stuck. I've seen it before."

They approached a spot in the road where two more dirt roads intersected it when Jackson spotted something ahead to the left.

"There," he said. "Ten o'clock."

Shaw slowed down and looked where he directed. "What do you see?"

"There was something bright colored over there. Red or orange, something like that."

Shaw turned onto the road that ran out that way, driving through a cluster of trees. On the other side, floating in a shallow pool of water, was a red kayak.

"Good spotting," Shaw said.

She pulled up next to the kayak, and the three of them got out. The kayak was empty, bobbing in what looked to be a small, narrow pond.

"I'm guessing whoever's kayak that is, they didn't come all the way out here just to sit in a little puddle," Bear said.

Shaw looked to the other side of the truck. Jackson followed her gaze. On the opposite side of the road lay more marshland and, in the distance, the channel.

"It's low tide," Shaw said. "At high tide, the area would be flooded. And with a storm tide? It'd probably flood over the road here."

She started walking further down the road. Jackson and Bear followed. They went no more than a few dozen yards when the dirt road suddenly became a muddy depression. She looked to the left. Snaking its way through the marsh grass was a little sliver of water.

"There," Shaw said. "That little inlet probably flooded over, taking the kayak with it."

Shaw stepped off the road and started plodding cautiously into the marsh. Jackson followed her in, stepping exactly where she'd stepped. Bear stayed at the edge of the road, scratching at his chin.

"I'll, uh, look around over here," he said.

Jackson and Shaw ignored him. They walked parallel to the little sliver of water, looking all around them. Shaw was only a few feet ahead of Jackson when she suddenly stopped, her eyes fixed on something just in front of her. Jackson came up alongside her to see what had caught her attention. There, in the marsh, a man lay face down. Jackson began to move ahead, but Shaw put her hand out.

"Don't," she said.

She reached into her back pocket, pulled out a pair of nitrile gloves, and snapped them on. She stepped carefully over the man's body to the other side, then bent down and rolled him over. A mud-smeared face, frozen with fear, looked up at the clouded heavens above them. Muddy water ran down his chin and into a gaping wound in his neck.

"What the hell is going on?" Shaw muttered.

TWENTY-TWO

A SMALL SWARM OF BOATS, trucks, and first responders
descended on the boggy marsh where Tom Marshall had been found.
By late afternoon, the sun had nearly set over Chincoteague, casting
the entire scene in long, skewed shadows. Despite them, Jackson was
beginning to see things for what they really were. Someone, or some
ones, were on a killing spree across the two islands.

He sat on the lowered tailgate of Shaw's truck, Bear beside him,
watching Shaw as she stood on the dirt road talking with Lederer.
Every few minutes one of them would look Jackson's way. It didn't
take a detective to figure out Lederer probably wasn't praising his
initiative.

"If they give you any shit, it's just because you were right all
along," Bear said. "Now, they can't deny it."

"It's not about being right, Bear," Jackson replied. "It's about
stopping whatever... this... is." He looked over his shoulder at two
crime scene technicians lowering Marshall's body into a bag.

Bear snorted. "Maybe not to you. But to them? It's politics. Politics always matter."

Jackson didn't say anything more. He turned around to see Shaw and Lederer end their conversation and approach him and Bear. When they got close enough for Jackson to smell the mint gum on Lederer's breath, Lederer folded his arms.

"We'll be looking into any possible connections between Mr. Marshall and Ms. Jensen. If you know of any, it'd be good if you cooperated," Lederer said.

Bear smirked and shook his head. "You mean other than the fact that both of them ended up filleted by some psycho on your park lands?"

Lederer leered at him. "Yes, the manner of their deaths are very similar. But that's all they are at this point. Jumping to any other conclusion is counterproductive. And going around telling tall tales of some phantom serial killer is only going to cause undue panic."

Bear cocked his head. "Well, more likely, you're lookin' at a spree killer here, not a serial killer. Less Son of Sam, more DC Sniper."

Jackson glared daggers at Bear.

Bear shrugged. "What? I've gotten really into true crime podcasts."

Jackson returned his attention to Lederer. "Any idea when Mr. Marshall was killed?"

"Rigor Mortis puts his time of death likely twelve to twenty-four hours ago," Lederer said.

"If it is a spree killer like Bear said," Jackson replied, "that means we have twelve to twenty-four fewer hours until they strike again."

Lederer shook his head. "*Whatever* this is, *we* are handling it. As in, those of us with a badge. I've spoken with Chief Diaz, and I understand he gave you all the same lecture and you were warned about obstructing the investigation *before* you decided to come out this way."

"By the looks of things, I'd say we've aided your investigation far more than we've obstructed it," Jackson said.

"Be that as it may, we've got it from here." Lederer gestured to Shaw. "FWO Shaw here will take you back to your truck at the beach. I also understand Chief Diaz encouraged you to leave town, and that suggestion has clearly fallen on deaf ears. Due to the incoming hurricane and the recent homicides, the refuge is now closed to the public. So, I don't care where you go, but you'll get off Assateague."

Jackson knew there was no pushing Lederer to change his mind, so he said nothing more. Deeming the matter put to rest, Lederer left to tend to matters at the scene. When he was gone, Shaw centered herself between Jackson and Bear.

"I get he's being a bit of a prick, but he's not wrong," Shaw said. "You guys should head for the mainland."

"This hurricane is all the more reason to have all hands on deck," Jackson said. "We can handle ourselves."

"You know how many people I've heard say that very same thing before needing to be rescued?"

Jackson gave a slight shake of his head. "I appreciate the concern but we're not going anywhere."

Shaw looked to Bear for a second opinion on the matter.

Bear nodded. "You heard the man."

Shaw took a deep breath in and sighed. "Why do I get the feeling you've given many in law enforcement gray hair?"

"Persistence is our specialty." Bear hopped off the tailgate. "That and quality outdoor gear at ridiculously low prices. If you're ever in the Martinsville area, look us up."

Shaw rolled her eyes. "Come on, get in. I'll drive you all back."

———

SHAW PULLED up to the back of Bear's Suburban and threw her truck into park. She took off her sunglasses and looked over at Jackson.

"I don't have to follow you out, do I?" she asked. "Make sure you actually leave the refuge?"

"No, we'll leave," Jackson said. "For real."

"And you're sure I can't convince you to keep on going and head for the mainland?"

Jackson shook his head. "Not until I know this is over."

"For what it's worth, we had a meeting this morning. They're expecting us to be placed under a Hurricane Warning any time now, at which point town leadership will upgrade the evacuation advisory to a warning."

"Short of placing me in cuffs and driving me off the island personally, I'm not going anywhere. Not yet anyway."

Shaw huffed. "Just... be careful, okay? It seems like you can handle yourselves, but these storms are no joke."

Jackson nodded. "Copy that."

With that, he and Bear got out of Shaw's truck and into Bear's Suburban. Shaw pulled away enough to give them room to back out, then seemed to linger, seeing if they would. Jackson obliged her, backed out, and left the parking lot, waving at Shaw as they passed in front of her and headed down the beach road.

"You heard what that other guy said?" Bear asked. "They think that guy was killed sometime yesterday evening or early this morning."

Jackson grunted in the affirmative.

"We rolled up on Russell Hanz just after midnight. Like we said this morning, that's a pretty narrow window for him to have done it."

"I know," Jackson muttered.

"So?"

Jackson kept his eyes on the road ahead. "We'll wait to see what Bailey finds out about Hanz's alibi."

TWENTY-THREE

THE BULL SHARK had spent the entire day trolling the channel for signs that the authorities had found his latest victim. It had been unplanned, and with that, far riskier than he'd intended, but everything had worked out remarkably well. No witnesses, and the body had been left in an area that couldn't be traced back to him. It had given it all a new kind of exhilaration, adding to the thrill of the hunt.

Late in the afternoon, as he motored south for the sixth time, he finally spotted signs that his work had been discovered. Fish and Wildlife Service and National Park Service trucks were parked rear-to-nose on a service road just off the marsh where he'd left the kayaker. A couple of Virginia Marine Police boats sat idle in Janey's Creek. Ahead of him, he saw a small Coast Guard Response Boat heading toward him. As it neared, it slowed down. The Bull Shark's chest tightened.

A Coastguardsman in a blue uniform and red life jacket stood off the boat's stern and waved at him. He waved back. Another Coastguardsman behind the wheel cut the throttle to the engine altogether, and the boat floated up easily next to his.

"Good afternoon," the Coastguardsman said. "Petty Officer John McKey with the U.S. Coast Guard. How are you today?"

"Good," The Bull Shark replied, smiling. "And you?"

"Good, thank you. Do you have your Government ID and Boat Registration with you?"

"I do." He reached back for a wet bag next to the boat's motor. He fished out the necessary documents and handed them to the Coastguardsman. "Can I ask what this is about?"

"Just a routine safety check." The coastguardsman examined the ID. "What are you doing out here today?"

He thought for a moment. "I guess you could say I'm fishing. Just looking for my next spot."

The coastguardsman tipped his head. "Then I'll need to see your fishing license as well, please."

He found that in the bag, too, and gave it to the Coastguardsman.

The coastguardsman studied the paperwork a moment longer, then handed everything back to him. "Are you coming out of the harbor down here?"

He nodded. "Yes, sir."

"Don't know if you've heard, but there's a Hurricane Watch for the area. The harbor will cease all nonessential operations at sundown this evening. You make sure you're in by then, okay?"

He nodded again. "Got it. Thank you, sir."

"No problem. Stay safe." The coastguardsman motioned for the officer inside the cabin to go.

A moment later their boat rumbled back to life and pulled away.

Irritability rose within The Bull Shark. The waterways were how he hunted, how he moved about. Even if he found a different point to launch from after the harbor closed, the area would be crawling with law enforcement ushering people back to shore. His anonymity would be gone.

But The Bull Shark fancied himself a cunning predator, as adaptable as he was fierce. He'd read about bull sharks being found as far up the Mississippi River as Illinois, adapting for the sake of the hunt.

Now, it was time for him to do the same.

Adapt.

Heading back to shore, The Bull Shark prepared to continue his hunt.

TWENTY-FOUR

JACKSON KNEW they would have to go back tonight and decide what to do with Russell Hanz. Things with the inbound hurricane were happening fast, and there was no guarantee they'd be able to return to the hunter's cabin the following night. No matter what Hanz was or wasn't guilty of, Jackson wasn't willing to let him be swallowed by the storm.

He desperately needed Bailey to get back to him with information on Hanz's alibi. He spent most of the late afternoon and early evening waiting for that phone call. Bear eventually went out to the back deck to grill some of the duck they'd shot the other day. Finally, just after six, Bailey called.

"Tell me you've got something," Jackson said.

"We really need to work on your manners," Bailey replied. "Yes, I've got something."

Jackson waited a beat for her to continue. "Well?"

"It looks like your boy Hanz walked into the 7-Eleven in Ocean City just as he claimed." There was the tapping of a keyboard in the background. "He goes in, walks up and down a couple aisles, then buys himself breakfast and leaves."

Jackson's eyes narrowed. "What do you mean looks like?"

"I mean, to me, it looks like the guy in the photo you sent me, only twenty-five years older and with a beard. But you wanted this kept between us, which means I couldn't have any techs run it for facial recognition."

Jackson's shoulders dropped. "But you're pretty sure it's him."

"I'd bet a substantial chunk of my paycheck it's him."

"Can you send it to me?"

"Sure, hold on." There was more typing on Bailey's end. "There. Should get it soon. From my personal email, obviously."

Jackson went to the dining room table where he'd left his laptop and opened it up. It chimed with an incoming email. Jackson opened the video attached to it. It was from a camera behind the store clerk's right shoulder. A man Russell's size and build plodded leisurely into the store, looked at a few things, then made himself a cup of coffee and grabbed a sticky bun just as he'd told Jackson. When the man came to the register, he looked up briefly, showing enough of his face. It was, without a doubt, Russell Hanz. Hundreds of miles away from Will's Creek and the duck blind when Captain Terry was killed.

"That's him," Jackson said in little more than a whisper.

"Meaning, he's not your guy," Bailey clarified.

Jackson cleared his throat. "Correct."

"For what it's worth, I'm sorry."

Jackson clicked back and replayed the video. "Yeah. They found another body today, Bailey. There's someone or a group of people here going on a killing spree for God knows what reason."

Bailey's voice spiked. "Another body? Who?"

"A kayaker who had gone out last night and never returned. He was found in the marshes in the refuge with his throat slit."

"Jesus Christ."

"Yeah."

Bailey paused. "Be careful out there. Not just the storm, but this —whatever *this* is—too."

"Will do. Anything yet on the DNA sample?"

"Last time I checked with my Bureau guys there wasn't any update. I'll touch base with them again in the morning."

"Appreciate it. How's my dog doing?"

Bailey snorted. "You know, the usual. Continuing to terrorize me and my cat."

"If you need to board her, I get it."

"Don't be ridiculous. She's being a pain, but we'll manage. I've got things here. You just finish up and get back here to her, preferably in one piece."

Jackson leaned back in his chair. "That's the plan."

"Have a good night, Clay."

Jackson hung up and tossed his phone onto the table. Bear opened the screen door to the deck and came in with a basting cup and brush. "Bird's almost done," he said, heading toward the kitchen. "Who was that on the phone?"

"Bailey," Jackson said.

Bear looked back, an eyebrow raised. "Yeah? Any news?"

Jackson nodded. "Hanz's alibi checks out. He was in Ocean City when Captain Terry was killed.

Bear huffed. "Shit. That's what I was afraid of."

Jackson didn't say anything.

Bear turned and began rinsing off the dishes in the kitchen sink. "I guess he's not our guy then. Unless you think one person killed Captain Terry and someone else the other two."

Jackson shook his head. "Too many bodies are stacking up for these all to be a coincidence. They have to be connected. Besides, the timeline on Tom Marshall doesn't really work for Hanz, either."

"We ought to go back and kick him loose, then."

"Yeah, tonight, after it gets dark. We'll eat and we'll go."

Bear finished cleaning the dishes, shut off the faucet, then turned around to face Jackson. He leaned against the counter and folded his arms. "And then what?"

Jackson thought, then cocked his head to the side. "Then we do what we came here to do. We hunt."

TWENTY-FIVE

JUST BEFORE TEN THAT NIGHT, Jackson and Bear split up. Bear headed down the dock behind their house and out to where they'd stashed Russell's boat and Jackson over to the harbor in Bear's Suburban. As he pulled into a parking spot overlooking Captain Terry's boat as it bobbed in its slip, a knot formed in his stomach at what he saw. A law enforcement boat sat at the mouth of the harbor, its blue and red lights strobing the darkened marina around it.

Jackson got out of the SUV and tried not to pay it any mind, acting the part of any other boater here to take his vessel out. As he stepped onto the dock, though, a vehicle pulled up behind the Suburban. When the driver aimed a spotlight on Jackson, he realized it was a patrol car.

"You're not planning on going out, are you, Mr. Clay?" said a male voice.

Jackson held a hand in front of his face to block the spotlight. Even still, he could only see broad shapes, but he saw enough of the cruiser's wrap to tell it belonged to Chincoteague Police.

"As a matter of fact, I was," Jackson replied. "Is that a problem?"

"I'm sorry, sir, but that won't be possible. The harbor is closed to all non-essential activities by order of the mayor and town council."

"I'm guessing I can't persuade you to pretend you didn't spot me here?"

"Even if I could, that boat out there is the Coast Guard. They definitely won't be as accommodating."

Jackson tried to think of another angle but came up empty. "Fair enough." He left the dock and walked up to the patrol car. When he stepped clear of the spotlight, he could see the officer's face, illuminated by his laptop screen. Jackson didn't know his name but had seen him around the police headquarters.

Jackson extended his hand into the cabin of the patrol car. "You know my name, but I don't believe we've met."

The officer took Jackson's hand and shook it. "I've seen you around the police station with Bowden and the chief. Jon Perry, pleased to meet you."

"Same here. Listen, I really need to get out tonight. I left some gear in a blind. Any chance you could talk to the Coast Guard for me?"

Perry shook his head. "I'm afraid not. They've been trying to get everyone off the water all afternoon. Might be best for you to get out of Dodge while you still can."

"If I had a dollar for every person that told me that these past couple days, I'd have enough to buy my own place on the island."

Perry flashed a big smile. "Then maybe you ought to think about heeding their warning."

"I'll think about it," Jackson held a hand up as he backed away. "You have a good night."

"You do the same."

As soon as Jackson climbed into the Suburban and shut the door, he called Bear, who picked up immediately.

"You on your way, Jacky Boy?" Bear asked.

Jackson could hear the motor idling in the background. "No. We have a problem," he said. "Harbor's closed. They're not letting anyone out who isn't essential."

"Alright, you want me to double back and come get ya?"

"No. Chincoteague PD was here just in time to tell me not to go out. Could be a coincidence or they could have tabs on me."

"Then how do you want to play it?"

Jackson fired up the Suburban. "You keep going. Get Hanz and bring him back to the house. I'll take the scenic way home to check for a tail."

"What if they're watching the house?"

"I doubt they are, but we'll have to risk it. Go slow and stay close to the coastline. Coast Guard was posted at the mouth of the harbor. I'm sure they'll be patrolling the area, too."

"Gotcha. I'm on it."

Jackson heard the motor of the boat roar to life as the call disconnected.

———

JACKSON ZIGGED and zagged his way back to their rental. Using a mixture of back roads and main thoroughfares, he drove anywhere from ten under the posted speed limit to five over. Even when he was convinced no one was following and headed to the house, he doubled back down the street on foot to see if anyone else came. No one did.

Jackson flipped on a bedroom light that shone out the front of the house, then walked around the side in the dark and down the boardwalk to the dock. The night was still and quiet. Jackson had spent enough time out here over the previous evenings to know islanders were usually treated to an orchestra of crickets and cicadas calling out to one another. Tonight, though, as a chill coursed through the air, all was still. *The calm before the storm*, Jackson thought.

A distant motor broke the silence and slowly grew louder. Then, in the low light of the crescent moon, Jackson made out a small boat with two figures aboard, one larger than the other. It cruised up to the dock where Bear cut the engine. He stood up, and Jackson offered him a hand onto the dock. Russell stayed seated in the boat. He looked at them, then at the house in the distance.

"What is this?" he asked. "The place you kill me? Goodfellas-style?"

"Not so much," Jackson replied. "You're free to go."

Russell shook his head. "I don't get it. You hold me captive for a whole day... just to kick me free?"

"Like I told you last night, no one was stopping you from going anywhere."

"Yet you took my boat."

Jackson shrugged. "You're welcome to file a report with the police if you feel that strongly about it."

Russell hissed. "Asshole." He scanned Jackson's face. "You no longer think I killed those people."

Jackson squatted down so he was almost face-to-face with Russell. "Your alibi checked out."

"So, it's over? Just like that?"

"Just like that. Actually, there is one other thing I've been thinking about since last night. You said you never made any attempt to reach out to any of the Meachems, even Stephanie."

Russell nodded. "That's right. Why would I? Last I dealt with them, they tried to fucking kill me."

"But you went over there that night because you'd heard Stephanie was pregnant. You were never curious if she actually was? Or if it was yours?"

Russell rubbed the back of his neck. "I thought about it. I don't know, I guess any wanting to know was outdone by my fear they'd come for me."

"What if she had a kid and it was yours? You didn't want to be in its life?"

"Of course I did! But... what choice did I have? You don't get it.

Me dating Stephanie Meachem was like a bum dating a princess. Yeah, maybe I was on the football team and that meant something back then, but I was a screw up. Shit, look at me. Of course I'd want to be in my kid's life, but I also wouldn't want them to have to deal with me and my bullshit."

Jackson folded his hands together. "The sins of the father and all that."

"Yeah, I guess. It just seemed better I stayed away. For a lot of reasons."

Jackson didn't say anything. He understood where Russell was coming from, but resented him nonetheless. He'd loved his own son fiercely, would have done anything up to and including laying down his own life for that boy, and still lost him. Here was a man who could've been given the same gift, and he'd willingly let it go.

"You said I can leave?" Russell asked, his voice heavy.

"Yeah," Jackson said. He rose. "There's a hurricane inbound. Authorities are stopping people out on the water and telling them to head in. I don't know what it's like north of here in Maryland, but I'd imagine it's a similar situation. I'd be extra careful if I were you, considering you don't exist and all."

"Don't exist." Russell snorted and shook his head. "That's a good way to put it."

He switched seats to sit next to the motor and started it up. Jackson used his boot to gently nudge him away from the dock. Russell pointed the motor's tiller all the way to the left and gave it just enough gas to make a tight U-turn. Before he opened the throttle all the way up and sped off, he looked back at Jackson and Bear, standing on the dock. Jackson nodded farewell as the two of them watched him disappear into the night.

"The only lead we've had so far just left on that boat," Jackson said.

Bear shrugged. "Only thing to do is to keep at it."

They remained standing on the dock, listening to the rumble of Russell's motor grow distant, when both their phones buzzed and chirped at the same time. They exchanged a look with one another before pulling their phones out separately and looking at them. An alert flashed across the screens.

HURRICANE EVACUATION ISSUED FOR EASTERN SHORE

Jackson looked up at Bear. "We just got put on a clock to end this thing," he said.

TWENTY-SIX

THE NEXT MORNING, Jackson and Bear got breakfast at Maria's, an island institution along the main drag of shops on Maddox Boulevard. It was located between a candy shop on one side, with which it shared space in a red brick and beige building, and a Sunoco gas station on the other side. Bear was keen on getting in as many hot meals as possible before the storm shut everything down, whereas Jackson figured it was as good a place as any to regroup and refocus their efforts.

They'd passed a tangled knot of cars bottlenecked at the bridge, heading off the island. All the local news outlets were leading with the Evacuation Warning for all barrier islands and about half of the Eastern Shore's mainland. Jackson couldn't help but notice many more of the vehicles now had Virginia plates or bumper stickers. Even the locals were heeding the warning.

Inside Maria's, the dining room was barren. Their server, a sturdy woman in her fifties with dark brown hair, had asked, before taking their drink order, if they'd heard about the evacuation and why they were staying behind. Now, she brought two plates heaping with food.

"Creamed chipped beef for you," she said, laying a plate of toast smothered in a thick white sauce in front of Bear. "And an egg white omelet with a side of fruit for you."

"Can you go back there and get my friend here some real food?" Bear asked.

"Bear," Jackson said through his teeth.

The server giggled as she walked away. Bear took his knife and fork and began slicing through his breakfast.

Jackson poked much more ploddingly at his fruit cup. "We've exhausted just about every angle I can think of when it comes to Captain Terry."

Bear gave a quick shrug. "Then let's focus on one of the other ones."

"We discovered Tom Marshall's body less than twenty-four hours ago. Police and that ISB agent will still be tight-lipped about him."

Bear loaded up another forkful of smothered toast. "That leaves the Jensen girl. It's been a coupla days, right?"

"Yeah, but her case hasn't exactly gone cold."

"Still, it's been a while. Maybe we could take a run at talking to her friends."

Jackson shook his head. "For all we know, they've gotten out of Dodge like everyone else."

"Didn't someone tell us they were staying at that hotel across from the McDonald's?"

"I think so."

Bear shrugged again. "All it takes is a quick little drive to find out."

———

THE DRIFTWOOD MOTOR Lodge was situated on three floors and just before the bridge over to Assateague Island. Painted a grayish tan, it had a covered veranda out front with its parking lot to one side and an outdoor pool on the other.

Jackson and Bear parked and walked into the lobby off the veranda. A young woman no older than thirty, with hair dyed black and purple, sat behind the desk. She smiled earnestly at them as they walked in.

"Hello," she said. "I'm so sorry, but we're unfortunately closing due to the incoming storm. I apologize if no one got a hold of you two about your reservation."

"That's alright, we actually didn't have one," Jackson said.

"I see. Well, as I mentioned, we are closing. We're just waiting for the last few folks to check out and then we'll be closing the hotel completely."

"None of the remaining guests are the friends of that young woman who was killed, are they?"

The hotel clerk blinked several times. "I'm sorry, I can't give out any information on hotel guests."

He'd known she likely wouldn't tell them anything, but they were on a ticking clock. "I can appreciate that. We'd heard about what happened and we're just hoping to pay our respects."

The hotel clerk nodded. "That's very sweet of you all. Unfortunately, I still can't give you any information." She paused. "Even for guests that have already left."

Jackson sucked at his teeth and shook his head. Another dead end. "Alright, no problem. Thank you, anyway."

"My pleasure. If you'd like, some people have created a memorial out on the other side of the veranda. Mostly locals. Everyone I know is just shocked and saddened that someone would do such a thing here." The hotel clerk shook her head. "And now this kayaker, too." She straightened her posture. "Anyway, if you wanted to pay respects in some way, we haven't moved anything. It's all still out there."

Jackson smiled. "Sure, thanks. We'll do that."

The hotel clerk waved goodbye as Jackson and Bear stepped

outside. Sure enough, up against one of the support beams for the roof overhead, people had propped flowers against the base, creating a floral teepee of sorts. Spread amongst them were candles and other various mementos. Jackson squatted down to get a better look at everything. As his eyes swept slowly over it all, he spotted something. A chill shot through him like a frozen lightning bolt. He popped up quickly, fished his phone out of his pocket, and dialed a number.

Bear frowned. "Who are you calling?"

"Shaw," Jackson said. He put his phone to his ear as he nodded at the memorial. "That toy shark there. I saw one just like it next to the remembrance ribbon on Susan Yarbrough's fence post."

———

SHAW WALKED into the administration offices first thing in the morning, looking to touch base with Special Agent Lederer before assisting with the evacuation and storm preparation efforts drew her elsewhere. As she traversed the corridor of workstations and came to the office Lederer had requisitioned in the back, she found it empty.

She spun around, looking to see if she'd passed him. Only a handful of people were in the office and none of them were him. Across the room, she spotted Bridger pulling paper from a copier, looking it over as he held it in one hand and a cup of coffee in the other. Shaw trotted over to him.

"Morning," she said. "Have you seen Lederer around?"

Bridger didn't look up from the piece of paper. "He's left the island."

"You're kidding."

Bridger shook his head. "He was quote 'falling back' to DC until the storm blows through. Can't say I blame him. All he'd be doing if he stayed here would be hunkering down."

"But he can't just up and leave in the middle of the investigation."

Bridger began to walk, still studying the document in his hand. "Like I said, what would you expect him to do in the middle of a hurricane?"

Shaw paused as she tried to think of a good answer, then when she couldn't, hurried to catch up to him. "Where does that leave the friends and family of Jensen and Marshall?"

"We're advising everyone close to them to heed the evacuation warning the same as everyone else, and we'll be in contact when we can."

Shaw huffed.

Bridger finally looked up and met her eyes. "Iz, we can't control what we can't control."

"I know." She huffed again. "It just…"

"Sucks, I know. But unless you know how to magically make a hurricane turn on a dime, we've got other things to take care of."

Shaw nodded without saying anything more. Bridger continued walking. Shaw was about to head out to her truck when her phone buzzed on her hip. She pulled it off its clip and answered.

"FWO Shaw," she said.

"Shaw, it's Jackson Clay. I need you to meet me at the Driftwood Motor Lodge."

"It's not a good time, Clay."

"This can't wait."

Shaw tapped her fingers on her leg. "What is it?"

"I think whoever's doing all this left something at a memorial to Taylor Jensen."

Shaw hurried toward the office doors. Clay was right. This couldn't wait. "I'll be there in five."

———

JACKSON AND BEAR were standing over the memorial when Shaw turned sharply into the parking lot, got out, and marched up to them.

"Show me," she said. "What is it?"

Jackson crouched down and pointed. "That toy shark there. I saw one just like it on the fence post in Susan Yarbrough's yard where people had tied up a ribbon for Captain Terry."

Shaw dropped down with him. "Maybe it's someone's weird way of paying homage to the dead."

"Or maybe whoever's doing all this is leaving their calling card."

Shaw pulled out a pair of nitrile gloves and put them on. "You're sure you saw one just like it on the Yarbrough's fence?"

Jackson nodded. "One hundred percent."

"Is it still there?"

"I don't know. I called you as soon as I spotted this one here."

"Snap a picture of the one here for me." She went to the back of her truck, fetched a plastic baggie out of the utility box, and brought it back over. She reached out and gingerly pinched the fin of the shark just enough to ease it into the baggie. "Let's go check the Yarbrough house."

———

THEY DROVE in a two-car convoy over to Susan Yarbrough's house and pulled off the road opposite it, where a large marsh led out to a little bay. In unison, they crossed the street and examined the fence post. The toy shark was still right where Jackson had seen it.

"You were right," Shaw said. "Same as the other one."

"It has to be whoever's doing this," Jackson said.

Shaw crossed the street back to her truck to get a fresh pair of gloves and another bag.

Bear looked over at Susan Yarbrough's house and its empty driveway. "Doesn't look like anyone is here."

Shaw came back to them. "Probably headed out of town, which is what you two should be doing, mind you."

Jackson ignored the comment.

Shaw slipped the toy shark into a baggie as carefully as she had the other one, then held it up and examined it closely. "It looks like one of those toys you can get at any of the souvenir shops around here."

Jackson's eye twitched. "It would take days to run down the place they were bought from, assuming they were even bought here. And recently."

Shaw shook her head. "Days we don't have."

"Can you have Lederer run them for prints and DNA?"

Shaw shook her head again. "Lederer skipped town, won't be back until the storm passes."

"Can you run them yourself?"

"We rely on Chincoteague PD whenever we need to try and pull a latent print. I can go over there and see, but I'm sure they're even busier than we are."

Jackson scratched his head. "I'd offer to take it, but I have a feeling they won't be happy to see me."

"It's fine. I'll take it over there." Shaw looked across the street at the bay. "The storm tide is rising." She looked back at Jackson and Bear. "I'm guessing I can't make one last sales pitch for you two to evacuate with everyone else?"

Jackson looked out at the water, then up to the sky. It'd been overcast all day, but the cloud cover had gotten darker, saturated with rain and the promise of the coming storm. "I'll make you a deal," he said. "Those prints lead to a positive ID, and we'll be the next ones out of town."

"You know it doesn't work like it does in the movies. Even if they drop what they're doing and get right to work, it'll take some time."

"Then I guess we're hanging out."

Shaw sighed. "Well, at the very least, pack up and head over to the Chincoteague Center. The town is establishing an emergency shelter for people who can't... or *won't*... evacuate."

Jackson nodded. "We'll do just that." He gestured at the toy shark in the bag. "Let me know what comes of that."

"I will."

Jackson and Bear turned and crossed the street, headed for their Suburban. Before they got in, Shaw called out to them.

"Hey!"

Jackson turned and looked at her.

"You guys be safe."

Jackson nodded again. "You do the same."

TWENTY-SEVEN

THE BULL SHARK cruised south down Main Street, a slow-moving slew of cars congesting the opposite lane as everyone made a last-minute push to leave the island. Not The Bull Shark, though. He was in his element. He wasn't going anywhere.

Driving the twenty-year-old Chevy pickup he'd paid cash for the night before his Awakening, The Bull Shark stalked the streets. The chaos on the island stirred the violent energy within him, bringing that hunger forth. To feed it now was risky—he wasn't stupid—but sometimes animals had to give in to their most primal instincts. Tom Marshall had been an example of just that.

He looked down the tiny roads that branched off Main Street looking for anyone staying behind, weak prey that had strayed from the relative protection of the community. He turned down the last road before the harbor. On the other side of a small waterway, the road split wide into four prongs like a mangled fork. Along the roads was an array of single wide motor homes neatly plotted on mani-cured lawns. Overhead, the tempestuous sky stirred as the wind whistled through the truck's open windows. The area was aban-doned, an absolute ghost town. Dismayed, The Bull Shark was cranking his wheel to turn around when he spotted someone. An elderly woman struggling to put up plywood boards on her screened-in porch amidst the gusting wind.

The Bull Shark grinned as he turned and pulled slowly onto the woman's gravel driveway. As the tiny rocks crackled under the tires, the woman turned around. Short and squat, but also frail-looking, her long gray hair was done back in a braid and her yellow flowery dress rippling in the gale. The Bull Shark got out of the truck and waved.

"Afternoon, ma'am," he said. "Didn't mean to startle you, but I saw you having a bit of trouble with those boards there."

The woman's cheeks flushed as she smiled. "Oh, yes," she said. "I'm trying to get these darn things up before the storm, but they're practically bigger than me."

The Bull Shark nodded. "I see that. You headed out of town?"

The woman shooed the thought away. "And go where? I've lived in this town every one of my eighty-two years, and I don't plan on going nowhere for no storm." She shook her head. "Not for Sandy, not for Erin, and not for... whatever they've named this damn one."

"I don't blame you." He looked around the block once more. "Seems like all your neighbors aren't as brave as you, though. Let me give you a hand getting these boards up."

"Oh, bless your heart!"

The Bull Shark ascended the woman's steps and onto her screened-in porch. He pretended to assess the matter, picking up the box of nails the woman had on her porch table, and turned to her. "Here's your first problem. These skinny little things are no good. They wouldn't hold up a birdhouse much less these boards in the storm coming."

"Oh!" the woman said, exasperated. "Oh, I don't know if I have any others."

"Well, why don't we take a look and see what we can find."

"Yes, please! This way." The woman opened the front door to her house and hobbled in. "Shut the door behind you, if you would, please."

"Absolutely." Smiling, he did as she asked before turning the deadbolt shut.

"I'm so sorry, I never asked you your name."

"The Bull Shark," he said, turning to face her.

"The wha—"

Before the woman could turn around, he shoved her forcefully from behind, throwing her into her kitchen counter. The sick crack of snapping bone cut through the space around them. The woman wallowed in pain, grabbing her arm. He grabbed her by her dress and pulled her to her feet. She tried to push him away, but he slammed her against her kitchen cabinets.

"Please! Stop!" she cried out.

He didn't. He couldn't. Pulling his hunting knife from its sheath on his belt, he plunged it into her abdomen. The woman let out a shriek before The Bull Shark threw her deeper into the house, his knife protruding from her belly. Trying to get her feet underneath her, she took two tumbling steps before crashing onto the wooden coffee table in the middle of her living room. He watched her for a moment, her chest heaving as her lungs begged for oxygen. She reminded him of a fish taken out of the water. Lord knows he'd seen plenty of that since coming to the island.

Closing the distance, he used his boot to push her off the table. She rolled face-up, and he straddled her, dropping to his knees. The woman's mouth moved, but no sounds came out. He slipped his hands slowly around her neck and squeezed. Gently at first, then harder, not stopping until his knuckles turned white. The woman didn't resist. The fight within her—the same determination that had apparently caused her to defy mother nature and the authorities alike—had drifted away like an ebbing tide. After several seconds, she stopped struggling for air. Her pupils became fixed, and her soul left its mortal vehicle.

Out of breath himself, The Bull Shark wiped his brow and

pivoted off the woman. He yanked the knife carelessly out of the woman's midsection, then rose and walked back to the kitchen. He found a kitchen towel folded over the handle of the oven and wiped off his blade, then replaced the towel thoughtfully over the oven door's handle.

The craving within him was sated again. How long would it last? He didn't know. He honestly didn't care. Truthfully, he looked forward to the moment when it would return.

The Bull Shark took one last look at the woman lying lifeless on her living room floor, unlocked the door, and walked out into the coming storm.

TWENTY-EIGHT

THE FIRST BANDS of rain began to fall across Chincoteague as Jackson and Bear pulled into the parking lot for the Chincoteague Center. Located directly across the street from the police station, the building was a single-story event center with the same red-brick facade and hunter green accents as its neighbor. Out front, public works crews were stacking sandbags in a rectangular perimeter around the covered entryway.

Bear climbed out of the passenger seat of the Suburban and looked at the shallow knoll the building sat on. "Not exactly the 'higher ground' I imagined us heading for," he said. "I don't know how much better we are here than at the house."

Jackson held his hand out with the keys in it. "Not too late to take the Suburban and go."

Bear waved him off. "Ah, to hell with that."

Jackson looked across the street and saw Shaw's service truck in the parking lot of the police station. He'd just pulled his phone out to call her when the doors opened, and she walked out. She headed for her truck when she spotted Jackson across the way looking at her. He raised a hand and waved. Shaw looked both ways, then trotted across and joined them. She held a hand to the bill of her ball cap to aid in shielding her face from the rain.

"Any luck with the toy sharks?" Jackson asked.

Shaw shook her head. "They weren't able to pull any prints. DNA isn't likely, given how long they were out in the elements. We're going to send them out to a lab when we can, but I'm not optimistic."

"At the very least, it's a tangible connection between Yarbrough and Jensen."

Shaw nodded. "I've got to run. I'm glad you all at least decided to come to the shelter. If I were you, I'd hunker down here."

"So why aren't you?"

"I'm still needed elsewhere, but I'll be coming back when I'm done."

Jackson nodded. "Sounds good."

Shaw trotted back across the street. Jackson and Bear went to the back of the Suburban and unloaded their gear, each carrying two large duffel bags. Jackson had their shotguns slung over his shoulder. Together they headed for the Chincoteague Center, stepping over and around the sandbags and workers when they got to the front door. They were just about to enter when Officer Perry stopped them.

"Can't have any guns in the shelter, Mr. Clay," he said with his hand raised. "Got to leave them at home."

"We're not local, you know that," Jackson said.

The officer shrugged. "I don't know what to tell you, sir. They can't be inside. Best I can do is offer to lock them up in the police station."

"I don't think so," said Bear. He pointed at the officer. "I know you wouldn't be denying a red-blooded American of their second amendment right!"

The officer crossed his arms. "Sir, the second amendment does not..."

"Is there a problem here, Jon?" asked a voice just inside the building.

All three men turned to see Chief Diaz step out and join them.

"Chief, I was just explaining to these men that guns are not permitted inside the emergency shelter," Officer Perry said.

"And I was just explaining to your boy here my constitutional rights!"

Chief Diaz held out his hands in a calming gesture. "Look, Officer Perry here is right. We can't have any firearms inside. People are on edge already as it is. Not only because of the storm but with everything else… happening."

"You mean the murders that you have no suspects for," Jackson said.

Chief Diaz leered at him. "The murders we are *actively investigating*, yes, among other things. And having people walking around armed will only serve to exacerbate matters. Please, if you don't want to hand your guns over, at least secure them in your vehicle."

Jackson and Bear looked at each other for a moment before Jackson nodded toward the parking lot. Bear sighed to note his protest, then took the shotguns off Jackson's shoulder and trotted out into the rain toward the Suburban.

"Thank you," Chief Diaz said, exhaling. "If you need anything else, I'll be around."

Jackson entered the Chincoteague Center. Immediately through the two sets of double doors was a cavernous ballroom with a tiled floor. It was filled with cots laid out in a neatly arranged matrix. Jackson spotted two empty cots in the near corner of the room, carried his and Bear's bags over to them, and set them down. He sat down on one of the cots and took in the rest of the space. People milled about in the aisles between the cots. He counted roughly two dozen people. The people seeking shelter were a varied bunch. Everyone from parents with their children to an elderly couple splayed out on two cots in the middle of the room. Jackson recognized one of the people as Hank Willis, the man that had chatted them up at the Jensen crime scene.

Branching off on either side of the ballroom were several smaller rooms, each with a sign plastered overhead.

MEDICAL

KITCHEN

BATHROOMS/SHOWERS

SUPPLIES

Bear came in, found Jackson, and settled onto the cot next to him.

"Home sweet home, huh?" he asked.

"I guess so," Jackson said. "At least for the next couple days."

Jackson continued to watch everyone. After a bit, he spotted Officer Perry step inside, locate Chief Diaz across the room, and hurry over to him. He got the police chief's attention and told him something. Chief Diaz clenched his jaw, then grabbed a chair in front of a folding table next to him. He stood on it, facing the room.

"Excuse me. Excuse me! Can I have everyone's attention, please?" the Chief called out.

Everyone quieted down and turned to face him.

"Thank you," he continued. "I have an important announcement to make. The storm surge has come in high enough that it has flooded the causeway to the mainland. As of fifteen minutes ago, the Accomack County Sheriff's Office has closed the road. We will be closing access to the causeway and the bridge on our end effective immediately. We will let you know when we can reopen the road, but the weather outside is only going to get worse before it gets better. If you were planning on staying here, that's fine. If you were still hoping to evacuate the island, I'm sorry, but that is no longer possible. Rest assured, we will do everything we can to keep everyone safe. Thank you."

The chief stepped off the chair as people began to talk amongst themselves.

"I guess whoever's here is who we're riding out the storm with," Bear said.

"Yeah," Jackson said. He scanned the ballroom full of people again. "The only question is whether this killer is among us."

PART FOUR
CABIN FEVER

"Monsters are real, and ghosts are real too. They live inside us, and sometimes, they win." -Stephen King

TWENTY-NINE

AFTER PARKING in the lot next to the Chincoteague Center, The Bull Shark jaunted through the steady rainfall to the building, soaking in the storm that had come as the wind gusted around him. A man out front offered him his hand in stepping over the battery of sandbags that had been constructed. The Bull Shark took it with a nod of thanks and slipped inside the building. He stood just inside the double doors and took in the shelter. The cacophony of conversations being had inside the ballroom reverberated off the harsh, bare walls, creating a roar of incomprehensible noise. A woman in a safety vest saw The Bull Shark pause and stepped toward him.

"My goodness, you're soaked!" she said with a warm smile. "Can I get you a towel?"

He shook his head. "That's alright, I'll manage," he said. "Don't mind being a little wet."

The women nodded. "Well, there's hot coffee in the kitchen over there if you'd like some."

The Bull Shark's smile widened as he nodded in thanks. He traversed the array of cots that had been laid out and staked his claim to an empty one near the far-right corner. Sitting down on it, he opened his bag, rifling through his things. Beneath his stack of clothes was his hunting knife. After double-checking that no one was watching, he pulled it out and slid it into his pocket.

The first bands of the hurricane may have arrived, but he had no intention of stopping his hunts. Nor could he if he wanted to. Sooner or later, the hunger within him would rise again, and he would be driven to satiate it. As he took in his surroundings, he felt the craving form inside him. Each subsequent attack had satisfied him less and less. It had only been a few hours since he extinguished the life of the old woman, and now here he was, already yearning.

No matter, The Bull Shark thought. The storm had corralled a buffet full of prey for him. Opportunity abounded. The pining would return, yes, but The Bull Shark would feed it as he always had. No storm would stop that. No storm would stop *him*.

He'd just lain back against his bag when the ballroom was plunged into darkness. He heard a few sporadic screams, and then, a second later, the power returned. People exchanged unsure glances with one another. The father of a family of three several cots over flagged down the volunteer that had offered The Bull Shark a towel.

"Excuse me, miss," he said. "What just happened?"

"The power must've gone out," the volunteer said. "But don't worry. We brought in an emergency diesel generator for this very reason."

Darkness, The Bull Shark thought. Like the fog on the beach. Low visibility made for the perfect conditions to hunt. He made himself comfortable, fantasizing about which of those around him he would take first.

THIRTY

JACKSON REMAINED in his corner of the ballroom as the lights came back on. The grid must've gone down, triggering a backup generator. It was early for them to lose power. He hoped the shelter had enough fuel to see them through the storm.

He stood against the wall and created a mental manifest of everyone there. By his count, there were twenty-seven people taking shelter outside of him and Bear. Ten female, seventeen male. Five were children—two girls and three boys—no older than twelve. Another five looked to be in their late teens or early twenties, all keeping to themselves, and nine more were in their thirties or forties. That left the final eight, who ranged from Hank Willis somewhere just north of fifty, to an elderly couple that must be approaching eighty. In addition to them, there were eight people running the shelter, four police officers—Chief Diaz, Officer Birch, Officer Perry, and Investigator Bowden—and Shaw alongside three civilians. The eight were all easily identifiable by their uniforms or the orange vests they donned. Jackson had also heard four firefighters, a skeleton crew for the Engine Company, were posted at the fire station a half-block away, still running calls as long as they could.

Bear had drifted off on his own cot and began snoring, much to the chagrin of those around him, including Jackson, but Jackson remained alert. He monitored everyone inside closely, unable to shake the feeling in his gut that one of them was responsible for the three murders over the last several days. He ruled out the five children as well as the elderly couple, but the remaining twenty were all plausible, as were the four Chincoteague police officers and three volunteers.

Jackson's phone vibrated in his pocket. He pulled it out and checked the caller ID. It was Bailey.

"Hey," he greeted.

Bailey remained silent on the other end.

Jackson looked at his phone to make sure it was still connected. "Bailey?"

"Sorry, I'm just not used to you answering the phone like a civilized person," she said. "I assume you're still on the island?"

"Correct. The causeway to the mainland has been washed out. We're here for the long haul now."

"Please tell me you're somewhere safe."

Jackson looked up at the rafters. "We're in a community center they've turned into an emergency shelter. Safest place on the island, I assume."

"Gotcha. Well, I figured you'd want to hear it from me first. That DNA sample pulled from the Jensen girl? It came back with a partial hit."

A shot of adrenaline spiked through him. "Partial?"

"Correct. It's not a positive ID, but the match shares DNA with your killer. Making them..."

"A relative."

"Also correct. The partial match can't tell you how they're related specifically, but it would have to be a close relative."

Jackson began scanning the room again. "Who's the partial match?"

"Hold on, I have it here." Bailey rustled through papers on her end. "A Scott Meachem."

A knot formed in Jackson's stomach.

"The partial match comes from blood work taken during a DUI arrest in '98."

"So, whoever killed Jensen and the others is a relative of Scott Meachem."

"Jensen for sure. Anyone else, you'd have to prove that connection." Bailey paused. "Also, your killer is male, based on the DNA."

Jackson looked around again. That knocked his suspect pool down to thirteen, plus the four officers. "Got it. Thanks, Bailey."

"I know you and know you're not going to just sit on this. So whatever you do, be careful, Clay."

Jackson cracked his neck. "Copy that."

Jackson hung up. He searched for Investigator Bowden and found him leaning against the open door to the kitchen before jostling Bear awake.

"Get up, we've got work to do," he said.

Jackson circumnavigated the outer perimeter of the ballroom and hurried over to Bowden. Bear, after stretching and yawning, trudged behind. Bowden saw Jackson approaching and turned to head in the opposite direction. Jackson didn't care.

"I know about the DNA sample pulled from Taylor Jensen's body," he said as he reached him. "I just learned it came back with a partial match. The infamous Scott Meachem."

Bowden didn't look up from his phone. "I don't know where you heard that, but Scott Meachem hasn't been here for a quarter of a century. Your DNA match might as well belong to the boogeyman."

"Did you hear me? I said *partial* match. Meaning it's a relative of Scott Meachem... and male." Jackson looked back at the group spread out over the ballroom. "Is anyone in here related to the Meachems?"

Bowden winced as if Jackson's question was ridiculous. He gave the room a cursory scan then refocused on Jackson. "No, there are no Meachems here. Nor would there be."

Chief Diaz strode over, clearly having noticed the tense conversation.

"What's going on over here?" he asked.

"The DNA that was pulled from Jensen's body came back. A partial match for Scott Meachem," Jackson reiterated. "Your killer is a Meachem, and male."

Chief Diaz folded his arms. "Where did you hear that?"

"My contact. That doesn't matter. What does matter is you need to prepare a warrant for the Meachems' property."

"Even if I wanted to, how would I serve it? And with who? I have four officers on the island, including myself, and over two dozen people here to look after."

Jackson stepped even closer to Chief Diaz and dropped his voice to a whisper. "And what if one of them is your killer? Do you think they're going to stop just because of the storm?"

Chief Diaz sighed. "Look, I hear you. But I don't have the manpower to spare. Hell, I haven't even seen these results myself yet."

"If my contact says they're legit, they are. Emily Meachem lives alone now on the property with her two children, correct? A daughter and son? That makes exactly one male Meachem on the island."

"I'm not spreading my manpower any thinner, Mr. Clay."

Jackson thought for a moment. "Fair enough." He turned to Bear. "Want to take a drive?"

Bear flashed a menacing grin. "Hell yeah, Jacky Boy!"

Chief Diaz held up his hand. "There's a hurricane inbound, Mr. Clay. It is far too dangerous for you to be running all over town."

Jackson ignored him.

"What are you going to do? You can't just barge onto their property!"

Jackson headed for the doors, Bear at his side. They were done sitting by and waiting. It was time to act.

THIRTY-ONE

RAINFALL DELUGED Bear's Suburban as Jackson and Bear sped toward the Meachems' property. Jackson took a hard right onto Main Street and headed north. As they neared the bay, he could see the water level had risen within inches of spilling over onto the road.

"We may need a damn boat to get back," Bear quipped.

Jackson didn't care. He drove on, occupying both lanes of the deserted road. Where Main Street turned into a dead-end private road, Jackson sped through. Coming through a cluster of pines, the marshes on either side had flooded the road.

"Easy, easy!" Bear said.

Jackson eased up on the gas just a little. As they splashed into the water, the wheels sent waves taller than the Suburban shooting outward. The SUV bogged down, but Jackson put his foot down on the gas pedal, bringing all two-hundred thirty horses under the hood to life, willing the Suburban to ford the waters. After several hundred feet, the road rose and cleared the flood. Just ahead were the gates to the Meachems' property. Jackson didn't let off the gas.

"Hang on," he said.

Bear grabbed the oh shit handle over the window. The Suburban slammed into the gate, kicking it wide, and roared through. Jackson veered hard right and took the drive for Emily Meachem's house.

Emily's Navigator was parked right where it'd been several days before. Jackson skidded to a stop, nearly crashing into the back of it. Bear reached into the back seat, grabbed Jackson's Beretta, and handed it to him before grabbing his own .357. Jackson, closer to the door, left Bear by the truck. He threw open the screen door and pounded with his fist.

"Emily Meachem!" he shouted over the storm. "Come to the door, please!"

He waited a moment. Bear, hidden by the back of the Suburban, kept an eye on the side of the house.

Jackson banged again. "Emily Meachem! Come to the door! We need to talk!" He waited again. Still no answer. He pounded a third time. "Emily Meachem! Come to the door now or I'm kicking it in!" Nothing.

Jackson took a step back and mule-kicked the door in. The nauseating, sickly sweet smell of death hit him in the face. Jackson turned wide of the door as if the stench might reach out and grab him. He put the collar of his shirt over his face and looked back at Bear and shouted over the growing howl of the storm.

"Someone's dead inside," he said. "Been there for a while by the smell of it." He peered into the dark interior. "Grab me a flashlight."

Bear grabbed two from the Suburban and trotted over to him, then drew his .357 and posted up on the opposite side of the open door. "On you, brother," he said.

Jackson nodded. One after another, they swept into the house, guns drawn.

The house had an open floor plan. The entry opened onto a living space with a kitchen across the way. On the tiled floor there, poking out from behind an island, was a pair of feet. Jackson moved toward them.

When he got to the island, he looked over. Sprawled on the floor between the island and the dishwasher lay an older woman. Much of her body had bloated and discolored from decay.

"Is that Emily Meachem?" Bear asked, coming to Jackson.

"I'm not sure," Jackson said. "Let's clear the rest of the house."

On the far side of the house, between the kitchen and the living space, a u-shaped staircase led upward. Jackson padded up the hardwood stairs.

Five doors opened off a wide hallway—four bedrooms and a bathroom. Jackson and Bear swept each room methodically. All of them were empty.

"Clear," Jackson said as he got to an en suite bathroom off the final bedroom.

Back downstairs, Jackson paused only long enough to snap a picture of the dead body in the kitchen. Outside in the fresh air, both of them spat repeatedly, trying to get the sulfurous taste out of their mouths.

"I'll bet ya anythin' whoever killed her killed the other three," Bear said.

Jackson didn't say anything, but feared Bear was right.

Bear cleared his throat and spit again. "If she's dead, what about her two kids?"

Jackson looked across the way at the other two houses.

"You realize we have to check those now, too."

Jackson cocked his head to the side. "*On you*, brother."

They got back in the Suburban, drove back to where the driveways split, and took the one leading up to the other two houses. As they prepared to enter the first one, they heard another engine behind them. Jackson motioned to Bear, and both men took cover behind the front of the Suburban.

After a moment, there came the sounds of a car door opening and shutting. Poking his head up, Jackson saw Shaw with her service truck. He rose up and lowered his weapon.

"Chief Diaz told me you two headed out this way against his

wishes," Shaw said, coming up to them. "I came to make sure you all didn't screw anything up."

"There's a woman we believe might be Emily Meachem dead in her house," Jackson said.

Shaw's jaw went slack. "You're kidding."

Jackson shook his head. "By the looks of her, for quite some time. My guess would be a week, maybe more. We were just about to check the other two houses."

"You think one of her kids was involved?"

"I'm not making any assumptions. Or taking any chances."

Shaw unholstered her service weapon. "I'll make entry. Official welfare check."

"We'll cover you."

Shaw hesitated. "Fine, but as soon as it's clear, you all step out."

Jackson nodded.

Together, the three of them searched both houses. Each time, they were greeted by the same stomach-turning smell followed by the eventual discovery of a body. Unlike the first, though, these two were in bedrooms. Shaw snapped pictures of the scenes. When they were done, they stepped out and took cover among the stilts of the second house.

"They have to be Adam and Hannah, Emily's children," Shaw said.

"Looks like they've been there as long as their mom," Jackson said.

Shaw nodded. "I have to call this in." She trotted through the torrential rain to her truck and hopped in.

Bear looked at Jackson. "If whoever killed the other three also did this, these three would've come before them."

Jackson nodded. "They've probably been dead as long as we've been here."

Bear shook his head. "It doesn't make any damn sense. Why take out three people in the same family—*your* family—and then three random strangers."

"That's what we have to figure out. And quickly, before anyone else gets hurt."

Bear huffed. "You've looked at this thing every which way. If there was a connection, you'd have found it by now."

"You said it yourself, it doesn't add up."

Bear shook his head. "It sure as hell doesn't."

Jackson folded his arms and leaned against one of the stilts for the house, looking out at Shaw in her truck. Gusting winds blew the rain sideways as trees in the distance swooshed back and forth. Lightning flashed. Jackson counted the seconds until he heard the thunder, approximating how far away the strike had been. It was a habit ingrained in him in the Boy Scouts. *Always be prepared.* A key to being prepared was knowing how close you were to danger. Regardless of the lightning, a sensation prickled Jackson's skin that he was as close as ever.

The door to Shaw's truck opened, and she hurried back over to them under the cover of the house. Shaking the rain off the windbreaker she had on, she looked up at Jackson. "The engine company at the firehouse was called out to a house on the south end of the island. Person down from unknown causes. When they got there, it was clear there'd been another attack."

"Holy hell," Bear muttered.

"How recent?" Jackson asked.

Shaw took off her cap and wrung it out. "From the sound of it? Sometime today."

"Then our killer is still on the island," Jackson said.

Shaw nodded. "That's my fear, too."

Jackson lifted the bill of his own cap and rubbed his face as he thought. "Alright, then we need to get back. Put the shelter on lock down. Either our person is there, in which case we can isolate and contain them, or they're not, in which case we can keep an eye on everyone. Keep them safe."

"Until what? Back up arrives? Look at the sky. This is just beginning."

Jackson shook his head. "It's the only play we have right now."

"Okay. I want to get eyes on this latest attack, though. You all go back to the shelter, meet with Chief Diaz and his officers, and come up with a game plan. I'll check out the scene the firefighters responded to then rendezvous with you all."

"Sounds good."

The three of them headed back out into the storm.

THIRTY-TWO

JACKSON, Bear, Chief Diaz, and the three other officers met in the Supplies room. A classroom-sized space filled with metal shelves in neat columns storing everything from extra event supplies to maintenance and cleaning equipment. The six men huddled in the open space just inside the door.

"You're certain it was Emily Meachem and her two kids?" Investigator Bowden asked.

"Shaw seemed pretty sure, and from what I understand she follows this sort of thing closely," Jackson said. He looked at each of the officers, trying to gauge their reactions to the news.

"Christ," Chief Diaz said. He put his hands on his hips. "Did we get an ID on the woman from the most recent attack?"

Bowden consulted his phone. "Ada Fitzhugh."

"Mrs. Fitzhugh?" Chief Diaz shook his head. "God almighty."

Bowden slipped his phone away. "With the three victims Mr. Clay discovered, that brings the total to seven. And it's safe to assume they're all somehow connected at this point."

"You think?" Chief Diaz's voice dripped with sarcasm. He looked over to a window that'd been boarded up, as if he could see through it. "And there's a very good chance they're among those here."

Bowden rubbed the back of his neck, then crossed his arms. "We need to start questioning people. Someone must know something. And even if they don't, we can start putting pieces together by process of elimination."

Bear huffed. "That's a dumb fuckin' idea."

"Excuse me?" Bowden scowled at him.

Jackson held a hand up. "I think what the Chief is trying to say is, you have a group of people in there who are already scared and on edge from the storm. You start asking questions related to the killings, you're only going to make things worse."

Bowden shook his head. "Fine, then what do you suggest?"

"We've got to limit the people who know about this to just us and Shaw. We tell everyone we need them to stay contained to common areas for safety. Then we monitor. Keep eyes on them. You all as the ones in charge, Bear and I as support. Worst case, people are grouchy, but no one gets hurt. Best case, whoever's doing all this makes a mistake and reveals themselves."

Bowden shook his head. "It's not definite that our suspect is here."

Jackson nodded. "Correct. But, like your chief said, it's a safe assumption."

Bowden slipped his hands into his pockets and leaned against the boarded-up window. "I don't know. Seems too passive."

"If we overreact, we risk showing our hand. The killer doesn't know how much we know yet."

Chief Diaz nodded. "Mr. Clay is right. You don't reel the line in before you have your fish on. We play this slow. Keep this between the six of us and have the firefighters stay at the station unless absolutely necessary. We watch everyone and see what comes of it. Our priority is to keep everyone safe." He looked at each person, his eyes asking for objections. He came to Jackson. "We know our suspect is a close blood relative of Scott Meachem. We need to start looking at everyone here for a familial connection... quietly."

Bowden shook his head. "The Meachems keep... *kept*... to themselves. The ones that stayed, anyway. If anyone here knew them, let alone was related to them, we'd know."

Jackson shrugged. "DNA doesn't lie."

"You want six of us—seven when Shaw returns—to keep an eye on everyone here *and* also run background checks on them all?"

Jackson turned to Chief Diaz. "Can you put together a list of everyone here without anyone asking questions?"

Chief Diaz nodded. "Probably."

"Then my contact can cross reference everyone for us."

Bowden huffed. "Terrific. The same person that's leaking you information on our investigations."

Chief Diaz held his hands out between Bowden and Jackson. "We're all on the same team here. Now, is there anything else?" He looked at Jackson.

Jackson shook his head.

"Then let's get to it," Chief Diaz said.

He opened the door, and everyone filed out. As Jackson and Bear returned to their cots, Bear leaned in close to Jackson and spoke quietly.

"That fish analogy the chief laid down," he said. "You realize we're the bait in that scenario, right?"

"I'm aware."

Bear shook his head. "Fishing never works out well for the bait."

"You get some rest. I'll take first watch." Jackson stretched out on his cot.

Bear laid down on his side and fluffed a spare hoodie to use as a pillow. "I told you, I fuckin' hate fishin'."

THIRTY-THREE

HE WATCHED from his cot as the six men came out of the supply room. Four members of Chincoteague's finest and two other men who kept showing up. The Bull Shark had seen them around the past few days, first with Captain Terry then on their own after he had dispatched the old man. Who were they?

Originally, he'd taken them to be tourists, out-of-town hunters here for a trip. But if that were the case, they should be long gone. Instead, they were still here, taking up cots in this shelter, same as him. What was their connection to the police? The two men had spoken briefly with the officers before hurrying out into the storm a couple of hours ago. Now, this second meeting. Were they law enforcement themselves?

The female Federal Wildlife Officer came through the double doors, scanned the room, and went over to the two men to speak with them. Whoever they were, he needed to keep an eye on them. It was rare, but bull sharks could find themselves prey to larger animals. Were these two rival predators? If so, they'd have to be put down.

The Bull Shark lay back and closed his eyes. As he did, he rested his hand on the hunting knife sheathed in his pocket. Tomorrow, this hurricane would make landfall. Conditions would deteriorate, and, with a little luck, chaos would rear its menacing head. It could prove to be a big day for The Bull Shark.

And should these two rival predators come for him in the middle of the night, he would be ready.

THIRTY-FOUR

THE HURRICANE INTENSIFIED OVERNIGHT. Jackson sat on his cot to watch over everyone, listening to the wind and rain probe the walls and roof of the building for weaknesses. Every so often there came a metallic whine or random bang. Jackson looked up at the large, tubular air vent over his head, imagining it being the last thing he saw before it came crashing down on him.

Inside, the night was relatively uneventful. Only four times did someone get up to use the bathroom. Three of them had been men, making it easy for Jackson or Bear to rotate following them, but Shaw was the only one who could cover the women. Jackson knew that would eventually become suspicious and, thus, a problem, but for this first night they'd gotten lucky.

At two in the morning, Jackson switched shifts with Bear but only got a fitful four hours of rest before the clinks and clanks of the kitchen coming to life woke him.

Jackson popped out of his cot and walked over to the front doors. Rain sheeted down from the angry gray sky. The lawn around the shelter was saturated but not flooded. He hoped if the floodwaters did come, the battery of sandbags would hold.

Stretching, he walked into the kitchen to find a cup of coffee. In the corner stood a buffet table with two coffee urns and a third with hot water. He got a paper cup and flipped the switch on one of the coffee urns, and a dark brew flowed into his cup.

Chief Diaz walked over to him and poured a cup from the other urn. "Good morning," he said.

"Morning," Jackson replied.

"Everything seemed to go alright last night."

"Nights are easy. People are sleeping. It'll be tougher tracking almost thirty people during the day as they get antsy with cabin fever."

Chief Diaz reached for a canister of nondairy creamer and poured some into his cup. "We'll make it work."

Jackson looked over his shoulder to see if anyone out in the ballroom was watching them. "Were you able to put that manifest together for me?"

"Yeah." Chief Diaz turned to him. "Before I hand it over to you, though. I need to know who your source is. I can't have some rogue party digging into the lives of people I took an oath to protect."

Jackson let the slightly acrid coffee smell wake up his brain. It reminded him of the burnt joe from countless dining facilities in the army. "Then I need your word you'll keep it to yourself. This doesn't blow black on them."

"I'm not interested in getting anyone in trouble, Mr. Clay. But I need assurances this information will be handled with the proper discretion."

Jackson looked at Chief Diaz a beat longer. "My *source* is a special agent with the Virginia State Police. Took the same oath to protect and serve as you. You'd probably have called them in to assist anyway if we didn't have this storm over us." He took a sip of his coffee, black and unsweetened. "But if you have reservations, you guys can do the legwork yourself. It doesn't matter how, it just needs to be done."

He looked into Jackson's eyes, saw the man's mind churning, arguing with itself.

Finally, Chief Diaz reached into his pocket and handed Jackson a paper folded over twice. "I'm trusting you on this one, Mr. Clay," he said.

Jackson nodded and slipped the paper into his own pocket. "I'll let you know when I have something."

Chief Diaz walked away. Jackson poured a second cup of coffee for Bear and walked back to his cot with both in hand. As he sat down, Bear rolled over.

"Coffee?" Jackson asked.

Bear growled with pleasure as he took the cup. "God, you're a beautiful man." He sat up.

Jackson checked his phone. Remarkably, it still clung to a single bar of reception with everything it had. "Chief Diaz gave me the list of everyone here. I'm going to call Bailey. Cover me, make sure no one except us and the police eavesdrops."

Bear nodded. "I got you, brother."

Jackson rose and headed into the supply room to make his call. On the second ring, she answered.

"Clay," she said. "How's everything going?"

"We're good for now," Jackson said, "but I need your help again."

"What's up?" Her voice sounded garbled.

"Bailey?"

"Clay? I can barely hear you. What's up?"

"Cell service must be taking a hit from the storm. Listen, I'm going to text you a list of names. I need you to run them all, specifically looking for familial connections to Scott Meachem, the partial match on the DNA profile."

Bailey paused a beat. "Why?"

"The Meachems were island royalty here before the Hanz scandal. They have a large property here with three houses. I went up there yesterday to get answers about the DNA match. They were all dead."

"Oh my God."

"And they'd been that way for some time, so none of them are our killer. I need to know if this person is in the shelter with us. The list of names I'm giving you is everyone here."

"Hold on, isn't this a small town? You said these Meachems are like the royal family?"

"Used to be."

"Then, wouldn't everyone know if someone around town was a part of the family?"

Jackson looked out to the ballroom through the skinny window in the door. "I'm starting to think it's not quite as simple as that. Can you run the names for me?"

"How many are we talking?"

"About thirty."

"Yeah. Send me what you have."

Jackson stepped away from the door. "As fast as you can."

"It'd go faster if I could delegate some of the work."

Jackson thought about what Chief Diaz said to him. "Keep it to people who you trust to be discreet."

"I can do that."

"I'll send everything now."

Jackson hung up, pulled the paper from his pocket, and punched in the list of names.

THIRTY-FIVE

SITTING against the exterior wall of the ballroom, not far from his cot, The Bull Shark poked at a plate of powdered eggs and plotted his next move. The hunger was rising inside him again. Not for luke-warm mush and weak coffee, but for pain and violence. It welled up inside him like the floodwaters rising all around the island. Soon, he'd need to quench his bloodlust.

The only problem was these police officers. Well, them and the two men that seemed to be working with them. Ever since that meeting the lot of them had yesterday, The Bull Shark had noticed they were keeping a keen eye on everyone inside, more so than he'd expected. He wondered if they were on to the truth—*his* truth—that such a beast lurked amongst them. He would need to draw their attention away to hunt again.

He'd overheard from the volunteers when he'd gotten his eggs that the shelter was now being powered by a generator situated just next to the back doors at the end of a long hall near the bathrooms and showers. He could get to it quickly, but not without being spot-ted. He needed a distraction.

The powdered eggs tasted awful. He'd known plenty of less-than-great meals in his time, but these eggs, if you could call them that, bordered on inedible. Looking around the room, he noticed most of the others shared his feelings on the matter. Situated two cots over from his sat a tall, husky man with a physique like a tree trunk. Having given up on the eggs altogether, he was now working on some jerky he must've brought himself. A young boy from the family next to him was running down the aisles between the cots, playing, when he spotted the jerky. He hurried over to the man.

"Can I have some, mister?" the boy asked.

The man put the bag behind his back. "Hell no, this is mine," he said. "Get lost, kid."

The boy's lower lip trembled as he turned and left.

The man continued snacking on his jerky until he spotted a female volunteer in an orange vest struggling to carry another coffee urn into the kitchen. Tucking his bag of jerky under some clothes on his cot, he hurried over to help the woman. Such chivalry. It probably didn't hurt that she was twenty-something, blond, and bosomy. But the abandoned beef jerky gave The Bull Shark his opening.

Rising quickly, he grabbed the bag of dehydrated meat off the cot. A couple of cots further down was the little boy's family. They'd just headed into the bathroom area with extra clothes, undoubtedly, to get washed and changed, leaving the rest of their stuff on their cots. The Bull Shark scampered over to one of the family's bags, slipped the jerky into it, then doubled back to his own cot.

There, he waited.

The tree trunk of a man took longer than the Bull Shark had expected. Regardless, it proved beneficial. By the time the man returned, the family returned to their area, freshly washed. The large man came back to his own area with a cup of coffee in his hand, savored a large sip, then reached for his jerky.

"What the fuck?" he stammered.

"Something the matter?" The Bull Shark asked in the most docile voice he could muster.

The man spun around. "I had a bag of beef jerky here when I left and now it's gone!" He pointed a finger at him. "You wouldn't know anything about it, would you?"

He shook his head. "Haven't seen it. But there's breakfast in the kitchen if you're hungry."

The man sneered, licking his teeth. He looked over at The Bull Shark's half-eaten plate of eggs against the wall. "The breakfast is shit and I think you know it. Where's my goddamn beef jerky?"

The Bull Shark put his hands out to his side. "Honest to god, I haven't seen it." He looked warily over at the family, then nodded for the man to come over to him.

The man stomped toward him.

The Bull Shark lowered his voice. "I saw that kid playing around your cot after you left."

The man looked over at the family sitting together. "Is that so?"

He nodded. "You didn't hear it from me."

The Bull Shark watched, a smile forming on his lips, as the man began marching toward the family. The dominoes had lined up just so, and The Bull Shark had effortlessly pushed the first one over. Now he waited with eager anticipation for the others to fall.

THIRTY-SIX

JACKSON CHECKED his phone every few minutes, fearing his reception would drop out. Right now, Bailey was his only way of getting the answers he needed.

He'd found busy work for himself by helping the volunteers collect trash from the bins around the ballroom. It also gave him an excuse to stay on the move and keep an eye on everyone. He had just taken a couple of bags to the supply room—where it'd been agreed to keep the trash instead of venturing out into the storm to the dumpsters—when he heard a loud commotion. He dropped the bags and hurried back into the ballroom. At the rear center of the massive space, a large man was in the face of a smaller man. Behind the smaller man stood a woman and two children.

"Give me back my jerky!" the large man shouted.

"I'm telling you, we don't have it!" the smaller man said.

"Really?" The large man knocked his adversary aside and began rifling through the family's things.

The woman shrieked, "Stop! Get away!"

Jackson zigzagged through the matrix of cots.

The large man turned a backpack upside down. Among the

things that spilled out of it was a bag of jerky. He grabbed it and held it accusingly in the smaller man's face.

"Then what the hell is this?!" he seethed.

"That's not... I don't know where that came from!"

"Bullshit!"

Jackson had almost made it to the fracas when the larger man cocked his fist back and swung.

THIRTY-SEVEN

THE DOMINOES FELL. The man built like a giant sequoia fired accusations wildly at the family next to him. In a matter of seconds, the drama had the attention of everyone in the shelter, including the men working with the police.

Perfect.

The Bull Shark slipped away from his cot and edged toward the wall. One of the men working with the police, the fit one, was hurrying over, no doubt in an effort to save the day. If he was going to hunt, he had to go now.

He skulked against the wall to the hall that led out back. Once there and out of sight, he turned and ran, throwing himself at the push-bar door and out into the wind and the rain. Right next to him was the generator, humming underneath the howl of the storm overhead. He did a lap around it, looking for its gas tank. He couldn't figure out where to access it, but a portion of the tank wall was visible behind metal bars to show its current level. That would have to do.

The Bull Shark pulled out his hunting knife, slipped it in between two bars near the tank's base, and placed the tip of the blade against the plastic tank. Then, with an open hand, he slammed it forward. The knife punctured the tank. He twisted the blade in every direction, widening the hole. Fuel began to trickle out around the blade, and when he removed the knife, a gurgling stream began to flow. He flashed his toothy grin, admiring his handy work.

His mission accomplished, he sheathed the knife and hurried back inside. He closed the door behind him and turned back toward the main room when he noticed a figure standing in the hall. An older man with leathery skin leaned against the wall just inside the doors, a freshly lit cigarette in his hand. The Bull Shark knew this man from around town. Hank Willis was always keen to chat up whoever was nearby him.

"You damn near scared the piss out of me," Hank said.

"And you me," The Bull Shark said. He scrambled to compose himself. "It's really coming down out there now."

"Seems so." Hank's brow furrowed. "What were you doing out there? Cops said they didn't want anyone sneakin' off."

The Bull Shark smiled bashfully. "Ah, it's this artificially cooled air. I just needed some of the fresh stuff, even if there is a hurricane going on." He nodded at the cigarette in Hank's hand. "What about you?"

"Just the opposite." Hank twirled the cigarette between his fingers. "Was hankerin' for a nicotine fix."

The Bull Shark chuckled. "Well, I won't narc on you if you don't narc on me."

Hank shrugged. "Fair enough."

The Bull Shark held a hand up in farewell and continued down the hall, leaving Hank to his smoke break. Maybe Hank really did intend on keeping his word, but The Bull Shark couldn't chance it. Sooner rather than later, the generator was going to run out of fuel. The building would lose what little power it had and plunge into darkness and disorder. In those churned-up waters, he'd strike at his next victim.

And now he knew who it would be.

THIRTY-EIGHT

JACKSON, Bear, Shaw, and Investigator Bowden stood over Carter Gray in the shower area of the men's bathroom, Carter's wrist shackled to a metal railing bolted to the wall. His large hand had bruised and was starting to swell after hitting a man named Peter Wright. Carter's punch had connected with Peter's jaw just before Jackson and Bear tackled him. After Shaw came in and slipped her handcuffs on the man, she'd checked both of their IDs. Now the three of them worked with Bowden to figure out if Carter had been up to more than just a donnybrook over shelf-stable meat.

"You like hurting people, Carter?" Bowden asked.

"People that mess with my shit, yeah," Carter said.

Jackson folded his arms and leaned against the wall the metal railing was bolted into. "Peter out there says he has no idea how your jerky ended up in his bag, and his whole family claim he's a vegetar-ian. He had no use for the stuff. Either way, doesn't give you the right to sucker punch the guy."

"Whatever." Carter spit onto the bathroom floor, his saliva smeared with blood. "That bag didn't up and grow legs. He knows what he did."

Shaw crouched down and looked Carter in the eye. "We're more interested in what you've done. Where were you before you came here yesterday?"

Carter's eyes narrowed. "My place in Tom's Cove. Why? What's it to you?"

Shaw pulled a notepad and pen out of the pocket on her vest. "Can anyone verify that?"

Carter snorted. "Yeah, ask Hurricane fucking Margaret out there."

Shaw gave a sarcastic smile. "What about the Meachems?"

"What about them?"

"Do you have any familial connection to them?"

Carter snorted again. "Yeah. That's why I bust my ass working construction and live in a fucking single wide. Because I'm a goddamn Meachem."

Chief Diaz stepped into the bathroom and cleared his throat to get the group's attention. He motioned for them to join him.

"Don't go anywhere," Bear said to Carter as he stepped away.

"Go fuck yourself," Carter snapped.

Chief Diaz waited for the group to huddle around him, then he spoke in a low tone. "We searched Gray's things. Nothing incriminating beyond a baggie of weed."

Shaw gave a shake of her head. "Doesn't mean he's not our guy."

"I've known Carter Gray since my wife and I came to town fifteen years ago. He gets in bar scraps and things of that nature, but he's not a killer. And he's definitely not related to Scott Meachem."

Jackson scratched his beard. "We shouldn't rule anyone out just because we can't connect them to the Meachems. Whatever the family ties are, it must be complicated if it isn't clear yet."

Bowden shrugged. "Still, the chief is right. Gray doesn't seem like the type."

Chief Diaz looked at Jackson. "Your contact running the names. They run Gray yet?"

Jackson pulled out his phone and checked it. Thankfully, he still had service. "I don't know, but I can find out."

He stepped out of the bathroom and walked down the long hall leading out back. When he got to the door at the end, he called Bailey.

"Jackson," she said. "Everything okay?"

"As good as can be expected. People are starting to get on edge," he replied. "I was calling to see where you were at with the list."

"Still working on it. These databases aren't exactly set up to prove familial connections. It takes some leg work."

"I know. I appreciate the effort. What about a specific name on the list?"

Keyboard keys tapped on Bailey's end. "Shoot."

"Carter Gray."

More keystrokes. "Yeah, we ran him. No known connection to Scott Meachem."

Jackson sighed. "You're sure?"

"Uh huh. He was born to Mary and James Gray October 9, 1984, at Riverside Shore Memorial in Onancock. Neither of them have any connection to Scott Meachem, either."

Jackson thought for a moment. "What about Peter Wright?"

"Also ran." Bailey typed away again. "Wright has a passport showing him to be a resident of Hamilton, Ontario. Came into the US via customs at Norfolk International eight days ago with his family. Pretty obvious there were no ties to Scott Meachem let alone anyone in Chincoteague."

Jackson shook his head. "Alright, thanks."

"Uh huh. We'll keep at it. Stay dry out there."

"I'll try."

Jackson hung up. He closed his eyes and tried to refocus when he heard footsteps coming down the hall. He looked over and saw Hank Willis.

"Everything alright?" he asked.

Jackson nodded. "Fine."

Hank chuckled. "Just wanted to make sure. I snuck a smoke down here when all hell broke loose. I didn't mean for it to cause anyone trouble. I know, strictly speaking, I'm not supposed to smoke in here."

Jackson shook his head. "I'm not the police. And even if I were, I wouldn't be worried about someone sneaking a smoke with everything going on."

He pulled his pack and clapped it in his hands. "Then I guess you don't mind if I have another?"

Jackson pried himself off the wall and headed back toward the ballroom. "Your secret's safe with me."

"Appreciate it." Hank took a cigarette and slipped it between his lips. "These things'll kill me one day, but I just can't help it, you know?"

THIRTY-NINE

HURRICANE MARGARET officially made landfall a quarter after three in the afternoon as the eye of the storm, thirty miles in diameter, came ashore in Berlin, Maryland, just south of Ocean City, clipping the northernmost points of Assateague Island. For Chincoteague, that meant they'd catch the brunt of the eyewall, the most ferocious part of the storm. One hundred-twenty-mile-per-hour winds ripped through the island with an onslaught of rain. The Chincoteague Center, squat and made of all cinderblock and steel, held firm, but those inside could hear the wind as it roared around them like a locomotive. The children and more fearful adults looked to their family members for comfort.

The normal talking and general noise had never been as loud as it had been before Carter Gray punched Peter Wright, but now the ballroom was nearly silent, with most conversations drowned out by the howling squalls.

Jackson posted himself near the front doors, keeping an eye on the flooding situation outside — so far, just shallow pools from the torrential rainfall — and keeping himself ready to act should the doors need to be hastily barricaded. He scanned the room, his mind constantly churning, trying to decide who among them had killed Captain Terry and the others. His gaze shifted from Peter Wright, tending to his jaw with an ice pack, to Hank Willis chatting up his cot neighbors, to the elderly couple, whom he learned were Curt and Leona Porter. Allowing a spree killer to sit amongst them felt like playing with a matchbook over a canister of gasoline. Jackson didn't like it.

Shaw stepped out from the kitchen, also looking around, but locked onto Jackson and headed toward him with two bottles of water in her hands. When she got to him, she held one out. Jackson untucked an arm and held his hand up, saying, "No thanks". Shaw slipped the extra bottle of water into a cargo pocket in her duty trousers, opened hers, and leaned against the wall next to Jackson.

"Chief Diaz said they're going to keep Gray in the shower area for now," she said before taking a sip. "They're not convinced he's ready to play nice with everyone else."

"We've been in here little more than twenty-four hours," Jackson replied. "People are only going to get more restless, more agitated. And that's without them knowing about our main problem."

Shaw took another sip of her water. "Any word from your contact at VSP?"

Jackson shook his head. "Just that Wright and Gray seem to be clear."

"It'd be nice if we could just make everyone submit a DNA sample and be done with it, not that we have any way to run samples." Shaw capped her bottle. "But it'd make this all a lot easier."

Jackson cocked his head, conceding her point.

Shaw looked over at him. "You have any suspicions? Anyone you're keeping a particular eye on?"

"It's not helpful to think that way. You start to zero in on someone for no reason, it makes you see things differently."

"Confirmation bias."

Jackson nodded. "Exactly. Then you don't see the danger even when it's right in front of you." The corner of his mouth turned down. "That's when people get hurt."

Shaw tucked her bottle under her arm and slipped her hands into her pockets. "You should be in law enforcement, you know. You think like us. Have our instincts."

Jackson shook his head. "I've never been one for donuts."

Shaw snorted. "Was that a joke out of the steely Jackson Clay?"

"Maybe." Jackson let a small grin form on his face.

Shaw was about to say something more when the fluorescent lights above them suddenly flickered, then dimmed.

"What on earth?" Shaw asked.

Jackson looked overhead, thinking. "The generator—"

Before he could finish, the entire building went dark.

FORTY

HE WATCHED Hank Willis the rest of the day, making sure he knew where the old man was at all times. He moved around him. Stalked him.

Truthfully, he didn't know when the generator would run out of fuel. He figured it would be in the next twelve hours and hoped it would happen before everyone settled in for the night. The confusion it would cause when people were still milling about would only aid him in remaining unidentified.

He looked up at the clock on the wall. It was almost a quarter after six. At best, there were only three or four more hours before people started to turn in. Anxiety crawled under his skin as the minutes ticked by. The craving within him begged to be sated.

That's when it happened.

The lights flickered, then dimmed. The Bull Shark was the only one in the shelter that knew what was about to happen. Slipping off his cot, he moved to the back wall of the ballroom, zeroing in on Hank as he did. Hank walked along the outside of the ballroom, past the door to the supply room, and headed in the direction of the hall that led out back.

The building went completely dark. As people screamed from the abrupt loss of power, The Bull Shark was already moving, skirting the outside wall and homing in on where Hank had gone. As he got to the far wall, he reached out. His hands found the collar of Hank's shirt. The Bull Shark felt for the knob to the bathroom door beside him, then grabbed Hank and yanked him into the bathroom.

He wrapped his arm around Hank's neck. The man went to scream, but only a dry gagging sound came out. With The Bull Shark behind him, Hank drove the two of them backwards into the wall. The Bull Shark's grip didn't falter. Hank turned and tried to load up another go at it, but his feet slipped. He fell forward.

The Bull Shark lay on top of him now, his grip on Hank's neck as tight as ever. He heard screams and shouting coming from the ballroom, people panicking as the police and volunteers no doubt tried to restore calm. Hank's hands slapped at the tile floor, trying desperately to get any leverage. They never did. And a second later, Hank's entire body went limp.

Pivoting to flip his limp victim over, The Bull Shark drew the hunting knife from its sheath. He knew it was a risk. Knew that any blood splatter found on him would surely out him as the man's reaper, but he couldn't resist. He plunged the knife into Hank's torso, slipping the blade between two ribs. Hank, the life all but extinguished from him, took one last gulp of air. The Bull Shark rose. Just before he stepped away, he slowly pulled the knife out and tossed it aside. He imagined a stream of blood flowing onto the tile floor. In the pitch-black, he bared his teeth.

The Bull Shark prowled out of the bathroom, his hand on the wall to guide him, to rejoin the others before anyone noticed he was gone.

FORTY-ONE

ALL AROUND JACKSON came the screams of panicked people. Loud crashes as people tripped over cots and other things at their feet. In the kitchen, somewhere to his right, came the metallic clangs of cookware falling.

Next to him, Shaw drew a personal flashlight from her duty belt and clicked it on. Sweeping across the ballroom, the two of them saw the scene in a single spotlight. Peter Wright holding his hand to his face. A little girl, standing between two cots, crying. A volunteer in an orange vest picking herself up off the floor. Moments later, a couple more flashlights cast their beams into the pitch-black void.

"What the hell was that?" someone asked the darkness.

"It had to be the generator," answered another.

Shaw led Jackson through the chaos to the hall that ran out back. As they did, a meaty hand reached out and grabbed him.

"On your six, Jacky Boy," Bear said.

The three of them made their way to the hall and broke into a jog. Pushing the doors open to the outside was like stepping out into a turbulent underworld. Jackson's eyes, already adjusted to the darkness, could see the silhouettes of everything around him. Trees shook violently as the strong squalls howled through them beneath an aubergine sky. Rain pelted his face. He looked to his left and saw the generator.

Bear stepped past him and ventured out, using his hands to both brace himself and diagnose the possible problem. Shaw came up behind him and focused her flashlight on the matter. When they got to the far side, Bear pointed to a puncture wound in the side of the generator between two metal bars.

"The tank has a hole in it," he shouted over the wind.

"What can we do to plug it?" Shaw asked.

Bear thought for a second. "One of you give me a sock."

Before Shaw could ask why, Jackson untied one of his boots, pulled the sock off his foot, and gave it to Bear. Bear took it and worked it into the gash. It wasn't a perfect seal, but it would stymie most of the leak.

"I need something flat to hold it in place," Bear said.

Shaw patted around her utility belt, then pulled her notepad from the pocket in her vest and offered it to Bear.

Bear shook his head. "Something stronger and waterproof. Or more waterproof than that."

"This is all I've got," Shaw said.

Bear hesitated, then took the notepad and sandwiched it against the sock. He turned to Shaw and Jackson again. "I need something to hold it all in place."

Shaw looked at the matter, then pulled a knife from her utility belt, folded it open, and handed it to Bear. "Wedge it between the two bars."

Bear did as she suggested, maneuvering the knife so it was pinned between the bars on one side and the protruding sock and notepad on the other. "This should hold for now. But we'll need some more fuel."

"I saw them put canisters in the supply room," Shaw said. She turned to Jackson. "I'll go get a couple."

"Hurry," Jackson said.

Shaw disappeared inside. Jackson and Bear took cover in the alcove cut into the building.

"Do you think something hit the tank?" Jackson asked. "Debris?"

Bear shook his head. "If it did, that was a one in a million shot. Looks more like someone punched a hole in the damn thing. But who would want to do that?"

Jackson had the same question. Then, in one epiphanous and horrifying moment, it came to him. They'd fallen for a diversion. Their killer was, in fact, here—or here *now*—and they'd sabotaged the generator on purpose. Jackson opened the door and ducked inside, temporarily blinded by Shaw's jostling flashlight, illuminating two diesel cans from where they were tucked underneath her arm. Jackson took a can from her and held the door open.

"It's them, Shaw," Jackson said. "Whoever's killing everyone, they did this. They wanted the power out."

"Shit," Shaw uttered. "We have to warn everyone."

Jackson nodded toward the dark hall. "You go. Find Chief Diaz and tell him. Bear and I will get the generator back up and be right behind you."

Shaw grabbed the flashlight beneath her arm. "Here. You'll need this."

Jackson shook his head. "You'll need it more. Go."

Shaw gave him the second can, turned, and ran back down the hall. Jackson grabbed both cans of diesel and turned to Bear, who must have ducked inside during their conversation.

"Let's go," he said.

Bear led them back out into the storm, stepping between the generator and the building and coming back to the punctured tank.

"Where do we fill it?" Jackson asked.

Bear felt out around the side of the generator before his hands found a small door just over his head. He opened it, finding a gas cap over the fuel filler.

"Here!" Bear said.

He unscrewed the cap, and Jackson lifted a can up to the open hole. The sound of fuel sloshing barely cut through the squalling wind. After several moments, Jackson felt the can go empty and lifted the second one to pour in. When that too was empty, he backed away, and Bear put the cap back on and shut the door.

"We'll need to prime it to get the air out before we turn it back on," Bear said. He took a step toward the far end of the generator to what looked to be the control panel and began feeling around.

"Here," Jackson said.

He pulled out his phone, turned on its light, and handed it to Bear. Bear ran his hands over the various buttons before pressing and holding one. The generator groaned like a large creature waking from a long slumber. After several seconds, Bear released the button, looked around again, and pressed another one. The generator whirred and hummed to life.

Bear looked at Jackson with a shit-eating grin. "MacGyver ain't got shit on me!"

Jackson rolled his eyes and started for the door. "Come on, we've got to go!"

Soaking wet and with only one shoe on, Jackson hurried back down the hallway to the ballroom, Bear following. The lights had come back on and everyone was strewn about the space, just starting to gather themselves and whatever things had been knocked over during the power outage. Jackson's eyes jumped from person to person, watching them closely, looking for anything suspicious.

Across the room, Chief Diaz climbed onto a chair trying to get everyone's attention. Shaw stood next to him, watching his efforts go in vain. Finally, she put her fingers to her lips and whistled.

A stunned silence followed. "Listen up!" she bellowed, then yielded the floor to Chief Diaz.

"There's no need for alarm. As you all can see, we've got the generator back up and running. It just ran out of fuel," he said.

People still milled about, talking amongst themselves.

"Is everyone okay? Does anyone need medical attention?" Chief Diaz asked.

The talking petered out. Everyone looked around the room, curious if anyone had, in fact, gotten hurt.

"Over here!" A man called out. "This lady's split her head open."

"Alright, we'll get her help. Everyone else, please, if you would, return to your cots, and we will——"

A blood-curdling scream filled the room as Peter Wright's wife came running past the open door to the men's bathroom.

"Oh my God!" she shrieked. "In there! Someone's hurt in there!"

Shaw and the other police officers ran for the bathrooms, but Jackson and Bear were much closer. In a second, Jackson barreled through the propped-open door to the men's room, following the woman. She stood near the sinks, pointing and crying. Ten feet from her, he saw Hank Willis on the ground.

Jackson dropped to his knees at Hank's side, noticing a stab wound on the left side of Hank's chest. He ripped open Hank's button-down shirt and began searching the rest of his torso for injuries. Bear dropped down next to Jackson.

"What do you need?" he asked.

"Put pressure on the wound," Jackson said.

Officer Birch stepped into the bathroom, standing over them. "Holy hell," he said at the sight before him.

"He's got a puncture wound to the chest," Jackson called out. He felt for the radial artery in Hank's wrist. "Shit. No pulse." He put his ear to Hank's mouth and nose, listening for breathing as he looked for Hank's chest rising. "No breathing. Starting CPR. I need someone to start rescue breathing."

Shaw came into the bathroom, stepped around them, and knelt down next to Hank's head on the other side. Jackson began doing chest compressions. After thirty of them, he nodded to Shaw. Shaw bent over and blew two deep breaths into Hank's mouth as she pinched his nose closed. When she was done, Jackson checked Hank for signs of responsiveness. There were none. Jackson started compressions again.

They continued like that for several more minutes until, after two more breaths, Jackson checked again for a pulse. Shaw could see in his eyes he hadn't found one. She shook her head. When she did, Peter Wright's wife cried out again from the corner of the bathroom.

"Oh God!" she said. "Is he... is he *dead*?"

Officer Birch gently put his arm around the woman, trying to usher her away. "Come on," he said. "Why don't we step out here?"

As she was leaving, she gasped and frantically stabbed her finger at the corner of the bathroom. Jackson followed her gesture. A few feet from Hank, under the sinks, lay a knife, its blade covered in blood.

"Oh my God!" Peter's wife screamed. "Did someone in here kill him?!"

"Get her out of here, now!" Shaw ordered.

Officer Birch led her away, but it was too late. Several people heard what she'd screamed. From inside the bathroom, Jackson, Bear, and Shaw could hear everyone descend into a frantic, fear-fueled uproar again.

Jackson looked at the knife, then at Hank. "This doesn't make sense," he said. "He shouldn't have bled out that fast, unless it hit an artery, in which case there'd be a lot more blood."

Shaw, too, studied Hank's body. "His neck is red," she pointed out. "Marks similar to being choked or strangled." Her voice dropped to a whisper. "Just like Ada Fitzhugh."

Chief Diaz stepped into the bathroom and took in the scene. "Is it true? Someone attacked Mr. Willis?"

Shaw rose to her feet, pointing at the knife under the sink. "It would seem so."

Jackson and Bear stood as well, their hands and pants covered in Hank's blood.

"Someone out there did this, Chief," Jackson said. "They've done *all* of it. No more watching, we need to act."

Chief Diaz's gaze moved from the knife to Jackson and Bear's blood-soaked pants. Investigator Bowden appeared in the doorway. Chief Diaz turned to him.

"Get everyone to their cots," he said. "Check everyone for blood."

FORTY-TWO

THE BULL SHARK watched as a mass of people crowded around the doors to the bathrooms. The wife of the man he'd framed earlier slipped through the fray. She was sobbing and muttering something about a person being killed. It was all just coherent enough to spark a powder keg of pandemonium in the ballroom. Some began to cry as others held their loved ones close, looking at those around them with fear and suspicion. Gossip and rumors spread amongst them as quickly as the fear had.

The crowd at the bathrooms split in two and out stepped the police chief and a couple of his subordinates, one of the uniformed officers and the investigator dressed in a polo and slacks with his badge and gun on his belt. The chief held up his hands, asking for everyone to quiet down.

"Is it true?!" a man snapped. "Is someone dead in there? You have to tell us if we're in danger!"

"Please," the police chief begged. "Let's just take the temperature down in here for a moment."

"Oh my God!" A woman cried. "Someone did get killed, didn't they!"

"They're covering it up!" the first man shouted.

His accusations sparked more shouts and cries. The chief tried pleading with them before sticking his fingers in his mouth and whistling loudly. It brought the room back to order.

"Yes, a person is deceased in the bathroom," he said. "And, yes, it appears someone attacked him. But I assure you, we are going to keep everyone safe as we figure out exactly what happened. For right now..."

A flurry of groans came forth.

"*For right now*, I need everyone to return to their cots until a member of my police department speaks with you."

People still seemed skeptical, but they slowly obeyed the chief's commands. The Bull Shark, already sitting on his cot, stayed put. Two more officers came out, including the wildlife cop. They each took a person on the row of cots nearest the bathroom and began interviewing them. This would put The Bull Shark as one of the last to be questioned.

He casually checked over himself, making sure there was nothing incriminating. His clothes had dried in the hours since he'd stepped out to sabotage the generator, now he just needed to double check there was no blood or anything else that could tie him to the attack. He didn't see any.

The two men working with the police stepped out of the bathroom next. Their pants were stained with blood, and the sight of them stirred more gasps from throughout the ballroom. The Bull Shark had to put a hand over his face to hide his smile.

He noticed that the two men were not participating in questioning people. *Interesting.* They must not be law enforcement. Then what was their role in all this?

It took forty-five minutes for one of the officers to come to him. An Officer Birch, based on his nameplate. When the officer approached him, he gave his best disarming smile.

"Please stand for me, if you don't mind," Birch said. "I need to check you real quick."

"No problem." He stood, spinning slowly at the direction of Birch. Birch gently fanned his shirt and pants out from his body, spreading them so he could see more clearly.

"You can take a seat for me again."

The Bull Shark did as he was asked.

"The man who was attacked was Hank Willis," Birch said. "An older gentleman with long gray hair. His cot was right over there." Birch pointed to the center of the ballroom. "Have you had any interaction with him since you arrived here?"

"If it's who I think you're talking about, I've seen him smoking down the hall over there once or twice. Just smiled and said hello in passing."

Birch nodded as he jotted things down on his notepad. "Anything else?"

"Mm, not that I can think of." He turned his gaze to the two men. "Maybe it's a little obvious, but have you asked the two men with blood on their pants?"

Birch gave a cursory look over his shoulder before returning to his notepad. "They got that blood on them trying to resuscitate Mr. Willis."

"Oh, I see. Are they doctors or something?"

Birch shook his head. "In any event, they were also with another officer fixing the generator when we believe Mr. Willis was attacked."

The Bull Shark made himself frown. "What happened to the generator?"

"Not sure. Just know it kicked out, and they fixed it." He looked up from his notepad. "Did you see anyone have any strange interactions with Mr. Willis? Anything stand out to you?"

He paused an extra moment for effect, pretending to think. "Can't say that I have. What about that large man who swung at the other guy? He seemed awfully angry."

Birch shook his head again and returned to his notepad. "He's been detained since that incident."

"Good, we don't need any more trouble."

Birch finished what he'd been writing and slipped his notepad into his pocket. "Alright, well if you think of anything else, just grab a hold of one of us."

"No problem. Can I ask you one thing, officer?" He lowered his voice. "Are we safe?"

Birch nodded. "Yes, sir. Just like the chief said, we're going to get to the bottom of this and, while we do, we're going to be extra vigilant and keep everyone safe."

The Bull Shark grinned. "Just had to ask."

Birch returned his smile and stepped away. When he was gone, The Bull Shark grinned wider, baring his teeth.

FORTY-THREE

IT TOOK NEARLY an hour for Shaw and the Chincoteague police officers to check and interview everyone. Jackson, with Bear by his side, posted up in the corner of the ballroom, keeping a keen eye, looking for anyone trying to shirk from the officers. No one had.

When they were all finished, they reconvened with Chief Diaz in the supply room, save for Officer Perry who was tasked with holding down the fort outside.

Chief Diaz rested his arm against a shelf filled with jugs of water. "Where are we at?" he asked.

Shaw shook her head. "Back where we started," she said. "Everyone has at least someone that seems to remember they were in the ballroom when the power went out and when it came back on."

Investigator Bowden frowned. "Power was out for a good few minutes. Anyone could've attacked Mr. Willis and come back."

Shaw shrugged. "It's the only kind of corroboration we can get. Plus, that'd be pretty hard to do in the dark."

Chief Diaz nodded. "Hard but not impossible. What about blood? Anyone have any on them?"

"Only one, sir," Officer Birch said as he checked his notes. "A Willow Grace. She was the one with her head split open. She says she fell during the blackout. Two others corroborated this."

"It was pitch black," Bowden said, "how could they confirm her story?"

"Because she fell into them," Birch said.

Bear snorted and shook his head.

Chief Diaz shifted his weight from one leg to the other. "What about the knife? Can we connect it to anyone?"

Bowden shook his head. "No one remembers seeing it before. It might have prints or DNA on it, but we have no way to test it right now."

"How did it get in, though?" Chief Diaz asked.

Bowden slipped his hands into his pockets, shrugging. "We didn't exactly search everyone upon coming in. We stopped whatever weapons we spotted, but someone could've easily stashed that knife in their belongings."

Chief Diaz frowned. "Alright, fine. But we need to check everyone now. Any weapons get confiscated until this thing is over."

"Can we do that? Legally?"

"I may get an angry letter from the ACLU somewhere down the line, but I don't give a damn. We're not letting another attack happen in here. If anyone has a problem with it, they're welcome to be detained alongside Mr. Gray."

A silence came over the room, everyone seemingly taken aback by the chief's brusque attitude.

"Alright," the chief continued, "what about a possible motive? Does anyone in the shelter have any reason to want to hurt Mr. Willis?"

Investigator Bowden shook his head again. "Not that we have found."

Shaw looked around at the group, stupefied. "Are we really pretending this isn't our serial killer?"

"Spree killer," Bear corrected.

"*Whatever*," Shaw hissed. "Are we really pretending this isn't their latest victim?"

Chief Diaz pursed his lips. "It's very likely, but we can't make any assumptions. That's how mistakes are made."

Shaw looked at Jackson. "Did you tell them about the fuel tank on the generator?"

At that, everyone turned and looked at Jackson.

Jackson met Chief Diaz's eyes. "Something, more likely *someone*, punctured the fuel tank on the generator. That's why the power cut out. The generator was bleeding fuel."

"Are you kidding me?" Investigator Bowden stammered.

Chief Diaz pursed his lips. "Is it repaired?"

Bear folded his arms, taking a wide stance with his legs. "We got a quick fix on it right now, but it won't hold forever. Someone'll need to work on getting a better patch job on it."

Chief Diaz thought for a moment. "Alright. We're locking this place down. We'll leave the lights in the ballroom on for tonight. No one leaves the cot area unless they absolutely need to, in which case they're escorted by one of us. No more than one at a time. People may not like it, but they'll be safer for it. In the meantime, Jackson and Bear will work on engineering a better patch for the generator. And we check it every hour, regardless. The last thing we need is for the power to go out on us again."

"If we do this, we all but confirm to everyone there's a killer amongst them," Bowden said. "People are already uneasy. This may push some over the edge."

"They're not dumb," Jackson pointed out. "They'll realize that no matter what we do, if they haven't already. This will help us get a better handle on the situation."

Bowden threw his hands up in a gesture of surrender. "Just wanted to make sure we're all on the same page."

Chief Diaz nodded. "I appreciate it, but Mr. Clay is right. They've likely already put two and two together. We need to control the environment in here." He looked around at the group. "To that end, Mr.

Clay and Mr. Beauchamp, why don't you get to work on coming up with a fix for the generator."

"Best place for us to start is looking for parts in here, Chief," Bear said.

"Noted," Chief Diaz replied. "Let's give them some room to get to work."

Shaw and the other police officers opened the door and stepped out. Jackson and Bear started picking through the shelves, looking for whatever might be useful. When the officers were gone, Bear looked over at Jackson.

"You really think this is going to work?" Bear asked. "Have everyone sit crisscross applesauce until the storm is over?"

Jackson moved a large bag of rice on a shelf. "It's the smart play. Control the situation as best we can until we can get some more help."

Bear gave half a shrug. "I don't know. Seems like this guy's been at least one step ahead of us the whole time. We could just be making ourselves sitting ducks."

"The chief is right. We do this, and whoever's behind it all will feel boxed in. They'll want to make a move, and that'll lead to them making a mistake."

"Yeah, but what if that move is attacking someone else?"

Jackson shook his head. "We won't let it come to that."

Bear sighed. "Tell that to Hank Willis."

PART FIVE
MIDNIGHT SUN

"Thunder is good, thunder is impressive, but it is lightning that does the work." -Mark Twain

FORTY-FOUR

THE NEXT SEVERAL hours felt like a tense standoff. Very few in the ballroom gave in to sleep, and those who did lay down seemed restless. The filtered, air-conditioned air inside the building grew thick with many emotions, but trust wasn't one of them. Diaz and Bowden moved Hank Willis's body to a walk-in freezer in the kitchen that had only been storing a couple drums of ice cream leftover from a banquet held a few weeks prior. Not wanting it to go to waste, the volunteers had offered up sundaes to people in the shelter, but no one had been in the mood for a sweet treat.

Now Jackson sat against the ballroom wall between the doors for the supply room and bathrooms. He, too, was restless. Hank Willis had been in his pool of thirteen possible suspects. So had Carter Gray, who was now cleared because he'd been cuffed back in the shower area of the men's bathroom when Hank was attacked. That brought the group of possible suspects down to eleven. Watching the ballroom, Jackson ignored everyone else and focused on them exclusively.

Shaw, fresh off making a slow lap around the ballroom, took a seat against the wall next to Jackson. "Where's Bear?" she asked.

"Out at the generator," Jackson said. "Finishing up the repair job on it."

"Alone?"

"No, Birch is out there with him."

Shaw smirked. "You guys figure out something better than a sock and my notepad?"

"We found some metal shingles and epoxy putty in the supply room. We patched it up as best we could and covered the whole thing with a spare rain parka Bowden had." He gave a half shrug. "Not ideal, but it should buy us some time."

Shaw sighed. She scanned the ballroom. "This is all so surreal."

Jackson just nodded.

"To tell you the truth, it reminds me of the midnight sun."

Jackson looked at her. "The what?"

"Midnight sun." She met his eyes and pointed above her head. "North of the arctic circle. You ever been?"

Jackson shook his head. "Can't say that I have."

"I was up at Kobuk Valley National Park for a couple years."

Jackson raised an eyebrow.

"My ex left the Air Force and wanted to become a bush pilot. I followed him out there." Shaw chuckled. "Don't ask."

"Dating someone from the Chairforce was your first mistake."

Shaw chuckled again and scanned the ballroom. "Anyway, that far north, the sun doesn't set around the summer solstice."

Jackson looked up at the large, fluorescent lights above them. "Meaning you get light in the middle of the night, like this."

"Well, it's much more beautiful up there, no disrespect to the Chincoteague Center, but yeah." Shaw paused, reflecting. "It messes with people, though. Changing their circadian rhythms. People's behavior changes. They can get more... erratic. Unpredictable. It was a real thing we had to watch out for."

Jackson brought his knees up and rested his arms on them. "Are you trying to impart some wisdom for our current situation?"

Shaw cocked her head to the side. "Just stay sharp around everyone. Don't drop your guard."

Jackson nodded. "Copy that." Not like he'd planned to.

FORTY-FIVE

PRETENDING to sleep on his cot while he came down from the high of snuffing out Hank Willis's life and getting away with it in a building full of people, including almost a half-dozen cops, The Bull Shark found the craving forming inside him again.

The problem he faced now was that he was without a weapon. He was confident in his abilities to take on just about anyone in the shelter, but the attack would have to be quicker and stealthier than his previous one. That required a weapon.

He lay there, gaming out a way to acquire just that. A series of metal clangs came from somewhere past his feet, and The Bull Shark opened his eyes just enough to peek at what was going on. One of the volunteers was pushing a cart with two large cooking pots into the kitchen and it had caught on an extension cord running across the floor. The abrupt stop had sent the empty pots spilling over.

The kitchen.

How had he not thought of it earlier? It must be filled with knives and heavy objects, a commercial cornucopia of cookware that would easily aid him in his attack. The Bull Shark rolled off his cot and trotted over to the volunteer who had begun to clean up the mess.

"Let me help you with that," he said.

The volunteer, a middle-aged woman with brown hair woven into a long braid, smiled. "Thank you. I've seen that darn cord there since we got in here. I don't know how I forgot about it. I'm just... tired, I guess."

"I think we all are."

Together, the two of them got the pots back onto the cart, and he helped the woman guide it over the extension cord and wheel it into the kitchen. Afterwards, the woman placed a hand on his arm.

"Thank you so much," she said. "Why don't you go try and get some more rest."

"It's no problem," The Bull Shark said. "Is there anything else I can help with?"

"Oh, you're so sweet." The woman shook her head. "That's really alright."

The Bull Shark looked around the kitchen. He had found his in and he was eager to capitalize on it. "Nonsense. There has to be something I can do around here. Dishes or something?"

The woman raised her eyebrows. "Actually, you know, that'd be a big help."

He beamed. "Terrific."

The woman led him to the sink and showed him which dishes were dirty and how to load the commercial-grade dishwasher. He listened intently, while also canvassing the counter for armament. When she finished giving her instructions, the woman left him to begin washing and began preparing some pancake batter.

Left alone, The Bull Shark worked quietly, looking for an opportunity. The dishes that needed to be cleaned were mostly bowls and spoons from the impromptu sundae bar that had been offered up in the middle of the night. There were also some large baking pans that were cumbersome but not particularly heavy. None of it was useful.

It took him about twenty minutes to finish up the dishes. When he was done, he slapped the faucet off and stepped toward the volunteer. She had moved on from pancake batter to rehydrating powdered eggs.

"Need any help with that?"

The woman smiled. "You're really eager to make yourself useful, aren't you?"

"There's not exactly a lot to do around here."

The woman chuckled. "Sure, here, why don't you whisk these eggs if you don't mind."

She stepped back and opened a drawer full of cooking utensils to grab a large whisk. That's when he spotted it. Tucked up against the right side of the drawer was a set of kitchen shears. Before he could grab it, though, the woman pushed the drawer shut and stepped in front of it. She passed the bowl of eggs and the whisk to him.

"Here you go," she said. "Thanks!"

He nodded and began whisking the eggs. The woman turned and leaned against the counter directly in front of the drawer.

"I don't think I've seen you around town," she said.

The Bull Shark didn't look up from his work. "I'm fairly new," he said. "Moved here just a few weeks ago."

"Ah." The woman nodded, then extended a hand. "Well, I'm Jesse."

The Bull Shark looked at her hand and hesitated. He'd tried to stay as anonymous as possible. In the time he'd been on the island, only a handful of people had asked for his name, and most of those were only by way of him showing his ID. He was an afterthought. Immediately forgotten as people went on with their day. This felt too personal. Too memorable. An awkward silence formed between the two of them when Officer Birch walked in, wet and shivering.

"Any coffee on?" he asked.

"Oh, I meant to brew some!" Jesse said. "I'm so sorry, I'll get it going right now."

She hurried across the kitchen to the large coffee urns where Officer Birch stood, not realizing his back was to the predator he searched for. The Bull Shark moved fast. He opened the drawer next to him and slipped the shears into his pocket. When Jesse came back to him, carrying one of the urns over to the sink, The Bull Shark was back to whisking the eggs.

Jesse smiled at them as she filled a pot with water. "Those look killer. Thank you!" she said.

The Bull Shark grinned at the turn of phrase and kept stirring.

FORTY-SIX

BEAR AMBLED into the ballroom just after six in the morning. Dripping wet and sucking wind, he walked over to Jackson. A couple of the volunteers stared daggers from across the room at him and the watery snail trail he left behind him.

Jackson looked up at him. "You finish up with the generator?"

"Best I could," Bear said. "Conditions are still pretty bad out there, but I think we might be past the worst. Either way, I'll keep an eye on it." He looked around the ballroom, wiping his nose on his drenched sleeve. "How are things in here?"

"Quiet so far."

"That's good." Bear sniffled. "Why don't you try to get some rest? I'll change into dry clothes and spell ya."

Jackson arched his back and cracked his neck. He'd been awake for almost twenty-four hours now, and his body had started to remind him of that. "Thanks. You go get changed and then we can switch."

Bear nodded and headed for his cot. As he grabbed his clothes and doubled back, Jackson's phone buzzed in his pocket. That he still had reception was encouraging. He pulled it out and looked at the ID.

"Morning, Bailey."

"Hey," Bailey said. She sounded rushed. "Sorry it took me so long to get back to you. I had to let my guys go last night and finish the list myself."

"I appreciate you burning the midnight oil. You got good news for me?"

"I'm afraid not. We ran everyone on the list, Clay. We couldn't find any connection to Scott Meachem."

Jackson's head dropped. "Okay. I assume you ran background checks on them. Anyone with a violent history?"

"A couple. I can email you the info."

"Text might be better. I don't know how long we'll have data."

"Storm that bad, huh?" Bailey's voice crackled like thunder as reception waned.

Jackson looked at his phone. "Yeah, our killer struck again. Here, in the shelter."

"Jesus Christ. Are you okay?"

"I am. We've got a body in the freezer, though."

"So, whoever's doing all this is really with you all in the shelter."

Jackson's eyes jumped around the room between his possible suspects. "Seems so."

"How are you all holding out?"

"Four members of Chincoteague's finest. We've got the place locked down as best we can, but whoever's doing this already sabotaged our generator once."

Bailey was quiet on the other end of the line. "What can I do?"

"You already did what you could running down the list of names. Whatever the familial connection to Scott Meachem is, there must not be a paper trail of it."

"What about Scott Meachem himself? You run him down?"

Jackson scratched his chin. "Scott Meachem disappeared after that incident in '99 I told you about. Mark Meachem, his brother, apparently was run out of town. The prevailing theory here is Scott left as well."

"Hold on." Doors opened and closed on Bailey's end of the line, followed by typing on a keyboard. Then, a pause. "You're right. That's bizarre. Scott Meachem just fell off the face of the earth at the turn of the century. No addresses, no employment, nothing."

Jackson sat upright with an idea. "What about Mark Meachem? Can you run him?"

More typing. "Mark Meachem ended up in Lynchburg it looks like. Owned an LLC there. Then... passed away in 2020. Death certificate puts it right at the height of the pandemic."

Jackson thought some more. Checking for living Meachems off the island hadn't crossed his mind. He looked around the ballroom for Shaw. She sat in a chair near the front doors with her head back. Jackson snapped his fingers to get her attention as discreetly as he could. When she looked up, Jackson waved her over.

"Jackson? You still there?" Bailey asked.

"One sec," Jackson said. When Shaw came to him, he lowered the phone from his ear. "No hits on the list of names, but we didn't think about running the Meachems that have left town," he said to Shaw. "Scott Meachem is a ghost, and Mark died five years ago."

"And Emily is dead up the road," Shaw added.

"What about Scott's family?" Jackson asked. "Did he have kids?"

Shaw shook her head. "No, I thought about that when we learned about the DNA match. He never married, never had kids."

Jackson's mind worked. Emily's kids were dead along with her. But... Russell Hanz. He had dated Mark's daughter. "What about Mark Meachem? He had kids, right? Stephanie?"

Shaw nodded. "She went by Stephie, yeah. And her brother, Zach."

"Yeah, I see that here," Bailey said. "Zachary and Stephanie Meachem." More typing on her end of the line. "Okay, I don't get any in-state hits for a Zach, but it looks like Stephanie Meachem moved to Lynchburg like her father. Virginia DMV comes back with an address there."

"That's near you. I need you to go up and talk to her, Bailey. I'd do it myself, but..."

"No, I get it. I'm on it."

"I owe you one."

"You owe me two. Don't forget about your dog."

Jackson hung up. Shaw stared at him with her brows raised.

"Stephie Meachem is in Lynchburg," Jackson said. "Bailey's going to try to run her down for us."

Shaw folded her arms. "What do we do in the meantime?"

"Like you said. We don't let our guard down."

FORTY-SEVEN

SPECIAL AGENT JEN BAILEY got in her unmarked Ford Interceptor, a law enforcement variant of the Explorer, and took US Route 460 out of Roanoke. The outer bands of Hurricane Margaret had blown into the Shenandoah Valley in western Virginia, casting the landscape in a dreary gray drizzle. She drove northeast to Stephie Meachem's last known address, pulling up to an up-down duplex painted sunflower yellow with a red brick basement and a waist-high chain-link fence around the cozy, overgrown yard.

Stepping out of her cruiser, Bailey shrugged into the charcoal blazer of her pantsuit, untied her auburn hair, and clipped her service weapon onto her hip. Tall and athletic, she took the stairs up to Stephie's porch two at a time, eager to get out of the misty rainfall, then knocked twice on the Craftsman-style front door.

After several moments, the door slowly opened a couple of inches, and half a face peered at Bailey.

"Hello. Ms. Meachem?" she greeted with a smile. "Stephanie Meachem?"

"It's just Stephie," Stephie replied.

"Stephie, got it. My name is Jen Bailey with the Virginia State

Police. I was hoping to talk to you." Bailey flashed her badge and credentials.

"What about?"

"A homicide investigation. I had a few questions I was hoping you could answer."

Stephie didn't say anything.

"Would it be possible to speak inside? I promise it won't take long."

Stephie remained quiet, looking at Bailey with worry behind her pale green eyes. After several moments, she opened the door wide. She was a head shorter than Bailey and slender. Blond, wavy hair ran down both sides of her round face, coming to a rest on her shoulders. She studied Bailey for a moment longer before stepping back from the open door. Bailey noticed a sadness behind her expression.

"Okay," Stephie said softly.

"Thank you." Bailey smiled again and stepped inside.

Immediately off the entryway was a large living room painted the same sunflower yellow as the exterior. The room was tastefully decorated, but Bailey noticed right away there was nothing personal to the decor. A large art print of the Golden Gate Bridge. Smaller prints of famous paintings. Starry Night, The Kiss, and Nighthawks. It looked more like a generic Airbnb and less like a home. The room featured two armchairs and a sofa, with a coffee table in the middle.

"You said this was about a homicide?" Stephie asked.

"Yes," Bailey said. "You used to live in Chincoteague, out on the Eastern Shore, correct? You grew up there?"

Stephie's eyes dropped to the floor, but not before an emotion flickered behind them. Bailey couldn't put her finger on it. Despair? Dread? Hopelessness?

Stephie reached for the armrest of the chair nearest her and slid into it. "You know," she said, "I've waited over twenty-five years for the police to come knocking on my door like you just did. I must've pictured it a thousand times, but I never quite imagined it the way you came just now."

Bailey cocked her head. "I'm sorry," she said. "I don't follow."

"This is about my uncle, right? Scott Meachem? About that night?"

Bailey was caught off guard by Stephie offering up his name but didn't understand what she meant. "You mean the night Russell Hanz disappeared?"

A tear formed in the corner of Stephie's eye. She dabbed at it and shook her head. "Yes, among the many things that went wrong that night. It was the night my life turned into a total nightmare."

Bailey fought to keep confusion from showing on her face. The Stephie in front of her now wasn't a forty-three-year-old woman. It was a young girl, desperate and scared and needing to tell her story. Bailey wrapped her arms around her midsection and leaned toward Stephie.

"Stephie," she said, her voice softer. "What else happened that night?"

Stephie squinted at her. "Isn't that why you're here?" she asked. "Because my father killed my uncle?"

FORTY-EIGHT

THE NEXT FEW hours were spent waiting for the right moment to put the next part of the Bull Shark's plan into action. People filed in and out of the bathroom area as everyone in the shelter started to wake up — or at least gave up on sleep. He needed the men's room to be as empty as possible. The police wouldn't let him go in and use it alone, but that was fine. One extra person could be managed.

The Bull Shark walked along the perimeter of the ballroom. As he neared the bathroom, Officer Birch looked over from the chair he slouched back on and called out to him.

"You need an escort to go anywhere, sir," he said.

"Ah, yeah," he replied. "Sorry, I have to hit the head."

The officer got up and met him at the entryway to the bathroom. He jerked his chin, a go-ahead gesture.

"Do you need to go first?" he asked.

Birch shook his head. "No, just need to keep an eye on you."

"You got it."

The Bull Shark went into the bathroom, slipped into the stall furthest from the door, and shut the stall door. Sitting on the toilet, he pulled out the shears he'd lifted from the kitchen earlier. He popped off the plastic cap over the pivot screw. The screw needed a flathead. The Bull Shark didn't have one, but he had something that he thought might work. He pulled out his car keys, slipped the bitting into the screw's slot, then applied pressure and turned. The screw didn't budge. He pressed harder when his grip slipped and the keys slid across the bathroom floor.

Officer Birch took a couple of steps into the bathroom. The Bull Shark could see his feet from underneath the stall. He wrapped his hand around the handle of the shears, ready to strike if he had to.

"Everything alright in there?" Birch asked.

"Yeah, my keys just fell out of my pocket," he said. "Darn things."

The keys had fallen just outside the stall. No doubt Birch saw them.

"You want me to grab them for you?"

"That's alright, I can get them."

"I'll kick them over." Birch approached the stall.

"It's no problem, I've got them."

Birch didn't stop. The Bull Shark brought his arm back, shears in hand. Birch's shadow grew as he squatted down. The Bull Shark had to make a decision. He leaned forward, lunging with his free hand, grabbed the keys, and pulled them back into the stall.

"Got 'em," he said. "Thanks."

Birch's shadow shrank as he stood tall again. "No sweat." He returned to the other end of the bathroom.

The Bull Shark lined up the key's bitting again, pressed, and twisted. After a couple seconds, the screw gave. He chuckled quietly to himself as he turned the screw until he could grab it with his fingers. Unscrewing it the rest of the way, the shears slid apart into two pieces. Two separate blades.

He'd needed a weapon. Now he had two.

He rose, slipped a blade into each of his front pockets, and stepped out of the stall. Officer Birch leaned against the wall near the door, looking utterly exhausted. The Bull Shark washed his hands. As he did, he imagined plunging one of his new-fangled blades into the police officer's neck.

FORTY-NINE

BAILEY WAS STONE-FACED, but it wasn't a conscious decision. Stephie's sudden and spontaneous admission had stunned her like an uppercut. Straightening up, she smoothed out her blazer to recompose herself, then leaned forward again. When she met Stephie's eyes, though, she could see Stephie had realized her mistake.

"Oh God," she whispered. "You didn't know."

"Stephie..." Bailey tried to say.

Stephie stared into the distance. "For twenty-five years I kept that with me just to blurt it out to some cop I met two minutes ago. All that time... for it to come out like this."

Bailey could see Stephie was a world away from the living room they were sitting in, her mind overrun with a lifetime of concealing a horrible truth. Bailey reached out and placed her hand on Stephie's, bringing her back to the here and now.

"Stephie," Bailey started again, "you're saying you actually saw your father, Mark Meachem, kill your uncle Scott Meachem in 1999?"

Stephie's eyes focused on Bailey now, and tears cascaded down her cheeks like tiny waterfalls as she began to sob.

"Because of me," Stephie said.

Bailey was as confused as ever. She spotted a box of tissues on the coffee table, reached out, and offered it to Stephie. Stephie plucked one from the box and dabbed at her eyes.

"Walk me through this all," Bailey said. "Tell me what happened that night. From the beginning."

Stephie took a deep breath in, composing herself, then let it out. "I was pregnant," she said. "Eighteen years old and pregnant like a stupid TV drama." She shook her head. "My parents didn't know yet. I knew I couldn't hide it forever, but they were going to blow a gasket when they found out." She sniffled, balling up the tissue in her hand. "My whole family had their annual cookout following the pony penning. After we ate, I went for a walk to clear my head. I was standing out on the little fishing dock we had when my brother came running up to me. He told me that dad knew. That he knew *everything*."

"Your brother knew you were pregnant?"

Stephie gave a jittery nod. "He and I were very close back then. When I found out, I felt like I needed to tell someone, so I told him. He was the only one who knew until that night. When he told me dad knew, I knew my dad wouldn't understand. Really, *I* didn't understand. It just... happened. So, we ran back to the house knowing I had to explain it all somehow. That's when we heard the first gunshots."

"Gunshots?"

Stephie nodded again. "One after another. *Bang... bang.* I can still hear them like it just happened. I thought we were too late. We ran as fast as we could. Just as we got to the house, I saw my boyfriend Russell's truck. I thought that my father had shot and killed Russell. But then he stepped out of his truck."

"Your dad was shooting at your boyfriend?"

"No. It was my uncle shooting at my father."

Bailey shook her head. "But why would your uncle shoot at your father?"

Stephie stared down at her Kleenex. When she glanced back up, Bailey saw regret flooding her eyes alongside her tears.

"Your uncle was the father of your unborn child," Bailey whispered.

Stephie smiled sadly as she tapped the tip of her nose with her finger. "I can only imagine what you must think of me."

Bailey's voice was soft. "Did he assault you?"

Stephie shook her head as if it was a preposterous thought. "No. At least, not how you mean. Obviously, I know now it was some form of that. I've spent years and tens of thousands of dollars for therapists to tell me I was taken advantage of. I wish I could believe them, but I don't think I ever will."

"Then what happened?"

"I need to back up to explain. Several weeks earlier, the whole family went out on the water for Memorial Day. All of us between three boats. We'd go out to the middle of Chincoteague Bay and spend the entire afternoon out there. My uncle was taking people out two at a time, towing them on the inflatable. I wanted to go one last time, but my mother insisted we all head in. My Uncle Scott offered to take me out for one last run before bringing me back. My mother relented. Everyone else headed back on the other two boats, and my uncle took me around the bay one last time. When it was done, he brought me back to the boat. I was having a fun time, and I was really buzzed — my parents would let us drink some when it was just the family."

Bailey nodded. "Okay."

"So, we were pulling the inflatable in, and he was joking with me, and next thing I knew, he leaned over and kissed me. I... didn't know what to do at first. It happened so fast, but he did it like it was so natural, I guess a part of me told myself it was. I had a really poor image of myself back then. Girls would tell me I was too skinny, that I was a prude because I hadn't had sex yet, that my boyfriend Russell was only with me because he felt sorry for me. Then here was my uncle, an adult who was rich and handsome and always had pretty girlfriends over... and he was kissing me. I know it sounds crazy, but it made me feel special."

Bailey plucked another tissue out of the box and offered it to Stephie. "It doesn't sound crazy. It sounds like you were preyed on and didn't know any better."

"Well, I don't know how, but my father found out the night of our family's party a few months later. While I was at the dock, I guess he went and confronted my uncle at his house, right next to ours. My uncle ended up getting his gun and shooting at him. My father went back to our house to get a gun himself. Right as I got there, my father was walking out of the garage with one of his shotguns."

"This is when your boyfriend, Russell, arrived?"

Stephie nodded. "I don't know why he'd come, but there he was, in the middle of everything. He asked me what the hell was going on, and that's when my uncle started shooting again. He came out onto his front deck and shot at my father. My brother and I ran for cover. I lost sight of Russell. I wanted to call out for him, but Zach dragged me into the house. We found my mom, and we all went up to her bedroom and locked the door. By then the shooting had stopped, but we were all terrified. We stayed in there until my father knocked on the door and said it was over. I still remember seeing him when my mother opened the door. Blood smeared across his khakis and seersucker shirt. All over his hands and arms."

"No one called the police?"

"My mom wanted to, but my father refused. He'd said, 'What's done is done' and the police can't fix it, that they can only make things worse for us. He told us all to go to our rooms for the night. When we came down the next morning, he told us all that my Uncle Scott was gone. That he was never coming back and made us promise never to speak about it to anyone."

Bailey shook her head. "But what about your boyfriend, Russell?"

"He and his car were gone just like my Uncle Scott. Later that day, he was reported missing. By then I was all but certain my father had killed my uncle. I wanted to ask about Russell, but I was terrified of the answer." Stephie brushed at a tear on her cheek. "As time went on, I told myself I already knew the truth."

Bailey knew she needed to steer Stephie back to what she'd come here for. She took a deep breath in and out. "Stephie, have you had any contact with anyone in Chincoteague since you left?"

Stephie shook her head emphatically. "Everyone in town assumed we had something to do with Russell's disappearance. Most thought we'd killed him. It made going anywhere impossible. The store, school, any of that. Months later, my dad moved us away. We were practically run out of town. We left and never looked back."

"The thing is, there's been a recent string of homicides in Chincoteague. I'm sorry to say, but your Aunt Emily and her children, your cousins, are among the victims."

Stephie's lips trembled. She tried to hold back more tears, but she was losing the battle. Her eyes welled up as they met Bailey's gaze. "Do you know who did it?"

Bailey tilted her head to the side. "That's what I'm here to ask you about. If you know anything about it."

Stephie flinched and backed away suddenly. "It wasn't me if that's what you're saying."

"No, I know. I don't think you hurt anyone. But we got a partial DNA sample from one of the other victims. We know it's someone closely related to your Uncle Scott. We believe they're most likely a man."

Stephie's eyes drifted away from Bailey and out the window.

"Your father, Mark Meachem, passed away a few years ago, is that right?"

Stephie nodded vaguely, her voice distant. "Yes. He got COVID during the pandemic and never recovered."

"I'm sorry to hear that. And your brother, Zach? Where is he?"

"He left as soon as he turned eighteen. He never forgave my father for that night. He lives in New York now."

Bailey put the tissues down on the coffee table. "Do you still talk to him?"

"Some. He has a family now. He doesn't like to think about any of us. Or any part of his past. I can't say I blame him." Stephie looked back at Bailey and shook her head. "He wouldn't hurt anyone, and he sure as hell wouldn't go back to Chincoteague."

"That's the problem, though. We know for a fact that it's someone closely related to your uncle, but we're running out of family members. Is there someone we're missing?"

"No, there's no one else."

Bailey was about to press the matter when Stephie's jaw went slack. Her eyes widened and welled up with another spate of tears.

"Oh, god," Stephie whispered. "Caleb."

Bailey leaned forward. "Who?"

"My son. Our... son." She put a hand to her face. "Oh god. What did he do?"

Bailey stared at Stephie, her eyes wide, as she struggled to find her next words.

"You have to understand, I wasn't ready to be a mother, but my parents forbade me from getting an abortion. I carried him to term and then gave him up for adoption. It broke my heart. I couldn't stand the thought of seeing someone else raise him, so I gave up all my rights. Never tried to contact the couple who adopted him or anything. But a couple months ago, I got an email. I had done one of those ancestry things when my father got sick. I guess I was curious to find out where we really came from. Before Chincoteague and everything that happened. The email said I had a new connection. It said that our probable relationship was parent and child."

Bailey took out her phone, opened up her notes app, and started typing. "You said his name is Caleb. Caleb Meachem?"

"No. Caleb Ayers. That was the name on the account that connected to mine, anyway."

Bailey checked the list of names Jackson had given her. There was no Caleb or Ayers. "Could he have another name?"

"I don't know. Maybe. When I saw that email, I panicked and deleted my account. I couldn't imagine facing him. What he would think of me after all these years."

"So, you've had no contact with him. Just the alert that you two had been matched through the ancestry site."

Stephie rubbed her bottom lip. "I saw him. His profile picture. It was on the email. But other than that, no."

"Do you still have the email?"

"I don't know. I might have deleted it."

"Can you check for me?"

Stephie pulled her phone out of her pocket and began tapping at it with her thumbs. After several moments, she turned the screen to show Bailey. A young man in his twenties with a full head of dirty blond hair and a diamond-shaped face stared back at Bailey with an emotionless expression. Bailey held up her own phone and took a picture of the screen.

"I really appreciate you sharing all this with me, Stephie," Bailey said as she stood up.

Stephie remained seated. "Do you really think he hurt those people? My aunt and cousins?" she asked.

"I don't know, but I'm going to find out." Bailey reached into the breast pocket of her blazer and pulled out a business card. She gave it to Stephie. "If you think of anything else, please reach out."

Stephie nodded. "I will. Thank you."

Bailey went to the door and opened it. Before she left, she looked back at Stephie. "I'm sorry for everything that happened to you."

Stephie gave a sad smile. "Me, too."

FIFTY

BAILEY TROTTED down the steps and out to her cruiser. Hopping in, she pulled out her phone and called Jackson. He answered right away.

"Did you find Stephanie Meachem?" he asked.

"I did," Bailey said. "Listen, your killer might be her son."

"What do you mean?"

Bailey reached over to the passenger seat for her laptop and booted it up. "The night Russell Hanz supposedly went missing, there was a big fight between Mark and Scott Meachem, one that escalated to the two shooting at each other. That argument was about Stephanie being pregnant with Scott Meachem's child."

Jackson was silent for a moment. "Russell Hanz said he went to the Meachem's property that night because he'd heard rumors Stephanie was pregnant."

"She was, but Russell wasn't the father. Her uncle, Scott Meachem was."

"He assaulted her?"

"Not forcibly, but yes. Mark, Stephie's father, found out and lost it. When he confronted Scott, Scott got a gun and shot at him. That led to Mark getting a shotgun and eventually shooting and killing Scott. That's why it's like Scott Meachem fell off the face of the earth after that night. Because he did."

"And that's why Mark marched in a team of lawyers. It wasn't to cover up Russell's murder, it was to cover up his brother's."

Bailey put Jackson on speakerphone and began typing on her laptop. "The pregnancy, though, Jackson. She had a son she immediately gave up for adoption. She'd gone full no-contact from the beginning, but her son found her on one of those ancestry sites."

"When?"

"Just a couple months ago."

"What's his name?"

"Caleb Ayers."

Jackson conferred with someone on his end. "There's no one here by that name. Any known aliases?"

"I'm running him right now. Hold on." Bailey ran the name through the DMV database. "Found him. Caleb Ayers, born March 2, 2000. Last known address is in Virginia Beach."

"Any criminal record?"

"Checking now." Bailey ran Ayers through the Virginia Criminal Justice Information Services database. "Nothing crazy. A couple charges for simple battery. One disturbing the peace."

"You have a picture though, right? Try sending it to me."

"Okay, hold on."

———

JACKSON WAS in the hallway that led out back. He'd gotten Bear and Shaw's attention when Bailey called and waved them over to him. Now, the three huddled around Jackson's phone. Jackson's eyes stared at the top corner of the screen, eagerly waiting to see an alert for an incoming text. A moment later, his phone buzzed.

He opened the text. A circle whirring over a black square as the phone tried to load the image.

"Did it go through?" Bailey asked, her voice staticky through the phone.

"Hold on, it's trying," Jackson said.

Finally, the picture loaded. A young man with hair cut high and tight leered up at Jackson from the screen. It took him a second, but he recognized him. The man had longer hair now, but the same sharp jawline and disdainful look in his eyes.

"I've seen this guy before," Bear said. "He was the new guy on Bert's fishing trawler."

"Is he there?" Bailey's voice crackled through the air.

Jackson had already started heading for the ballroom when he heard Bear curse under his breath. He'd committed the faces of his eleven possible suspects to memory, including the one Bailey had just sent him. "He is."

FIFTY-ONE

CALEB AYERS SAT with his legs crossed on his cot. His eyes jumped from person to person in the ballroom, fantasizing about which one he'd attack next. The beast within him craved another hunt. As he looked to the far side across from him, the two men who had been helping the police came out from the back hallway with the wildlife officer in tow. There was something different about them, though. The way they were walking. With purpose. His eyes moved from their feet to their faces, and he was surprised to see all three looking at him.

He locked gazes with the one leading them, the fit one with a graying, short beard who always wore his ball cap. Something had changed in the man's eyes. He wasn't just looking in his direction, he *saw* him. Not Owen Barlow, the name he'd assumed from his forged ID ever since coming to Chincoteague, but *him*. Caleb Ayers.

The Bull Shark.

Behind the man, the wildlife cop waved to get the attention of the plain-clothed police officer near the front doors, then pointed at Caleb. That removed any doubt. They were coming for him.

Caleb knew he was in a bad spot. His cot was in a corner with no outlet. The two men and the wildlife officer were coming from one direction, the plain-clothes cop from the other. Caleb would have to go through one of them. He figured he had a better chance against one than three.

Rising, he started along the outside of the room. The cop rounded the array of cots and headed straight for him, his hand resting on the grip of his service weapon. Caleb slipped his hands into his front pockets and grabbed both kitchen shear blades. The cop was fifty feet away and closing. Caleb prepared to strike.

He sped up when Jesse, the volunteer in the orange vest, walked out of the kitchen and crossed between Caleb and the cop. Just what Caleb needed. He flashed a menacing smile. The cop looked between him and the volunteer and drew his service weapon.

"Caleb Ayers!" one of the men shouted somewhere behind him.

Too late.

FIFTY-TWO

JACKSON STOOD TOO FAR AWAY to stop what he saw was about to happen. A shelter volunteer, a woman, was walking out of the kitchen directly between Ayers and Investigator Bowden on the other side. He was a helpless spectator of what came next. Ayers pulled some sort of blades from his pocket and pounced on the volunteer. Instinctively, she cowered, turning her back to him. Ayers reached around and grabbed the woman by the neck then pressed his back to the wall. He held one of the blades to the woman's throat and the other threateningly out in front of him.

"Everyone get back!" he hissed.

Screams filled the air. People scattered, putting distance between themselves and the situation. Jackson rushed into the fray, Bear and Shaw behind him. They fought to cut a path through the rip tide of terrified people. Bowden and Chief Diaz were clear of bystanders and had drawn their service weapons. They crept forward, guns pointed at Ayers and his hostage. Ayers, back to the wall, put the woman between him and the police.

Jackson, Bear, and Shaw finally maneuvered through the uproar. Shaw also drew her pistol, but Jackson and Bear were unarmed.

Together, the five created a half-circle around Ayers, giving him space but leaving him nowhere to go.

"You know I'll gut her like the rest of them!" Ayers said. "Get back!"

"There's nowhere to go, son," Chief Diaz said. "Let Jesse go."

Jackson stood closest to the wall on Ayer's far right. Slowly, he tried to close the distance between him and Ayers, but Ayers spotted him and pivoted his way.

"Uh uh!" Ayers said. "No one's playing hero today."

"Let her go," Jackson said. "She's got nothing to do with you."

Ayers started sliding to his left. The perimeter they'd formed moved with him. As people scurried to the far side of the ballroom, Officers Birch and Perry came up and joined the others in surrounding Ayers.

"Look around," Chief Diaz said. "Where are you going to go?"

"I'm going to go right out that front door, and you're going to let me," Ayers growled.

"You know I can't do that."

Ayers pressed the blade on Jesse's neck into her skin. "It's either you all letting me go or Jesse here bleeding out on the floor. Your choice."

Chief Diaz and Bowden, the two furthest to Ayers's left, didn't move. Ayers pressed the blade even harder into Jesse's neck. She shrieked as a stream of blood started dripping down her neck.

"Not much more and I hit her carotid artery," Ayers said. "Think you can save her from bleeding out? Move!"

Chief Diaz hesitated a moment longer before looking over at Bowden and nodding at him to give Ayers space. As Bowden did, Ayers resumed sliding to his left. He got to the corner of the room and turned, all the while keeping Jesse, blade to her throat, in front of him. He was no more than thirty feet from the exit.

"There's nowhere to go, Caleb," Jackson said. "Maybe you haven't noticed, but there's a hurricane outside."

"You let me worry about that," Ayers said.

Jackson continued to move with him. "You want to venture out into that storm, you go ahead. But you leave Jesse here. Chief Diaz is right. She has nothing to do with this. It's not fair to her."

Ayers pointed the blade out in front of him accusingly at Jackson. "Don't lecture me about fair!"

The whole group continued to edge toward the door. Jackson's mind scrambled for an angle to play, a weakness to exploit. He didn't see one.

Ayers got to the door and pushed into it with his backside. He only needed to open it a few inches before the wind caught it and threw it wide open. A deafening howl blew into the ballroom. Ayers backed outside, stepping out into the elements. The gusting wind whipped at his clothes.

"You got what you wanted," Chief Diaz shouted over the wind. "Now let Jesse go."

Ayers ignored the command. Taking slow, steady steps, he maneuvered over the sandbags around the covered entryway, Jesse fumbling to do the same. A stream of floodwater flowed down the road between the Chincoteague Center and the police station like an estuary, filling the parking lot beyond and turning it into a shallow pond. Ayers guided himself and Jesse, still walking backward, toward its concrete shore.

"All of you stay on the other side of the sandbags!" Ayers ordered.

Seeing no other alternative, the police obeyed. Jackson came around them so that he was the furthest away from the building. He braced himself against the steel beam that supported the roof overhead. He looked out, watching helplessly as Ayers practically dragged a now sobbing Jesse further and further away from them.

Ayers's feet found the curb and stepped down gingerly into the flooding parking lot. To his left, pickets of the wooden fence that surrounded the building held onto their rails for dear life.

"What's the plan here, Ayers?" Jackson shouted. "You can't just walk on forever with her."

At that, Ayers stopped walking. He stood there, floodwater flowing around his and Jesse's ankles.

He tilted his head at Jackson, then flashed a smile. "Good point," he shouted back.

In one swift motion, he slashed the blade across her neck and ran. Jesse collapsed into the water. Everyone—Jackson, Bear, Shaw, and the four police officers—hurdled the sandbags and ran out into the storm. Bowden and Birch got onto balanced footing and fired at Ayers as he disappeared behind the dilapidated fence.

Without a gun, Jackson knew he'd be most helpful tending to Jesse. With Bear at his hip, he sprinted for her, dropping to all fours and splashing into the water when he got there. He tore off his shirt and pressed it to the wound on Jesse's neck. Jesse looked up at him, her eyes wide with terror.

"Stay with me," he said. "You're going to be okay."

Shaw came up, standing over him with her weapon raised and aimed at the long side of the building. She fired two shots. Jackson looked up, hoping to see Ayers go down.

Instead, he watched as Ayers entered the field next to the building and disappeared into the woods beyond.

———

JACKSON WAITED, expecting to see Shaw or the others pursue Ayers. When no one did, he looked up at Shaw. She had holstered her weapon, her shoulders sagging. She'd conceded that Ayers had gotten away. Jackson couldn't accept that.

"Keep pressure on Jesse's wound," he said to Shaw. He stood up and started trudging through the standing water toward Bear's Suburban.

"Where the hell are you going?" Shaw asked.

Jackson didn't answer her. He went to the door behind the driver's seat and grabbed his shotgun. He loaded several shells into it and slung it across his torso, then grabbed a loaded magazine for his

Beretta, fed it in, chambered a round, and tucked it into the waist of his jeans. Loaded up, he shut the door and headed for the field.

Bear, standing with the officers, saw this and headed out after him. "Jacky Boy, it's no use!" he called out. "He's gone."

Jackson ignored him. He trotted high-kneed through the water until he got to the curb on the far side, then broke into a run. His pants, completely soaked, rippled like wet rags in the wind as torrents of rain cascaded over his chest. A gust caught the bill of his ball cap and ripped it from his head. But that didn't slow him down. He just ran harder into the storm.

When he got to the tree line where Ayers had disappeared, he unslung his shotgun and pumped a round into the chamber. The woods in front of him were a verdant abyss. Branches and foliage swung and shook in the blustery gales, warning Jackson not to enter.

"Don't!" Bear shouted somewhere behind him.

Jackson brought the shotgun up to his shoulder and marched forward.

Stepping underneath the canopy of the trees was like stepping into a fever dream. Sticks and leaves swirled around him as the trees chattered angrily overhead. He moved forward, trying to spot any sign of where Ayers had gone, but the world around him now was disorienting.

He found a path through the trees and started to follow it. He struggled to get his bearings, pretty sure he was headed north. The constant howl of the wind and snapping of branches made it impossible to hear Ayers' movement through the woods. He had to rely on his vision. Even that was limited.

Jackson continued along a game trail through the trees when a loud, sickening crack rang out. He scanned his surroundings, looking for Ayers. He saw no one. He resumed his path when an eerie whine cried overhead.

Jackson looked up. A massive pine tree had snapped in two, the top half now falling toward him. Jackson turned to run and was hit from the side as if by a charging animal.

The shotgun flew out of Jackson's hands. The tree crashed into the ground at the same time Jackson did. He reached back for his pistol and pointed it at the shadowy figure that had hit him. He expected to see Ayers's menacing smile, but instead he saw a panting Bear resting on his elbows.

"This is stupid, brother," he said. "You're going to get yourself killed out here."

As the adrenaline ebbed out of him, Jackson realized just how reckless it had been chasing after Ayers. He nodded at Bear.

"You're right," he said. "I'm sorry."

"Let's just get the hell out of here," Bear said.

Jackson got his feet under him and helped Bear up. Together, they followed the passage through the trees back the way they'd come.

"I oughta kick your ass for making me run. And put on a shirt, will ya?" Bear huffed. "This ain't Abercrombie."

FIFTY-THREE

JACKSON AND BEAR stopped by the Suburban on their way back. Bear popped into the back seat quickly, then came back out with a Piedmont Ammo & Supply ball cap just like the one that Jackson had lost. He tossed it over to Jackson.

"Luckily for you, I keep a few of these on hand at all times," he said. "Marketin' opportunities."

Jackson tucked his hair back and pulled the cap down low to shield his face from the rain. "Thanks," he said.

"You lose another one and I'm going to have to start chargin' ya."

They entered the Chincoteague Center wet and covered in mud, carrying their guns with them. As they did, Bowden, posted just inside the doors, came up to them with his hands out in front of him.

"There's still no guns allowed inside," he said.

"You've gotta be shittin' me," Bear said.

Bowden shook his head. "Nothing's changed. We've still got to keep everyone safe in here."

Bear huffed. "Why don't you tell that to Hank and Jesse."

Bowden began loading up a retort when Shaw stepped in between the two sides.

"I think we can make an exception for Clay and Bear," she said. "They've proved to be assets, haven't they?"

Bowden glowered at her, but Shaw raised a brow, telling him she wasn't backing down. Bowden stuck his finger into her chest.

"They get someone else hurt, it's on you," he said before walking off.

Shaw turned to Jackson and Bear. "What the hell happened to you two?"

"Jacky Boy here played chicken with a falling tree and damn near lost," Bear said.

Shaw shook her head. "It was reckless to go out there." She disappeared into the medical room briefly before reemerging with a couple of towels. She walked over and tossed Jackson and Bear one each. "I wasn't bullshitting Bowden when I said you two were assets. If you get hurt, or worse, in the name of some cowboy crusade, you'll put everyone here in more danger."

Jackson wiped at his clothes. "I couldn't just stand there and watch him disappear," he said.

"No one wanted to let him go," Shaw countered, "but it was too dangerous. If you're dead or incapacitated, you're no use to anyone."

Jackson changed the subject. "How is Jesse?"

Shaw folded her arms. "We were able to get her on a backboard and bring her into the medical room. I think we've stabilized her, but she's lost a lot of blood. They're talking to the fire boys across the street now, seeing if they think they can get over here to assist."

Jackson didn't say anything. He continued to wipe himself down.

"Ayers?" Shaw asked quietly.

Jackson shook his head.

Shaw nodded as if she expected as much. "Well, he's no longer in here, which is a win. Take it."

Jackson looked out at the ballroom. Just about everyone was either sitting or lying on their cots. Most of them were looking at Jackson and Bear, watching the two men that had thrown themselves into the fray against a knife-wielding killer.

"How about the rest of them?" Jackson asked. "How are they?"

Before Shaw could answer, Peter Wright stood up. "He got away, didn't he?" he said loud enough for everyone in the ballroom to hear. "The guy who killed Hank and hurt Jesse. He's still out there."

"Yes, but the important thing is he's no longer in here with us," Shaw countered.

Carter Gray stood up alongside Peter. Jackson was surprised to see someone had released him from where he'd been shackled in the shower area.

"For now, but what happens if he comes back?" Carter grunted. "He's probably twice as determined to hurt us in here now, and we don't even know where he is or how he'll come at us."

Peter nodded emphatically. "Exactly!"

Jackson found it ironic how the two that had come to blows were now seemingly allied in their distrust of him and the police. Chief Diaz, hearing the loud exchange, emerged from the medical room, raising his hands over his head to get everyone's attention.

"I know you all are worried," he said. "Rightfully so. But there are only two entrances that are not boarded up. We will lock them from the inside and post an officer at each door at all times. The storm is almost over. We've made it this far, I assure you we will make it the rest of the way."

Murmuring broke out across the ballroom as everyone jumped into little conversations with their cot neighbors. No one, however, rebutted the chief. Looking satisfied, he nodded at Shaw, Jackson, and Bear then disappeared back inside the medical room. Jackson and Bear continued to wipe themselves down until their towels were little more than drenched, filthy rags. Shaw held her arms out and gestured for the towels.

"Here, I'll take them," she said. "You guys are still gross. Go get showered and changed. Chief Diaz wants to talk about what just went down."

———

CLEAN AND DRY, Jackson put on a fresh pair of jeans and plaid button-down shirt. Emerging from the bathroom area, he found Bear on his cot, grooming his beard. He sat down on his own cot to lace up his boots.

"I'm going to be pulling pine needles out of here for weeks," Bear griped.

Jackson ignored him. Both of them continued to put themselves back together when Bear spotted Chief Diaz and his officers approaching them from over Jackson's shoulder.

"Here comes the principal," Bear said. "Time to find out if we get detention or not."

Chief Diaz stood over them. "You gentlemen are looking better than when you came in," he said. "I've posted Officers Perry and Birch at each of the doors. We'll maintain a rotating guard, but I think we ought to have a quick word about what went down."

Bear shrugged. "We found the killer, did your guys' job for you, and ran him off," he said. "No need to thank us. But if you insist, a case of Miller High Life will do just fine."

Chief Diaz gave a gratuitous smile. "I was thinking something a little more in-depth than that." He motioned to the supply room. "Maybe we should continue this in private."

Jackson and Bear followed Chief Diaz into the room where Investigator Bowden was already waiting. Shaw brought up the rear and shut the door behind her. Bear moved to the far wall, leaned against it, and rested his arm on a shelf filled with canned goods.

"If we keep meeting in here, you guys should at least get some snacks or something," he said. "A bag of pretzels wouldn't kill ya."

Chief Diaz took a wide stance and folded his arms. "So, it appears our man was Owen Barlow. Any idea what his connection is to Scott Meachem?"

"Owen Barlow was an assumed identity," Jackson said. "His real name is Caleb Ayers, and he's Scott Meachem's son."

Chief Diaz shook his head. "Everything I've heard about him said he didn't have any children. He was the eternal bachelor of the family."

"He groomed and assaulted his niece, Stephanie Meachem. She was pregnant with his child the night Russell Hanz supposedly disappeared in July '99. Mark Meachem, Stephanie's father and Scott's brother, found out about it that night and confronted Scott. Things got so heated the two ended up shooting at each other and Mark Meachem killed Scott."

Bowden's eyes narrowed as an incredulous smirk stretched across the bottom of his face. "How do you know this?" he asked. "How do we know this all isn't just rumor and innuendo?"

"My contact," Jackson said. "She tracked down Stephanie Meachem and spoke with her. Shaw can verify. She was with us when I had Special Agent Bailey on speaker phone."

Bowden scratched his forehead. "And she just up and confessed? Out of the blue?"

Jackson shook his head. "I don't know. I wasn't there. But she supplied a name and photo of Ayers without knowing anything about what was going on here. She's telling the truth."

"Then how does Russell Hanz fit into all this? It's just a coincidence he disappeared the same night?"

Jackson hesitated, debating whether or not to tell everyone he'd found Russell Hanz alive and well. He knew now Russell was little more than an unfortunate bystander that night twenty-five years ago. A kid simply in the wrong place at the wrong time. If he didn't want to be found, Jackson decided it wasn't his place to give him up to the authorities.

"I don't know," he said. "I know as much as you do now."

Chief Diaz sucked on his teeth. "It doesn't change the situation here. We had a threat, identified it, and rooted it out. Now, we batten down the hatches and make sure he can't come back."

"With all due respect, sir," Jackson said. "I don't think you're considering the bigger picture here."

Chief Diaz turned and faced him, an eyebrow raised. "Oh? And what might that be?"

"You said it yourself. The situation hasn't changed. Caleb Ayers has been preying on this town for the past several weeks, letting the unassuming community provide safe harbor from which he carried out his attacks. This obviously all started with his family, but he's made it clear he's not stopping there. For whatever reason, it's become something more to him. Just because we've run him off doesn't mean he's going to quit." Jackson looked around at the group, looking in each of their eyes. "He's not going to stop until we stop him."

Chief Diaz shook his head. "You just tried that, didn't you? And since you're back here, I'm guessing that means you lost him. Not for nothing, but there is still a full-blown hurricane outside."

"A hurricane that almost just took you out," Shaw added. "Besides, if the rest of the streets are anything like the one outside, they're currently impassable. We couldn't go after him even if we wanted to."

Chief Diaz pointed at her. "Precisely. Our mission right now is to keep everyone in here safe. We're running a skeleton crew as it is, and with Jesse hurt we're even more shorthanded. We're going to do exactly what I said, the plan from the very beginning. Secure this place and ride out the storm."

The other police officers nodded in agreement. Even Shaw seemed convinced by the plan. Jackson wanted to object, but he realized the numbers weren't in his favor.

"Fine," Jackson said.

Chief Diaz sighed. "Good. Like I said, we're shorthanded. If I let you two help us secure this place, can I trust you?"

Jackson nodded.

"Then that makes eight of us total between my officers, Shaw, and you two. We'll have four people on watch at all times — one at the front doors, another at the back, and two more patrolling the building. We'll break into two teams. Four-hour shifts."

Investigator Bowden folded his arms. "And if this Ayers guy comes back? What then?"

Chief Diaz took a deep breath in, then out. "We handle it."

FIFTY-FOUR

AS THE ISLAND darkened from the sun setting somewhere beyond the storm overhead, the four firefighters made their way over to the Chincoteague Center from the firehouse down the street. Two of the men sat in one of the department's swift water rescue boats, securing their gear, as the other two guided the boat on foot through the flooded street. Instead of bunker coats and breathing apparatuses, they wore life jackets and bright red whitewater helmets.

The floodwater running down the street had crested over the curb and began inundating the lawn around the building. So far, the sandbags were doing their job. The firefighters utilized the overflowing water to guide their boat right up to the sandbags and disembarked. Shaw and Bear held the doors open for them as they carried their gear inside. Jackson led them to the medical room where they got right to work on Jesse.

Chief Diaz stepped into the doorway, watching the crew closely as they hung a bag of fluids and started an IV. "I assume you all know what you're doing," he said.

One of the firefighters, taller than the others with a bushy mustache, looked over his shoulder at the chief. "Hicks and I are cross trained as paramedics," he said. "She's in good hands."

Chief Diaz nodded. "She's lost a lot of blood. Do you guys have any with you?"

The firefighter turned his focus back to Jesse. "We don't carry blood. We'll give her fluids as well as TXA. That should help with clotting. We'll also control her body temperature as best we can, but that's about all we can do until we get her to a hospital."

A knot formed in Jackson's stomach. No one had any idea when that might be. A wave of guilt washed over him. Had he acted faster, had he been quicker to out Caleb Ayers, maybe Jesse wouldn't be lying in a makeshift medical ward fighting for her life. If he'd acted faster, maybe Hank Willis would still be alive. He replayed his only previous interaction with Ayers over and over again in his mind. The evening Ayers had bumped into Captain Terry as he got off Bert's fishing trawler. It'd been as innocuous an interaction as any. Yet hours later, the young man had killed Captain Terry. Had he missed any warning signs?

Jackson felt the sudden need to breathe in something different from the recirculated air of the shelter. He made his way to the front doors and stepped outside. He took a deep breath in through his nose, held it for several seconds, then let it out between his lips.

Shaw was out there, tying a line from the boat to one of the steel beams supporting the overhang.

"You okay?" she asked, looking over at him.

Jackson nodded. "I'm good."

Shaw finished tying off the line and sat on the wall of sandbags. "They working on Jesse in there?"

"As best they can. She really needs a hospital."

Shaw sighed. "Yeah." She looked out at the flooded street, then at the sky overhead. "The wind isn't nearly as strong as it was even a few hours ago. Even the rainfall feels like it's letting up some. Maybe we can get her out of here pretty soon."

Jackson stepped to the wall of sandbags and looked out. Shaw was right, the conditions were improving.

"Maybe," he said.

His mind began to churn. They'd been under the thumb of Hurricane Margaret for over forty-eight hours. The storm had to be passing. It'd be much safer soon to venture out. The floodwater would continue to be a problem, but looking at the swift water boat moored to the building, he had an idea for that as well.

"Come with me," he said.

He opened the front door, and Shaw followed him inside. Bear was back at his cot. Chief Diaz was huddled with his police officers just outside the medical room. Jackson nodded with his head for Bear to follow him, then walked briskly toward the huddle. Officer Birch pointed at Jackson, and Chief Diaz turned to face him.

"We need to prepare to go after Ayers," Jackson said.

Chief Diaz's shoulders dropped. "Clay, I thought we discussed this. Now's not the time."

"The conditions are improving outside. Go see for yourself."

Chief Diaz pointed toward the front doors. "And it's about to be dark out. The whole island is without power. It would be far too dangerous."

"Then we go at first light. The conditions will be even better by then, and we'll be able to see."

"It doesn't matter if the rain lets up, most of the island is underwater. You'd have the five officers here try to scour the whole island on foot? In knee- to waist-deep water?"

"We'll use the fire company's rescue boats."

Chief Diaz rolled his eyes.

"You said it yourself. They don't need all three. Let us take a couple and run down Ayers."

"Us?"

Jackson shrugged. "You said you were shorthanded. Bear and I can handle ourselves."

Chief Diaz rubbed his temples. "Even if I wanted to, what would be the point? Caleb Ayers is out there somewhere likely dead. And if he's not, he's certainly somewhere where he's not a threat to us anymore. The rest of the island is a ghost town. Going out looking for him only puts more people in danger. The potential cost doesn't outweigh the possible benefit."

"Do you think he's just going to stop because of what's happened? You really think he's just going to pack it in and call it a day? Something in that man has snapped. And he won't stop until someone else stops him. You're right, the rest of the island is deserted, which means he can slip away without anyone noticing. What happens when you find out a month from now that he's hurt more people somewhere else? Or worse, comes back here, to a town with fresh wounds. How will you feel knowing you had the chance here and now to do something about it? What is the cost-benefit analysis of that?"

Chief Diaz didn't say anything. No one did. Jackson's words hung thick in the air like the humidity outside. After several moments, Investigator Bowden stepped toward Chief Diaz from the cluster of police officers.

"For what it's worth, Chief," he said, "I think Clay is right on this one."

Chief Diaz turned to face him. "Joshua, we have a duty to protect the people here."

"And that's exactly what we'll be doing, sir."

Chief Diaz folded his arms, thinking. "*If* we were to do this, it'd take all of us. Who watches everyone here?"

Bowden shrugged. "The fire boys are already here, let them run point."

Chief Diaz worked the inside of his cheek.

"Hell, they'd probably do better at it than we could. Not that I'd ever admit it to them."

The other police officers chuckled.

Chief Diaz remained quiet a moment longer. He shook his head. "Even if we wanted to, there's only two boats. It would take God knows how long to search the entire island. And that's assuming he's even still *on* the island."

"He's still here," Jackson said. "I know where he'll be."

Everyone looked at Jackson curiously. Chief Diaz put his hands on his hips and raised his eyebrows, asking for the answer.

Jackson nodded past them. He wasn't gesturing to the rest of the ballroom or the back of the Chincoteague Center. He was nodding north, beyond its walls, to the far end of the island.

"The Meachem property," Jackson said. "Whatever this is, it started with his family. He's going home."

PART SIX

THE BURDEN

"Evil cannot co-exist peacefully with goodness because it insists on being seen as right." -Archbishop Charles Chaput

FIFTY-FIVE

CHIEF DIAZ'S eyes met Jackson's, weighing his words. He turned and looked at the squad of police officers behind him. None of them raised an objection. Finally, he looked at Shaw, who nodded. Chief Diaz sucked at his teeth.

"Alright, fine," he said. "If the conditions continue to improve, we go at first light. Shaw, see if the fire boys will lend us their boats."

Shaw nodded and headed for the medical room.

Chief Diaz turned back to his officers, giving Jackson and Bear his back. "Assuming we can use a couple boats, we'll go in two teams. Andy and I in one boat, Joshua and Jon with Shaw in the other."

Bear cleared his throat. "You forgetting a couple of us?" he asked.

Chief Diaz turned around and shook his head. "There's no way I'm letting you two be a part of this."

"There's no way we're *not* being a part of this," Jackson countered.

"Mr. Clay, there are a dozen reasons why it's a bad idea. For one, you're not law enforcement officers, you're civilians. You have no power to enforce. And I meant it when I said my main mission was to keep everyone here safe. Bringing you two along will only put you in unnecessary danger."

Jackson folded his arms. "We know the danger. We're good with it and we're going."

"No, you're not. Two civilians mixed into a law enforcement investigation? Any defense attorney would have a field day picking this arrest apart in court. I'm not risking my men's lives to bring him in just so he can walk a month from now."

"You said it yourself, you're undermanned. There's risk in letting us go out there, but there's also risk in not letting us go. Say one of you does get hurt out there. How are you going to look their next of kin in the eye knowing you could've given them more backup."

Chief Diaz blinked. "You can be a real prick when you want to, you know that?"

"It's been mentioned once or twice."

Chief Diaz sighed. "Fine. I will allow you to accompany us, but only to operate the boats and free up my men to focus on bringing in Ayers. And you will not be armed."

Bear snorted. "Bull-fucking-shit we won't be armed with Jack the Ripper out there."

Jackson raised an eyebrow. "He's got a point, Chief."

Chief Diaz looked up and closed his eyes. "You two are going to be the death of me," he muttered. He dropped his head and looked at them. "Alright. You can carry, *but* you only use them as a last resort. I'm talking purely self-defense."

Jackson nodded. "You got it."

Shaw came out of the medical room and rejoined the group. Her face said she sensed the tension between Chief Diaz and Jackson.

"They're good with us using the boats," Shaw said. "Two of them will go back and get the other two, one of which they'll keep here. I offered to help." Her eyes darted between Chief Diaz and Jackson. "What did I miss over here?"

"We're going with you when you roll," Jackson said.

Shaw thought about it for a moment. "The more the merrier, I guess."

"Everyone try to get some rest," Chief Diaz said. "Come morning, we're going to need it."

———

SHAW LAY IN HER COT, but sleep didn't come. She turned to one side, then the other, before finally flipping onto her back and letting out a deep breath. She needed a drink in the worst way and longed for the bottle of vodka that stayed in her freezer. That is, assuming her kitchen and house were still intact.

She opened her eyes and looked up at the rafters overhead. Ayers was gone and, with that, lights-out hours had returned to the ballroom. But there was enough ambient light that Izzy could make out the metal framework above her. Taylor Jensen hovered in between two support beams, looking down at Izzy just as she had the night after Izzy had responded to the scene of her murder. She'd asked the specter of Taylor that night who had hurt her. Taylor had never answered. Now, there were other questions.

I know who hurt you now, Izzy thought. *We're going to try to get him, but he may already be gone. I hope knowing is enough.*

Just as before, Taylor didn't say anything. The only answer came when the others appeared lying down beside her. Terry Yarbrough, Tom Marshall, Ada Fitzhugh, and Hank Willis. Then Emily Meachem and her adult children. None of them said anything. They simply joined Taylor in watching Izzy. Blank expressions on all their faces, hollow eyes looking through Izzy.

"You're right," Izzy whispered. "It's not enough."

She blinked several times and the specters disappeared, but her anxiety remained. Restless, she sat upright in her cot, swung her feet around, and looked out at the darkened ballroom. Her cot pressed against the wall between the medical room and the kitchen along with the other law enforcement officers and volunteers. She looked to the back hall and the front doors, double-checking that others were on watch. Officer Birch sat in a folding chair at the head of the hall, but there was no one by the front doors. Concerned, Izzy got up and went to check.

As she opened one of the front doors, she was greeted by the hissing of a steady drizzle. Izzy took a step out but didn't see anyone.

"Couldn't sleep?" said a familiar voice.

She jumped, turning in time to see the shadow of Jackson Clay sitting with his back to the brick exterior next to the doors. His face lay hidden in the shadows, but the ball cap on his head gave him away.

"Clay," Shaw said. "Damn near scared the shit out of me."

"Sorry," Jackson said. "In my defense, I didn't expect anyone else to sneak out here in the middle of the night."

Shaw grinned. "I wasn't sneaking... I didn't see anyone by the doors. I was just coming to make sure someone was watching them."

Jackson's hand raised up. "On watch, sir."

Shaw stepped to the other side of the doors and sat down on the wall of sandbags, resting her elbows on her knees. "You're right, though, I can't sleep."

"Comes with the territory, I imagine."

Shaw raised an eyebrow. "Oh? Do you have a lot of experience chasing depraved killers through natural disasters?"

Jackson snorted. "Just the one. I meant seeing something wrong and not being able to do something about it."

"You mean like injustice."

Jackson was quiet for a moment. "If you want to call it that, sure. I mean that thing that drives some of us. Others see something happen, something wrong, and may think, 'Oh, that's awful,' and go about their lives. But then there's some of us that can't let it go. It eats at us. So, we chase it. We chase it until we catch it. Because we have to. Something in us won't let us quit, like a primal instinct."

"You make it sound so heroic."

Jackson rose and moved to one of the support beams away from the building. He leaned against it, looking out at the storm. "It's not. At least, I don't think it is. I used to think it was a weakness. When I lost my son, I couldn't let it go. I chased that... *injustice*, as you said, for years. It cost me my marriage and everything that came with that."

"If you used to think it's a weakness, what do you think it is now?"

Jackson's silhouette shrugged. "I'm not sure."

Shaw stood and joined him by the support beam. "But it's why you're here, chasing a guy you don't know, who hurt a bunch of people you don't know."

"I knew Captain Terry, but yes."

"There's a word for that."

Jackson looked at her, waiting for an answer.

Shaw grinned. "*Injustice.*"

Jackson turned back to the storm. "Maybe," he said quietly.

They stood like that for several minutes, listening to the rain fall around them. Jackson slipped his hands into his pockets.

"I've got a while to go before Investigator Bowden spells me. You should head back in, take another crack at some shut eye."

Izzy nodded. She stepped away from Jackson and headed for the door. Before she opened it, she turned back.

"For what it's worth," she said. "I think you're wrong."

Jackson looked at her over his shoulder. "About what?"

"That drive in you, it's honorable."

Jackson didn't say anything.

"And it isn't a weakness," she continued. "Caleb Ayers is going to learn that soon enough."

FIFTY-SIX

JUST AFTER SIX the next morning, Bear quietly woke Jackson up. Across the ballroom, Chief Diaz did the same for his officers and Shaw, everyone making as little sound as possible. The rest of the shelter remained asleep.

With slow, soft movements, they got ready. Jackson checked that his shotgun was loaded with a round racked, then slipped six extra rounds into the slots on the sleeve around the gun's stock. Shaw came over and gave them each bullet-resistant vests. Jackson and Bear slipped them on and strapped in. Lastly, Jackson checked that the magazine in his pistol was loaded, then racked a round into the chamber before grabbing two more magazines from his gear bag. He looked over at Bear, who simply nodded, indicating he too was ready to roll.

They stepped through the front doors out into a world bathed in lavender-gray. The rain had tamped down to a light drizzle, and the wind was little more than a stiff breeze. The conditions had improved.

It was time to go.

The firefighters had lined two of their boats up in the flooded street and were holding them steady for everyone to load into. Chief Diaz, with one leg up on the wall of sandbags, looked as though he'd been waiting for Jackson and Bear. He came over to them and handed Jackson a leg holster for his pistol as well as two radios.

"We were able to get into the station across the way and get some gear," he said. "Here's a couple radios. Everyone has one. We also had a couple of these universal holsters. It should work with your Beretta."

Jackson took it and began strapping it to his right thigh. "Thanks," he said.

"Remember, last resort." Chief Diaz looked at Bear. "Mr. Beauchamp, I would have grabbed one for you, but I don't think they'd work for that big revolver of yours."

"All good, hoss," Bear said. He lifted his shirt up on the side to reveal his ample gut and a conceal-carry holster tucked inside his waistband. "Stay strapped or get clapped. I believe George Washington said that."

Jackson smirked as he slid his Beretta into the holster.

Chief Diaz frowned. "Yes, well, like I said. Self-defense only. You boys ready?"

Jackson nodded as Bear shouted, "Let's posse up!"

Chief Diaz stepped over the wall of sandbags and led Jackson and Bear through the standing water to the boats. The other officers and Shaw were already in and waiting. Jackson got into the lead boat with Chief Diaz and Officer Birch. Bear was waiting to board the boat with Shaw, Investigator Bowden, and Officer Perry when he suddenly hollered, reaching down and grabbing at his leg.

Everyone turned and looked at him. The firefighter next to Bear reached out for him.

"You okay?" he asked.

"Goddamn fish!" Bear stammered. "I hate fucking fish."

"Whenever you're ready," Shaw said.

Bear climbed into the boat then looked back at the firefighter who'd helped him. "'Preciate ya letting us borrow your rides."

The firefighter nodded. "You stop that maniac and we're even."

Bear nodded back. "Consider it done."

Chief Diaz, sitting in front of the lead boat, looked back at everyone. They all met his eyes.

"Let's go get our man," he said.

Jackson and Bear cranked the motors to life and guided them out.

———

SEVERAL TREES WERE DOWN across the road that cut over to Main Street, forcing the team to backtrack to Maddox Boulevard. As they motored down the main strip, an eerie, surreal feeling washed over Jackson. The creek next to The Village Restaurant had risen and flooded over, creating an abandoned water world. Roofs and walls had been ripped off houses, leaving the debris floating across what had been one of the major thoroughfares on the island. A large giraffe figure that had been part of the decor of one of the putt-putts had its head lodged in a broken window of Maria's, next door.

"Don't think they're open, bud," Bear said from the back of the rear boat.

"Eyes up," Chief Diaz called out. "Keep a look out for any sign of Ayers."

Jackson and Bear kept the boats to the streets — or where the streets had been — knowing it would be the deepest water for them to travel through. When they got to the intersection of Main Street, Maddox Boulevard rose out of the water on the other side and out to the bridge that stood above the floodwaters. Several cars sat aground on its concrete beach and floated lazily in the water.

"Let's check those cars," Chief Diaz said. "Make sure no one is stuck inside."

Officer Birch looked up at the elevated bridge. "Maybe we should go back," he said. "Let the fire boys know there's a spot where a bird could possibly pick up Jesse."

"There's no guarantee a medevac is available or that they could land there," Jackson said. "If there's a way to get Jesse out, they can handle it. We can help her and everyone else by getting Ayers and stopping him."

They checked each of the cars and found them empty. The team turned north and headed up Main Street. They passed the high school, whose slight incline had spared it from the flood. The park across the street, however, was completely submerged, annexed by Chincoteague Bay on which it had been nestled.

They went from seemingly open water to narrow corridors as the road snaked through houses built close to the sidewalk and trees planted along its slender shoulders. Jackson kept his head up, looking for anything overhead that might suddenly give and fall.

It took them almost an hour to make it up the winding road before it branched off for the last couple of houses along the Meachem's private drive. The swamp nestled between the two roads now covered everything around it. Here, the road became the highest point on what had been land, forcing Jackson and Bear to divert and lead the team through the trees that dotted the swamp. As they got to the other side, they found nothing but open water ahead of them. Power lines traced where the road was and pointed to a cluster of trees in the distance, the vegetation that had veiled the Meachems from the rest of the world.

"Next stop, Psychoville," Bear said.

Jackson and Bear guided the two boats through the gate Jackson had smashed open days earlier with Bear's Suburban. As they did, Chief Diaz looked back at Jackson, his brow raised. Jackson looked past him at where they were headed.

The marsh at what had been the fork in the two driveways had inundated both roads and obscured everything with brackish, brown water. Only the heads of the narrowleaf cattails that filled the marsh noted its previous location. Ahead of them were two of the three houses, those that had belonged to Scott and Mark Meachem and had since been lived in by Emily Meachem's children. To their right was Emily Meachem's house.

"Okay, Mr. Clay," Chief Diaz said. "This is your working theory. Which door is our prize behind?"

Jackson looked at each house closely, searching for any sign of life inside. Each one as dormant as the next. His eyes settled on the middle house. He nodded at it.

"This all started with Stephanie, his mother," Jackson said. "She lived in the middle one. That's where he'd be."

Chief Diaz motioned for Bear's boat to follow the submerged driveway to Emily Meachem's house and flank the middle house from the side. When Bear turned his boat and headed off, Chief Diaz pointed forward and unholstered his service weapon.

"Take us in slowly," he said.

Jackson trolled forward. The ground rose just ahead of them, creating a small knoll atop which the two houses had been built. Jackson kept going until the nose of the boat grounded on the muddy banks of the knoll. Chief Diaz climbed out, followed by Officer Birch. Jackson started to get out, as well, but Chief Diaz held up a hand.

"No, you stay with the boat," he said.

Jackson clenched his jaw but stayed put.

In the distance, the three of them saw Bear take the others out toward Emily Meachem's house before circling around and approaching the middle house from the side. Just off it, the top half of what looked to be some sort of footbridge protruded from the floodwaters. Bear took them to it and tied a line to its railing. Investigator Bowden, Officer Perry, and Shaw all stepped out onto solid ground on their side.

Chief Diaz keyed the mic on his radio. "You guys ready?" he asked the other team.

Shaw radioed back. "Ready."

"Let's move."

Chief Diaz took a single step forward when movement caught Jackson's eye up above.

Before he could warn them, a rifle shot rang out.

FIFTY-SEVEN

THE BULLET WHIZZED over Chief Diaz and Officer Birch's heads and crashed into the water behind them. As it did, the two men jumped backward.

"Shots fired! Shots fired!" Chief Diaz called into his radio.

Caleb Ayers stepped out from the cupola making up the house's third level and onto the widow's walk. He aimed the rifle at Chief Diaz and Officer Birch and fired again. The shot grazed Birch in the shoulder.

He hollered. "I'm hit!"

Jackson jumped out of the boat and pushed it so its broad side faced Ayers and the house. Chief Diaz grabbed Officer Birch, and the three men took cover in the knee-deep water behind the boat. Across the way, Jackson heard the unmistakable boom of Bear's .357 returning fire.

"You guys okay?" Shaw's voice crackled through the radio.

Chief Diaz radioed back. "Second shot clipped Andy."

"Status?"

Chief Diaz looked at Officer Birch, who was applying pressure to his wound. He nodded at his chief. A third shot hit the boat.

"He's okay," Chief Diaz radioed. "Move in on the house while we're drawing Ayers's fire."

"Copy that."

A fourth shot hit the mud somewhere in front of them. Chief Diaz turned to Jackson.

"What do you think?" he asked.

"I think Ayers's inheritance includes a decent hunting rifle, and he's found it," Jackson said.

Chief Diaz shook his head. "I meant we're in a bad spot out here."

"There's too much open ground between us and the house to make a move and not enough cover. We draw his fire, the other team makes entry and takes Ayers."

Chief Diaz nodded and relayed the plan to the other team. Jackson drew his Beretta. Chief Diaz watched him. Another round hit the boat.

"I'd say this meets your self-defense criteria," Jackson said.

———

BEAR SUCKED wind as he hurried to keep pace with the other three. He knew he'd been directed to stay with the boat, but he didn't care. The boat was out in the open and Bear didn't feel like getting a new hole to breathe out of from Ayers.

The house had been built on stilts with two stairways up to the main floor. Bear's team got underneath the house and ascended the stairway nearest them. Shaw turned back to Bear.

"Cover the exit here," she said.

Bent over and gasping for air, Bear gave a thumbs up, all too happy to oblige.

"We'll draw his fire," Chief Diaz radioed. "You guys make entry and take him down."

"Copy," Shaw replied. "Moving in now."

Bear could see across the way where Jackson and the others had turned their boat sideways to give themselves cover. More gunshots rang out overhead. Bear got down on one knee and used as much of the stair's banister as he could for cover. A second later, several shots snapped off in quick succession.

"Ayers is right outside the only stairs up to the top level," Shaw radioed. "We can't get to him. We need someone to flank him, make him move."

"The second we move, he'll see us," Chief Diaz called back.

Bear looked overhead. Behind him was the large deck that wrapped around the main level. Ayers had to be somewhere above it on the widow's walk. He looked out to the back of the house. The ground ended at a seawall that dropped off into the Assateague Channel. A dock adjoined the sea wall with several of the Meachems' boats moored to its posts. There was just enough room to get out beyond the deck.

Bear keyed his mic. "Jacky Boy, I'll draw his fire toward the back of the house opposite you. That'll give you the time to move on the house."

"Copy," Jackson radioed back. "On you, brother."

Bear stepped out wide of the house, putting one foot on the seawall. Inches to his right were the surging floodwaters. He pointed his revolver up to the top level.

When he saw movement, he fired.

———

JACKSON HEARD Bear empty the entire cylinder of his .357 in rapid succession. In unison, he, Chief Diaz, and Officer Birch hurdled over the boat and sprinted for the house. As they raced across the muddy knoll, Jackson expected Ayers to emerge with every step they took, catching them out in the open, and firing.

Bear didn't allow that to happen.

The three men made it to the house and took cover underneath it amongst its stilts. On the other side, Jackson could see Bear reloading his revolver. Jackson gestured with his hands, asking Bear if he saw Ayers. Bear cautiously stepped out toward the sea wall again and looked above him. He ducked back inside and shook his head.

"We're going up," Chief Diaz said. "You stay down here with Bear."

"You could use an extra man up there, Chief," Jackson said.

Chief Diaz shook his head. "You're a civilian. I won't risk it."

Jackson looked at him long enough to note the set of his jaw. "Okay."

Chief Diaz moved to the base of the stairs on their side and pointed his service weapon up toward the deck above him. "You stay on my hip, Andy."

Officer Birch got behind his chief. "Roger that, sir."

Cautiously, the two of them ascended. Jackson moved toward the back of the house opposite Bear to cover them. As soon as he took a step from underneath the house, a shot rang out and a round smashed into a pine tree just over his head, splintering its bark. Jackson ducked down, then slowly rose again, his pistol raised in front of him. He could see Ayers taking cover behind the corner of the house.

"Caleb!" Jackson shouted. "It's over. You've got nowhere else to go."

"Walk away from this while you still can!" Ayers shouted back.

Jackson watched Chief Diaz and Officer Birch make it up to the deck that wrapped around the main floor. Ayers was one level above them. Jackson caught the chief's gaze then looked up to where Ayers crouched on the balcony. Chief Diaz nodded and started looking for a different way to get up to him.

"No one else has to get hurt here, Caleb," Jackson said.

Ayers cackled. "You think I care who gets hurt? You haven't been paying attention!"

"They were your family, Caleb. Why would you want to do this to them?"

Ayers laughter disappeared as he roared back. "No! They weren't!

They should've been, but they took that from me! They took it all from me! The life I should've had!"

"So that's what this is all about? Your mother giving you up?"

"Look around! They wanted for nothing. I should've been one of them! They had me and they threw me away like trash!"

Jackson shook his head. "It's more complicated than that, Caleb."

Now Caleb was screaming. "No, it's not! It's *very* simple! You don't know what it was like! They were just too busy living their rich, fancy lives! But now they know! Now they know because I've made them pay!"

"And what did the others have to do with that? They did nothing to you."

Chief Diaz's head popped up over the top of the roof to Jackson's right. The roof ran around to the cupola where the widow's walk cut into it. Chief Diaz stepped carefully around the corner of the roof, closing in on Ayers.

He was less than fifty feet away when Ayers looked up, spotted him, and opened fire. Chief Diaz fell, sliding down the roof and dropping onto the deck below. Jackson could hear him scream. Ayers stepped out to pursue him, but Jackson fired several shots, forcing Ayers back into cover.

Jackson heard Officer Birch's frantic voice call out. "Chief! Are you okay?"

Chief Diaz shouted. "I'm okay. My leg... is messed up though."

Jackson keyed the mic on his radio. "Birch, I'll cover you. Get the Chief to cover."

He stepped out wide again, pointing his Beretta at Ayers. Out of the corner of his eye, he saw Birch begin crawling on the deck below, trying to get Chief Diaz and pull him to safety.

"I told you!" Ayers shouted. "Go now! The next of you won't be so lucky."

"We're not going anywhere, Caleb," Jackson said. "You know that. We have you cornered."

Ayers didn't say anything. Jackson kept looking, but he no longer saw him. He looked across at Bear who stood away from the house, .357 raised. Bear's gaze asked Jackson if he saw Ayers. Jackson shook his head.

He keyed the mic on the radio. "Shaw, we lost Ayers. Does he still have the stairway pinned down inside?"

"Hold on," Shaw radioed back.

Several moments went by. The rain had stopped, and the wind died down, leaving a deafening silence. Jackson saw a head come up inside the cupola. He set his pistol's sights on the figure before seeing it was Shaw.

"Stairs are clear," she radioed. "I don't see—"

Bear started running toward the far end of the house before she could finish. He leveled his gun at something above them that Jackson couldn't see.

"Don't do it!" he shouted.

Jackson broke into a sprint, carving a path through the array of stilts. When he got to Bear, he glanced at where Bear was aiming. Ayers was out on the end of the widow's walk. Ahead and below him were the docks, the boats, and the bay.

"You won't make it, Caleb!" Jackson said.

Ayers climbed onto the banister and stood, leaving nothing between him and the earth below. The flybridge of the Meachem's yacht was equal height but several feet away.

"Shaw!" Jackson shouted.

She burst out of the cupola and ran down the widow's walk for Ayers.

It was too late.

Ayers jumped.

His torso bounced off the hardtop of the boat's flybridge as his legs slammed into the side of it and carried him over. He grabbed an antenna that swung him around where he fell onto the boat's fore-deck. Jackson ran to the dock and jumped onto the back of the boat. He had started making his way toward the front when Ayers got his feet under him, ran to the bow and jumped, disappearing underneath. Jackson, coming around the side, expected to hear a splash.

Silence.

A second later, a motor rumbled to life.

Jackson made it to the bow just in time to see a small outboard motorboat take off, Ayers at the tiller.

FIFTY-EIGHT

JACKSON WATCHED Ayers speed off around a rocky jetty and turn south down the Assateague Channel. The same helpless feeling took root in his chest as when he'd seen Susan Yarbrough weep in her home, Hank Willis lying on the bathroom floor, and Ayers slicing Jesse's throat. His body started to shake. It had to end.

"Jacky Boy!" Bear called. "Come on!"

Jackson looked over and saw Bear running for the swift water boat he'd tied to the flooded footbridge. He jumped onto the dock and ran after him. He looked out at Ayers's boat, getting smaller by the second.

Bear hopped into the seat by the motor, cranked it to life, and untied the line from the footbridge. Jackson was still fifty feet away. As he ran, he waved for Bear to go.

"Get around the jetty!" Jackson shouted. "I'll meet you on the other side."

Bear gunned the motor full throttle. The sudden acceleration caused the front of the boat to kick up in the air before slamming back down onto the water. Bear raced clear of the rocky outcrop then cut a turn so sharp it nearly threw him from the boat.

Jackson ran to the base of the jetty as fast as he could. The land there came to a natural point that rose above the floodwaters. Bear doubled back for him. Before he could slow down, Jackson leapt and landed in the boat.

"Go! Go!" he shouted.

Bear sped them into the channel, chasing after Ayers. Jackson looked ahead, turning his ball cap backward so it wouldn't fly off his head... again. Ayers, in his low-profile boat, had become a dot on the horizon. Jackson guessed he was at least several hundred yards ahead of them.

"Faster, Bear!"

"I've got it maxed out!"

As they approached the more populated parts of the island, the channel became increasingly littered with debris from the storm. Jackson saw Ayers go wide, hugging the Assateague shoreline, to bypass the mess. If he and Bear could make it through the clutter, they could close the distance between them and Ayers.

Jackson looked back at Bear. Bear grinned mischievously with the same idea.

"Hold onto that hat!"

They dashed headlong into the detritus. Entire sections of walls and roofs created little floating islands. Bear slalomed between them, gunning it before cutting the motor and banking into sharp turns before gunning it again. Jackson gripped the bench seat in front of him, kneeling as much for prayer as he was for safety.

Around a capsized pickup truck, they found a clear lane forward. Bear took it, but as soon as he did, a motor home the storm surge had confiscated collapsed onto itself. Its entire backside broke free and swung away as if it were on a hinge. Ahead and to the side was the top half of a submerged tree. The piece of motorhome was going to become pinned and shut like a door on Jackson and Bear's way through.

When Bear didn't cut the throttle and turn back, Jackson's eyes widened.

He looked back at Bear. "We won't make it!"

Bear nodded, his eyes fixed on the path before them. "Oh, we'll make it!" he said.

They zoomed down the narrowing corridor. Jackson got his feet underneath him, prepared to bail out. The debris from the motor home continued to swing out. Their path was nearly blocked.

Bear got them so close to the tree its branches raked at the boat as it whipped by. Jackson leaned right, and the boat tilted forty-five degrees. The motor whirred angrily as it left the water, but the boat skirted through. When they were clear, Bear threw himself left, righting the boat. The motor splashed back down and jettisoned them away.

Jackson looked back at Bear who was laughing with a shit-eating grin on his face.

"Told ya we'd make it," he said.

Ayers came around the debris field, and Bear cut a path straight toward him. When they got back behind Ayers, they were a fraction of the distance behind. Ayers swerved left then right, trying to shake them, but Bear stayed on his stern. Still, they couldn't chase him forever.

"Go out wide," Jackson said to Bear. "I'm going to see if I can take out his motor without hitting him."

Bear nodded and veered right. The boat rocked violently as it left Ayers's wake. Jackson got on one knee to steady himself. Ayers looked their way and started to swerve erratically again.

Jackson brought up his Beretta, aimed down its sights, and fired. Once. Twice. Three times. Each time he missed. He adjusted himself and fired again.

Bang! Bang! Click.

The magazine in the Beretta — his last magazine — was out. Jackson had the shotgun slung around his chest, but it only had bird-shot. There was no way he could hit Ayers's motor without also hitting Ayers. Jackson wasn't willing to risk it. He was about to ask for Bear's .357 when Bear shouted to get his attention and pointed ahead of them.

"We got a problem, Jacky Boy," he said.

The two boats were quickly approaching the bridge connecting Chincoteague to the refuge on Assateague. Normally, there would be plenty of space for a small boat to pass underneath, but in the surging floodwaters, that gap had narrowed to just a few feet.

FIFTY-NINE

CALEB AYERS'S boat skipped across the choppy channel like a stone. The men pursuing him had made their way through the mess the town had thrown out into the water and closed the distance. This was new territory for him. Bull sharks were predators. He wasn't used to being prey.

Ahead of him was the Sheepshead Creek Bridge. He'd passed under it dozens of times since coming to Chincoteague, always with ease. Now, though, the storm surge had narrowed the clearance under the bridge to no more than a foot or two. Even if he could make it through, he'd have to do so slowly, allowing the men pursuing him to get even closer, if not catch him altogether. He could turn back and head north again, but all that was waiting back there were more police.

Caleb had made a pact with himself before the night of his Awakening—the night he'd confronted the family that had thrown him away and got his pound of flesh for their misdeeds. He'd promised himself that he would not become a spectacle for the people that would never and could never understand him. He would not let them take him and put him on display in front of the courts and the media. Pretending he was something different from them. Allowing them to jeer at him like some sort of monster. Refusing to acknowledge he was simply a consequence of the world *they'd* created. No, Caleb would never give them the satisfaction.

He'd known this moment would come eventually. His Awakening had been a rebirth, freeing himself of the anger and pain he'd harbored for so long by inflicting it on others, to make them hurt the same way he had hurt. But he'd known this rebirth was not a new beginning so much as the beginning of the end. A pilgrimage to his own reckoning. Now, that journey was nearly over.

Caleb twisted the throttle on the tiller as hard as he could, trying to squeeze every ounce of horsepower out of the outboard motor. He sped on, headed for his own deliverance.

SIXTY

JACKSON WATCHED AYERS CLOSELY. He saw what they saw, yet he wasn't slowing down.

Jackson shouted as loud as he could over the roar of the two motors.

"Caleb, don't!" he said. "There's not enough room! You won't make it!"

Ayers looked over and met his eyes. He gave a wide smile, baring all his teeth. There was something animalistic about his smile. Like a wolf. Or a shark. Ayers didn't slow down. He faced the bridge and stood, tiller in his hand, the wind whipping at his clothes.

"Son of a bitch," Bear said. "The guy's gonna kamikaze himself."

Jackson unslung his shotgun from around his chest, disengaged the safety, and leveled it at Ayers's boat. Maybe he'd hit Ayers, but at least he'd have a chance of surviving. He definitely wouldn't survive crashing into the bridge at full speed. Ayers was a little more than thirty yards away. Definitely a makable shot.

"Caleb!" he shouted, not taking the gun's sights off of his target. "Stop!"

Ayers tipped his head back and stretched his arm out wide, still holding on to the motor's tiller.

Jackson took a deep breath in, held it, then let it out. His heart rate slowed to the optimal sixty beats per minute. Good to go. Jackson slid his index finger down from the body of the shotgun and onto the trigger.

He didn't squeeze it.

Jackson lowered the gun from his shoulder as Ayers sped toward the bridge. Bear turned and guided them away.

Jackson watched Ayers, begging him to stop. To turn or slow down or bail out. He never did.

The second before Ayers's boat slammed into the bridge, Jackson closed his eyes.

———

JACKSON SAT on the divider that separated the road across Sheepshead Creek Bridge and the walkway on its north side. The bridge crested out of the flooded channel all around it like the spine of a large concrete sea creature. Meant to connect the two islands to one another, it'd become an island all itself.

Two hours had passed since Caleb Ayers had crashed into the bridge and taken his own life. In that time, Shaw and the members of Chincoteague's finest had arrived on the other swift water boat. Jackson had watched, numb, as Investigator Bowden and Officer Perry pulled Ayers's body from the channel.

"You alright, Jacky Boy?" Bear asked, standing by his side.

"I'm good," Jackson said, his voice quiet.

Now, the firefighters had come with Jesse on the third boat, as Ayers was no longer a threat to everyone at the shelter. Chief Diaz had a badly broken ankle and had placed Bowden in charge. He and Jesse now waited on the bridge to be airlifted out.

"Coast Guard bird is ten minutes out," Shaw said, walking over to Jackson and Bear from where the firefighters had Chief Diaz and

Jesse on backboards in the middle of the road. "They're going to take Jesse. Maryland State Police are sending another nearby chopper from Salisbury for the Chief. There should be room on board for you and Bear if you want to get out of here."

"That's alright," Jackson said. "Thanks, though."

"You sure? It'll be hard to get another one to come out without a medical emergency."

Jackson nodded. "You'll be even more under-manned than before. Bear and I can help until you all re-establish connection with the mainland."

Shaw cocked her head to the side. "I won't say no to that."

She hopped up on the concrete divider, taking a seat on it next to Jackson. Together, the two of them looked out the channel to the south. The houses still standing marked where the shoreline used to be.

"I feel like I need to say thank you," Shaw said.

"For what?"

Shaw gave half a shrug as she looked at him. "I don't know. All this? For giving a damn? You were onto all of this before anyone else. Lord knows more people would have gotten hurt without you."

Jackson didn't look back at her. "There's nothing you need to thank me for. I'm just sorry we... I... wasn't faster. Jesse and Hank and the others that got hurt along the way. You can't help but wonder."

"But you know that's not on you, right?"

Jackson sighed as he nodded. "And yet, it never feels that way."

Shaw shook her head. "No, it doesn't."

The Coast Guard helicopter, an MH-65 Dolphin painted bright orange-red, appeared in the sky to the west, getting louder as it approached the waterlocked bridge. Deploying its landing gear, it landed on the top of the bridge's crest. Jackson and Shaw watched as a guardsman got out and helped the firefighters load Jesse into it. Minutes later, the helicopter climbed straight up, banked right, then turned back toward the mainland.

"What do you think will happen with the Meachem property?" Jackson asked.

"I don't know," Shaw said thoughtfully. "If it were up to me, they'd raze the area and give it back to mother nature."

Jackson didn't say anything.

"I still can't believe this all ties back to that. That night in '99 has been a blight on this town for years. The dark secret everyone thought they knew. We were all wrong. When people learn about Ayers, about why he did what he did, it's going to reopen a lot of old wounds."

"Sometimes you have to let old wounds bleed again to let them heal right. Maybe this will give those that have been carrying the past with them the closure they need. The permission to move on."

Shaw thought about that sentiment. "You almost sound like you speak from experience."

Jackson could feel Shaw struggle to say the next part aloud.

"Your son?" Shaw said quietly.

Jackson gave the slightest of nods.

"That's why you do things like this, isn't it? Chase the Ayers of the world?"

Before Jackson could answer her, one of the firefighters called out to everyone on the bridge.

"Next bird is fifteen minutes out," he said. "We need to get the police chief into position."

Two other firefighters joined him by the backboard Chief Diaz was strapped onto. Each one of them took a corner, leaving one corner unmanned. They looked back for their fourth colleague to see he and Bear were struggling with one of the swift water boats as the current worked to pull it away. Seeing this, Jackson hopped off the concrete divider and started over toward the firefighters and Chief Diaz. As he did, he turned back to Shaw.

"That's for a head more shrunken than mine to answer," he said. "For now, I'm just going to keep doing what I do."

"And what's that?" Shaw asked.

"Go where I'm needed."

Jackson jogged over to give the firefighters a hand.

SIXTY-ONE

TWO DAYS LATER, the storm surge receded, clearing the causeway to the mainland when it left. The rest of the Chincoteague Police and Fire Department rolled into town accompanied by a small army of other emergency responders. FEMA, the Red Cross, even the U.S. Army Corps of Engineers. The rebuilding process was beginning.

Jackson and Bear returned to Bear's Suburban where they were pleased to see the old SUV had been spared from serious damage. Jackson looked on, a grin taking shape as Bear happily slapped the dashboard when he turned the ignition over and, with a bit of reluctance, it rumbled to life.

Before they left, they went back to the refuge to say goodbye to Shaw. She met them in front of the education and administration building and gave each of them a hug as she thanked them again for their help. Both told her it wasn't necessary. As they climbed back into the Suburban, Special Agent Lederer got out of his vehicle in the employee parking lot and headed for the front doors. He spotted Jackson and Bear, stopped briefly, and nodded, similarly conveying his thanks. Jackson nodded back.

Shaw came over to Jackson's open passenger window and rested her forearm on it. She looked at Special Agent Lederer, then back at Jackson.

"He owes you more than that for basically closing his case for him," Shaw said.

"He owes *you*," Jackson corrected. "Make sure you get the credit you deserve."

Shaw grinned. "Copy that." She stepped back from the truck. "Get home safe."

"Will do."

Their final stop on the way out of town was to Mr. Whippy, an ice cream and coffee shop on Maddox Boulevard. The last time they'd gone by it, floodwaters were up to its front doors. Now, it was one of the first places to reopen.

"People can't get back on their feet on an empty stomach," the woman with short, curly salt-and-pepper hair said with a smile.

Drinks in hand — a chocolate milkshake for Bear and a black coffee for Jackson — the two turned right and headed onto the bridge across the various narrows and creeks that separated Chincoteague from the mainland. On the other side, the causeway banked left, circumnavigating NASA's Wallops Island Flight Facility. Jackson looked out his window at the vast field of massive antennas, all pointed toward the heavens. They'd spent days isolated from the world, and here was every connection imaginable, right in front of him, just a few miles from the shelter. He could feel Bear looking at him over his shoulder.

"Something on your mind, Bear?" he asked.

"Well, I wasn't gonna say nothin', but since you mentioned it... why'd you let him go?"

Jackson was quiet for a moment. He knew who Bear meant but needed to hear him say it. "Let who go?"

"Ayers. Out on the boats when we were chasing him. You had the shot and I damn sure know you could've made it. So... why didn't you?"

The road turned west again, and the field of satellites disappeared behind a swath of woodlands. Jackson kept his gaze fixed out the window.

"I was worried you'd fall out of your chair again," Jackson said.

Bear shook his head but couldn't suppress a grin. "No. For real."

"Honestly?" Jackson looked forward. "I'd made a decision. I wasn't going to shoot him, not unless I had to. I know myself better now, and I know that's a line I don't want to cross unless I have no other choice."

Bear shrugged and nodded. "Sure, but..."

"But I also decided if some sociopath that's killed nearly a dozen people wants to leave this world on his own terms, I don't have to get in the way."

Bear nodded. "Amen, brother."

They turned onto the highway, headed toward Roanoke, neither of them saying anything else.

———

SPECIAL AGENT BAILEY lived in southwest Roanoke in a two-floor red brick ranch home on a rolling road lined with oak and walnut trees. This late in October, the canopies over the homes were alive with color. Leaves that had turned golden yellow and bright crimson caught the late afternoon sun as it headed for the horizon.

Bear pulled up to the house's paved walkway and let Jackson climb out. Jackson's black Dodge D100 was parked on the street behind Bailey's unmarked Police Interceptor just where he'd left it almost a week prior. He grabbed his gear out of the backseat, then came up to the open driver's side window.

"So, maybe next time we just go fishing," Jackson said.

Bear frowned before both of them grinned and laughed.

"Listen." Jackson turned serious. "I know you don't think I have to say it, but..."

"You never will, Jacky Boy," Bear said, clapping him on the shoulder.

Jackson nodded. "I'll see you around."

"Don't you know it," Bear said through the open window. "And tell lady cop I say hey."

Jackson started for Bailey's door. "She has a name."

"Good for her!" Bear chortled. "I'll see ya."

Bear and his Suburban climbed up the hilly street.

As Jackson crossed the walkway to the house, Josie, his Golden Lab, leaped up in the picture window next to the front door. Bailey opened the door, and Josie bounded out, greeting Jackson with slobbery kisses and a wagging tail.

Jackson chuckled as he knelt. "Hey, girl! I missed you, too."

Bailey leaned against the door frame, arms crossed. She smiled at Jackson when he looked up at her.

"Good to see you no worse for wear," she said.

Jackson rose and walked over to her. "Thanks. I hope she wasn't too much more trouble. I'm sorry she overstayed her welcome."

"It's alright," Bailey said. "She grew on me." She pointed a thumb toward the picture window. "It's him that probably wants an apology from you."

Jackson took a step back and saw a brown tabby with judgmental eyes scowling at him and Josie from the highest perch of a tall cat tree. He dropped his rucksack onto the slab concrete porch, opened it, and fished out a plastic shopping bag with something in it.

"As it so happens, I brought a peace offering," he said.

Bailey took the shopping bag and looked inside. "A feather wand?"

"I'm told they're popular with cats."

Bailey smirked. "What about me? I had to feed and clean up after the two fur missiles."

Jackson reached back into his rucksack and pulled a bottle of Lagavulin out of a paper bag. "I wasn't going to leave you empty handed."

Bailey's smile widened as she took the bottle. She tucked it under her arm and looked back up at Jackson. "Then everything in Chincoteague is… over?"

Jackson nodded. "It's over."

"And Ayers?"

Jackson stood and slid his hands into his pockets. "He chose not to face everything he'd done."

Bailey raised her eyebrows. "Wow."

"Yeah."

"Well, as long as you and Bear are okay."

Jackson nodded again. "We are."

A quiet came over them and, together, they watched as Josie chased a squirrel up the towering oak tree in Bailey's front yard. Jackson whistled, calling her back. He looked back at Bailey.

"Well, we better get on the road," Jackson said. "Thank you again."

"Sure," Bailey said.

With Josie by his side, Jackson went over to his truck. He opened up the passenger door, let Josie jump in, then shut it behind him. As he went over to the driver's door, he looked back at Bailey once more and waved.

Bailey waved back. "Get home safe," she said.

"I will," Jackson replied. "First, I have a stop to make."

SIXTY-TWO

STEPHIE MEACHEM STOOD in the kitchen of her duplex, waiting for the teakettle to come to a boil. She looked at the calendar on the wall. October was almost over. Soon it would be Thanksgiving. A time for family. She used to love the holiday as a child, the wonderful feasts her family would have. Traditional Thanksgiving staples complemented with coastal cuisine like oysters and duck. Her family was always so happy then. Now, those memories felt like they belonged to someone else.

A knock came at her door, and Stephie jumped, startled out of her nostalgic trance. She went to the door and looked through the peephole. Backlit by the evening's twilight was a shadowy figure. A man, tall, wearing a ball cap and coat. She opened her door just a crack, the chain still attached, and peered out through the narrow opening. A column of light slipped through the door and illuminated a sliver of the man's face. A soulful eye looked at her, and a faint smile peeked out of a trimmed brown beard that had gone gray at the edges.

"Good evening, ma'am," the man said. "Are you Stephanie Meachem?"

"Stephie," Stephie replied. "Who is asking?"

The man removed his ball cap to reveal a head full of chestnut hair just long enough to show its natural curls. "My name is Jackson Clay. You don't know me, but I was recently over in Chincoteague."

The name of her hometown cut through Stephie like a knife, as it had for the last quarter century.

"I... was the one who found your aunt and cousins," Jackson added.

Stephie studied the man for a moment before shutting the door to unchain it, then reopened it. "Please, would you like to come in?" She opened the door wide.

Jackson nodded as he stepped in. "Thank you."

Stephie motioned to her sparsely decorated living room, the sofa and two chairs. "You're welcome to have a seat." The tea kettle began to whistle from the kitchen. "I was just making myself some tea. Would you like some?"

Jackson lowered himself slowly into the chair closest to the door. "Tea would be nice. Thank you."

Stephie stepped into the kitchen and quickly fetched two mugs from the cupboard, filling each with hot water and dropping a tea bag in each. Grabbing the two mugs by their handles with one hand and a jar of sugar with the other, she returned to Jackson in her living room.

"Here's some sugar," she said. "If you take cream or honey I can..."

Jackson raised a hand. "Plain is wonderful, thank you." He took one of the mugs and grasped it in his hands.

Stephie went to the chair opposite her guest and sat on the edge. "A police officer came a few days ago to tell me about my family."

"I know," Jackson said. "I was the one who asked her to find you and speak to you."

Stephie's lip trembled. "Was she right? Did Caleb... my son... hurt them? Hurt all those people?"

"I'm afraid so."

Stephie's head dropped, her hair flowing over her face like a flaxen waterfall. She put her cup of tea on the coffee table between them and wiped her face. "I knew it. I hoped like hell she —or *I*, I guess—was wrong. But deep down, I knew."

"From what I understand, you'd never met your son."

She brushed her hair back with her hand, dabbed at a tear on her cheek, and looked up at Jackson. "Yes. Which is the problem. Why this all happened."

Jackson leaned forward, resting his elbows on the chair's armrests. "What do you mean?"

"Isn't that what set him off? Finding me? Learning who I am? Who... my... *our* family is?"

Jackson shook his head. "No. Whatever reasons he had concocted in his mind to hurt all those people, those were his reasons. His delusions. You had no hand in them."

Stephie sniffled. "Thank you for saying that, but that just doesn't feel like the truth."

"It is. I've spent the last couple weeks there looking for just that, the truth. I can promise you it is. Caleb Ayers, and Caleb Ayers alone, is responsible for hurting those people."

Stephie rubbed her nose. "Where is he now? Caleb?"

"He's... gone as well."

Stephie shook her head as more tears spilled down her cheeks. "The police killed him? Or someone he was trying to hurt?"

"My friend and I were pursuing him, trying to stop him. But he chose to take his own life."

At that, Stephie's head dropped into her hands, and she began to sob, the top half of her shaking with the overwhelming sadness of losing the child she'd never known. Jackson put his own mug of tea on the coffee table, got up, and moved to the corner of the sofa nearest to her. He sat there and gently took her hand in his.

"I'm sorry," Stephie said. "It's just... this thing, this horrible thing has followed me for most of my life. I try to move on, and it won't let me."

"You have nothing to be sorry for," Jackson said. "In fact, that's what I wanted to come here to tell you. I know everything you've been through. With your uncle, then that night your father confronted him. The way everything went sideways. I know about it all and I know what it's like to carry that burden of tragedy. The guilt that comes with it. I wanted to tell you in person that it's not yours to carry."

Stephie wiped at her eyes with her free hand. She sniffled again. "It's all felt like a curse. Like this one horrible moment that has snowballed into a dozen more, getting bigger and bigger, running over everyone in its path."

Jackson's voice lowered. "Almost as if it haunts you."

Stephie nodded. She sobbed some more.

Jackson stayed quiet for a moment. "Several years ago, I lost my son. I mean, literally, lost him. One minute he was with me in a theme park. The next, he wasn't. A man had taken him and I... never saw him again. I fought to find him, first with the police and law enforcement, and then on my own. I found many things—many truths—but never him. It all cost me my marriage and, with it, everything I cared about. When you get to that point, it's hard to see how you can go on. But if you allow yourself, you can."

"I just have this over-arching guilt about it all. If I hadn't stayed on that boat. If I had stopped my father before people got hurt. If I had fought to keep my son the way I should have."

Jackson squeezed her hand. "Guilt is like that. Those that should carry it don't, so it leeches onto others. You were preyed upon, put in one impossible situation after another by people who should have known better. But their sins are theirs, not yours. That's the burden I'm talking about. The one you have to find a way to let go of."

Stephie took her hand back and ran it through her hair. She looked at Jackson, her vision blurred by her own tears. She could hear in his voice that he spoke from a familiar place. These were not platitudes handed out by a well-meaning stranger. She had heard those her entire adult life and come to recognize them. No, these were something different. Someone who saw how broken she was and recognized it, having been similarly broken himself.

"I'll try," Stephie said in little more than a whisper.

Jackson nodded. "That's all any of us can do." He paused a moment. "There's something else you should know, too."

Stephie wasn't sure she could handle anything more. She tried to meet his eyes but couldn't, focusing instead on the U.S. Army Ranger tattoo on his forearm.

"Russell Hanz is alive, Stephie," Jackson said.

Stephie shook her head, unable to process that news. "How? That's not... possible."

"He fled during the chaos of that night. Stole one of your family's jet skis and took it to family he had across the bay. He's been laying low ever since."

Stephie's voice was little more than a whisper once more. "Where?"

"Ocean City."

Stephie smiled sadly. More tears came. "He'd always loved it up there. He talked about us getting a place there after graduation. I imagined telling my family I wanted to do that would be the hardest thing I'd ever have to face." She shook her head. "How wrong I was."

"I've talked to him and he seems held down by the past, similar to you. Perhaps you two can move on together. Give each other the second chance you both deserve."

Now, Stephie found the courage to meet Jackson's eyes. "I think I'd like that."

Jackson nodded. "I can help you find him, if you'd like. I've been told I'm good at that. Finding things."

Stephanie nodded back. "I'd like that."

Jackson asked for her number, and Stephie gave it to him. He put it in his phone, then stood. Stephie stood with him, following him as he walked back to her door. When he opened it, Stephie could see his black pickup truck parked on the street over his shoulder. A golden lab was sitting in the passenger seat, looking at them, floppy tongue hanging out. Stephie grinned.

"Your dog?" she asked.

"Yeah, Josie," Jackson said.

"She's adorable."

Jackson looked out at the truck. "She is." He looked back at Stephie. "Everything you've been through is sad, but it would be even sadder if it prevented you from moving on. I hope you and Russell can find a way to do that."

"Is that what Josie is? A part of you moving on from your past?"

Jackson cocked his head. "Something like that."

Stephie's grin widened.

Jackson held a hand up in farewell before stuffing it in his coat pocket. "Take care," he said.

"You, too."

Stephie watched as the man she'd only just met walked back to his truck. In that short time, he'd seen and helped her in a way no one else ever had. Something told her it wasn't the first time he'd done that sort of thing.

She stood there, wondering about that, as Jackson Clay drove off into the night.

———

The story continues in *River Dogs*, click here to order your copy now!

https://a.co/d/0d5G9yZG

Join the B.C. Lienesch reader family and stay up to date on all the latest news!
https://www.bclnovels.com/newsletter

ACKNOWLEDGMENTS

Growing up, we had two family vacations every summer: a multi-week trip to our family cabin in Michigan and a long weekend to Chincoteague on Virginia's eastern shore. Each year, I looked forward to Chincoteague weekend. We stayed at the Driftwood Motor Lodge (before it became a Best Western and is now a Spark by Hilton). We would take the Wildlife Loop and visit the beaches on Assateague, shop at local staples like The Brant, and dine at places like Maria's and The Beachway. And I was always bummed when it was over.

Cut to a little over a year ago, I was on a video call with the team at Liquid Mind Publishing, pitching several proposals for my next novel. Amongst them was a half-baked idea for a twist on a locked-room mystery, set on an isolated island where a killer hunts the populace. If I'm being perfectly honest, it wasn't even my "best" pitch, but the team at Liquid Mind immediately saw its potential.

We just needed an island in the area that Jackson and Bear might visit. And I had just the one.

I consider myself extremely lucky to have landed with a publisher like Liquid Mind Publishing, which not only actively supports its authors but also helps foster and encourage their passion and creativity. Without them, *Safe Harbor* would never have been realized, let alone written.

Amongst the team at Liquid Mind, thank you to Holly Langfeld, whose tireless work and assistance helped shape and build this novel into something far better than I alone ever could have concocted. Thank you to Nancy Sampson-Bach, who stepped in under extraordinary circumstances and deftly edited the manuscript. To that end, I would like to thank Walter Curran, Suzanne Childress, and my beta reading team for smoothing out the rough edges and giving the manuscript its final polish. And thank you to the rest of the team – namely, Nicolette Maino, Nick Reedy, and L.T. Ryan – who actively manage not just this book but the entire Jackson Clay & Bear Beauchamp Series.

Thank you to my mother and late father, who not only introduced me to dozens of different places like Chincoteague, but also fostered my creativity and imagination, and they have been steadfast in their support for my writing career.

Thank you to my friends and writer colleagues – especially Austin Shirey, Zach Lamb, and Christyn (C.C.) West – who deal with my neurotic rants and ravings on a day-to-day basis.

Above all, though, thank you to my wife, Meg. Whether it is lifting me up, grounding me, pushing me forward, or just talking me off the ledge, you have been my number one supporter from day one and the only partner I want to take on this journey. You are my everything, and very much the Keeper of the Author.

THE JACKSON CLAY & BEAR BEAUCHAMP SERIES

The Woodsman

Country Roads

Chasing Devils

Happyland

Safe Harbor

River Dogs

ABOUT THE AUTHOR

B.C. Lienesch is an award-winning mystery, thriller, and horror author hailing from the nation's capital.

A former freelance writer, featured columnist, and editor for guysnation.com, he is an author-member of the International Thriller Writers and the recent recipient of three 2024 LitStar Book Awards including Outstanding Book Series for his Jackson Clay & Bear Beauchamp Series.

Born in Washington, D.C. and raised in Northern Virginia, he now lives in the same area with his wife, Meg, and their feline over-lord, Hitchcock.

Join the B.C. Lienesch reader family and stay up to date on all the latest news!
https://www.bclnovels.com/newsletter

facebook.com/bclnovels

x.com/bclienesch

instagram.com/bclienesch

threads.com/@bclienesch

tiktok.com/@bclienesch

bsky.app/profile/bclienesch.bsky.social

JOIN LIQUID MIND PUBLISHING'S MAILING LIST

Follow the link to join our newsletter and stay up to date with Liquid Mind Publishing!

https://BookHip.com/GTQPXSQ

You'll receive a **free** copy of

A Dangerous Game: A Jackson Clay Prequel.